MW01240542

Fighting With Him

Fire and Ice Book Two

Tara Conrad

You can find all of Tara's books (ebooks and signed paperbacks) on her website: https://taraconradauthor.com/shop/

Fire and Ice Series

Fighting with Him: https://geni.us/FightingwithHim

Living for Him: https://geni.us/LivingforHim

His Melody: https://geni.us/HisMelody

Her Nightingale: https://geni.us/HerNightingale

Shattered Dreams https://geni.us/ShatteredDreams6

Coming Soon: **Fractured Lives (pre-order today for .99)** https://geni.us/FracturedLives**Release Date: June 27, 2023**

Coming Soon: **Mended Hearts (pre-order today for .99)** https://geni.us/MendedHearts**Release Date: August 29, 2023**

Real Life Romance World

Real Life Romance: Gilbert and Elizabeth
https://geni.us/GilbertandElizabeth

Real Life Romance: Duke and Percy
https://geni.us/DukeandPercy

Contents

To my Sir,
Thank You for being my rock. The one who is there to hold me when i struggle. The one who is there to share in my successes. The one who picks me up when i fall down. You are the man of my dreams. i love You with all my heart.

Just a note...

What you read in these pages is not to be used for sexual education or as a substitute for seeking professional medical advice.

Alex

EVERY DAY WITHOUT NATALIE in my life was a living hell. Out of fear, I made decisions that broke us. But fear isn't an excuse for wrongdoing. What I did is on me, and I've been paying the price for it. I haven't been able to eat or sleep. My life has been empty—meaningless. I can never repay our friends for stepping in to help. If it wasn't for their intervention, I don't know what I would've done. I screwed up and came very close to losing Natalie for good—that's something I won't let happen again.

Last night, my mouth and hands explored Natalie's body as if it were our first time. I missed her quiet mewls of pleasure, the way her body comes to life from the simplest touch. Over and over, I brought her to orgasm until she was unable to keep her eyes open. I held her in my arms all night, fearing if I let go, I'd wake and find it was all a dream. But when I open my eyes, Natalie's body is still curled against mine. I watch my angel as she sleeps, her blonde hair fanned over her pillow as I gently rub my knuckles down her cheek. Natalie stirs and looks at me with a sleepy smile.

"Good morning," she whispers.

"Good morning, baby girl." I kiss her lips. "I missed waking up next to you." And I plan to show her exactly how much. Rolling her onto her back, I position myself over her before sliding my erection into her tight, wet body. Natalie's back arches, pushing her breasts up. Her pert nipples beg for attention, which I gladly lavish on each one. "Do you feel how much I missed you?" I ask as I pull all the way out.

She whimpers at the loss of contact and lifts her hips, trying to find me.

"Always my impatient sub. Tell me what you want." I rub the tip of my cock through her wet folds, teasing her.

"You." Her voice is breathy and wanting.

That's all the confirmation I need to push in, balls deep. "And this time, I'm never letting you go. Tell me you're mine." I need to hear her say the words.

"I'm yours, Sir," she says, wrapping her legs tight around me.

Her show of possessiveness fuels my desire, and I growl in appreciation. I roll us over. Natalie now straddles my body, giving me the most perfect view of her breasts as she rides me. I want her to come with me. My fingers find her clit circling it until I know she's getting close. Then, I grab her hips, taking charge of the pace.

"Come with me." It's all the permission she needs. Natalie throws her head back as her body tightens around my cock. One more thrust and I follow her into ecstasy. I hold her to me until our bodies come down from their high. I pull her next to me. She lays her head on my chest, and I run my fingers through her hair.

"What time is your dad being discharged today?"

She pushes up on her elbow. "How did you know?"

The loneliness from the past few months hits.

"I never went back to New York," I confess. "I moved in here and kept in touch with your parents."

"I had no idea."

"I couldn't leave."

Natalie lays her head back on my chest. "Thank you for not giving up on us." She places a kiss over my heart.

I don't know what I did to deserve this amazing woman, but I know I'm never letting her get away again. I play with her long blonde curls trying to postpone the inevitable. It might be our first day back together, but we won't be able to spend it how I'd like. There are things we can't ignore. "As much as I want to spend the day in bed. We need to get up and shower."

Natalie groans as I sit up. "Are you sure we can't stay here?"

Stanley hasn't been home since he was shot on Christmas morning. Last month he was transferred to the hospital's rehabilitation facility. They've been working tirelessly on his daily living skills—things he needs to be able to do to go home. It's taken a long time, but he's finally strong enough to be discharged. "Your parents are expecting you to pick them up. It's a big day for your dad. We don't want to miss it."

Natalie

ALEX LEADS ME INTO our en-suite bathroom. He offered a full house tour last night, but I opted out, preferring to spend my time getting reacquainted with his body.

Like the rest of the house, the bathroom has been skillfully renovated, combining a rustic farmhouse feel with a modern vibe. The ceiling is covered in wood planks that Alex tells me are reclaimed from a hundred-year-old barn that once stood in town. Across the room, under a large window overlooking the lake, is a freestanding soaking tub.

"The window's tinted from the outside. So we have complete privacy in here."

"I was wondering how that would work."

As much as I love the tub, it's the walk-in shower that steals the show. Ombre glass tiles that transition from a dark charcoal grey at the top and fade into pure white line the walls. It's exquisite. I lean against the counter and watch Alex turn on the water. His muscles flex with each move. Hot water rains down from the ceiling. Alex steps in, and I follow, closing the glass door behind me. I position myself under the hot water, so it cascades over my body.

"I missed you, baby girl."

"I missed you more."

The words barely leave my lips before Alex lifts me and presses my back against the tile. Instinctively I wrap my legs around his waist for support as he takes me in the shower. This isn't slow or gentle, and I don't want it to be. He's marking me, laying claim to my body and my heart.

"Promise me you'll never leave again." He rests his forehead against mine.

"I promise, Sir. I'm yours always and forever."

Alex lowers me, keeping his arm around my waist until I'm sure of my footing. Then, he reaches behind me and grabs the shampoo bottle squeezing some into his hand. "Turn around." Alex washes my hair, his fingers massaging my scalp. A soft moan escapes my lips. "Don't make those sounds, baby girl."

"Then don't make me feel so good."

He slaps my ass.

"Cheeky little thing today, aren't you?" His voice is playful and light.

After Alex rinses my hair, he washes my body with his hands. Taking his time to reacquaint himself with every curve before allowing me to step under the water to rinse.

"Go start getting ready. I'll be out in a minute."

"Do I have to?" I drag my finger down his chest and abdomen, teasing him.

"Natalie." He grabs my hand. "Go, or we'll never leave the house."

I step out of the shower and blow him a kiss. Without grabbing a towel to cover my body, I walk out of the bathroom, swaying my hips.

"Just wait until tonight, my little temptress."

Natalie

"I'M LEAVING NOW," I say to my mom. "I'll be there in about an hour."

"Please drive safely, honey. I hate the thought of you on the highway alone."

Alex and I decided to surprise my parents today. They'll be thrilled to see us together. Over the past few months, they haven't stopped begging me to call him—to work things out. It's a complete turnaround from several months ago when they begged me to stay away from him.

"I'll be fine. I could do this drive with my eyes closed."

"Don't do that," Mom shrieks.

"It was a joke." I laugh. "I'll see you guys soon."

Alex locks the front door, and together we walk the stone path to his car, which is now parked in the driveway.

"This wasn't here last night."

I know everything happened in a whirlwind, but I wouldn't have missed his car sitting in the driveway. Would I?

"No, it wasn't." Alex opens the door for me. "Brandon and Lana brought it over early this morning."

I'm relieved I didn't miss something as obvious as his car. I'm also thankful for Brandon and Lana. They went to great lengths to make sure Alex and I got back together. If not for them, I would've lost the best thing in my life. I need to find some way to thank them.

Alex slowly maneuvers the gravel driveway until we reach the main road. Then, we start the all too familiar drive to Branson. It's been a long three months of driving back and forth while juggling my responsibilities here. Knowing this is the last time we'll need to make this drive is a huge relief.

Dad cleared a significant hurdle when he was released from the hospital to a lower level of care. Unfortunately, there are no in-patient rehabilitation centers in Northmeadow. As a result, my parents were forced to remain in Branson while Dad continued his physical therapy. Mom insisted on staying to be near her husband. I don't know how they were able to afford the hotel room for all these months. Every time I asked, my parents changed the subject.

"I'm worried about how to help my parents pay off their credit cards. This stay in Branson must've cost a fortune."

"You don't need to worry about that."

"Of course I do, Alex. They're my parents. There's no way they can afford—"

"I was hoping this didn't come up." Alex glances my way. "I paid for her hotel room and expenses."

"You did?"

"Charlotte and Stanley are your family, which makes them my family. I couldn't stand by and do nothing when I had the means to help them."

"Thank you doesn't feel like enough."

"I have you. That's all I need."

We drive in silence for a few minutes. The knowledge of what Alex did is still sinking in. I safeworded. Ended our relationship. But Alex not only stayed, he took care of my parents for the past few months. I don't deserve this man sitting next to me.

Alex breaks the silence. "I'm sure once Charlotte sees us together, the first thing she'll want to know is if we set a wedding date yet. I'd like to get married as soon as possible."

The selfish part of me thinks we should elope, but the little girl in me wants the fairy tale wedding I've always dreamed of. And then there's the adult me who's holding back. My head and heart are at war with each other.

When I don't respond, Alex asks, "What's wrong?"

I fidget with my fingers in my lap. "I don't want to get married until my dad can walk me down the aisle."

Alex reaches over, grabbing my hand. "As much as I don't want to wait for you to be my wife, that's a compromise I can live with."

"Really?"

"baby girl, I want our wedding day to be perfect. But perfect isn't only about what I want. It's also what you want. Why don't we talk to his physical therapist and see if she has an idea of a timeline? Then, we can pick a date from there."

"Thank you."

"You don't have to thank me."

With my biggest concern addressed, we spend the rest of the drive sharing ideas for the wedding.

"I'd like to keep it simple and inexpensive."

"Money isn't an issue," Alex reminds me. "Whatever you want, we'll get."

When I was a little girl, I'd spend hours sitting on the floor in front of the magazine display at Dad's store. One by one, I'd go through every bridal magazine pretending it was me in one of the beautiful dresses. As an adult, my love of weddings hasn't changed. Now, instead of magazines, I use the internet to save pictures and wedding-themed ideas

"I don't want us to spend a fortune—"

"We get one chance at this. I want it to be everything you dreamed of and more."

He glances my way, a sexy smile on his face. Will there ever be a day this man won't cause me to feel like a school-girl with her crush? I certainly hope not.

"I've been wondering. Do you think Anthony would let us have the ceremony in his garden at the restaurant?"

"I'm sure he will. Once we have a date in mind, we'll give him a call to make the reservation. Have you thought about who you want in the wedding party?"

"Lana's my maid of honor." That's a forgone conclusion. "I'd like to ask Leo to be my man of honor. Would you be okay with that?"

"I couldn't see it any other way." Alex doesn't flinch at my non-traditional request. "Your parents might have some-thing to say about it, though."

"I'm sure they'll be shocked. But this is our wedding. They'll have to keep an open mind."

"Very open," Alex chuckles. "I've asked Brandon to be my best man, and I was thinking of asking Tony to be a groomsman."

"Two couples. That's perfect."

With the wedding party agreed on, I move to my next concern.

"Who's going to marry us?"

Neither of us subscribes to a particular religion, so having a minister wouldn't be a good fit.

"I have an idea about that," Alex says as he pulls into the rehab parking lot. "If you don't like it, we can come up with something else."

"What's your idea?"

"Viktor." He watches me carefully for a reaction.

"You want Viktor to marry us?"

"Yes. All he has to do is go online and fill out a registration."

Obviously, Alex has already thought this through.

"Do you think he'll do it?"

"I think he'd do anything for you."

Alex's face tightens. He gets out of the car and comes around to open my door.

"Are you jealous, Sir?"

"Insanely and irrationally."

I exit the car and smile at the alpha man standing next to me. "Let's ask him."

Hand-in-hand, we walk down the long hallway to dad's room. The door is shut, so I knock.

"Come in," Mom calls.

Alex steps aside, "You go first."

I push the door and walk in. A second later, Alex follows.

"Alex." Mom jumps up from her chair. "Does this mean you two are together again?"

Walking over to her, I kiss her cheek. "Yes, Mom. We're back together."

Mom brings her hands to her chest. "I'm so happy. Come here, Alex. Let me hug you."

Alex offers a warm smile before he wraps Mom in a hug. Dad sits on the bed, his eyes glimmering with excitement.

As I watch the scene unfurl before me, the progress we've made as a family shines clear. We've made great strides in our communication with one another. Instead of rushing to judgment, we've learned to listen with compassion. To try to understand the other's point of view. My parents don't always agree with my decisions. But instead of treating me like a child and fighting me at every turn, they've learned to respect my choices. As a result, we're a happy family for the first time in a very long time. That knowledge brings a smile to my face. Our family is finally functioning like the loving and supportive unit Michael and I wished for so many years ago. Yet, the pain of his death feels raw, as if he left only yesterday. Grief is a difficult process. It's something that really never ends. It just changes with time. How I wish Michael were here to experience our love.

Alex returns to my side and wraps his arm around my waist. "Are you okay, baby girl?"

With Alex by my side and my family in my life, I'm confident with my answer.

"I am."

Alex

WITH THE DISCHARGE PAPERS in hand, we prepare to leave the rehabilitation center. The sun shines bright, but a chill remains in the early spring air. I leave the Clarkes with Natalie while I get the car and pull it up to the main doors. Natalie pushes her father's wheelchair to the car while I open the front door. I try to help Stanley into the front seat, but he insists on sitting in the back with his wife. When we get them settled in, I fold his wheelchair and put it in the trunk before circling to the driver's side.

"Are we all set to go home?"

I never thought I'd say it, but the small country town and even its nosey residents have grown on me. It won't be our permanent residence, but our cottage in Northmeadow has become a comfortable second home.

"I've been ready for weeks," Stanley mutters.

He makes me laugh. Stanley's been pestering the doctors to discharge him for months. Although he initially seemed okay, he suffered quite a few setbacks. Stanley was readmitted to the ICU at one point because he developed pneumonia. The doctor's prognosis was grim, but the man is a fighter, and despite everything, he beat the odds. It's clear where Natalie gets her tenacity.

"Let's get on the road, then."

Almost as if on cue, Charlotte asks, "Have you two chosen a wedding date?"

Natalie and I look at each other and laugh. We took bets on how long it would take for the wedding questions to start. Looks like Natalie won this one.

"What's so funny? Can you blame me for being excited that you're finally getting married? Maybe I'll even get a grandchild."

"Mom." Natalie looks back at her mother.

I interrupt before that conversation gets out of hand. "I'd like to marry Natalie tomorrow. But we've decided to wait until Stanley can walk her down the aisle."

"I think that's a wonderful plan," Charlotte says, "In the meantime, Natalie and I can start planning the wedding. We'll need to go dress shopping, choose the colors, pick flowers, and decorations." She doesn't take a breath before continuing. "I'll call Reverend—"

"The wedding isn't going to be in Northmeadow," Natalie interrupts.

"What do you mean?"

Natalie looks at me with trepidation in her eyes.

"We're going to get married in New York," I say calmly. "We have a venue already chosen. I have pictures on my phone if you want to see them."

Anthony hired my firm to promote his restaurant and their new wedding venue. Our photographer sent me the shots the other day. The place looks incredible. Using the rearview mirror, I glance in the backseat. It's clear from the look on Charlotte's face she's struggling with her next move. I give her a few minutes to work things out for herself. I hope she'll tamper down her usually overbearing nature and allow Natalie the freedom to plan our wedding.

"That sounds like a great idea." Stanley jumps in. "All I need is a date, so I have a goal to work toward. There's nothing that can stop me from walking my little girl down the aisle."

"We wouldn't have it any other way. Let's talk with your physical therapist, and we'll set a date from there."

"That's fair, son," Stanley says, satisfied.

While I'm driving, I continue telling them more about the venue. "It's an Italian restaurant. They have a brand-new space in Manhattan."

"You're getting married in a restaurant?" Charlotte shrieks.

"Not exactly," I reply calmly. "Our friend, Anthony, owns the restaurant. Recently, he purchased a large outdoor space that he's transformed into an exclusive wedding venue. Natalie, will you pull up the pictures for your parents?"

She grabs my phone from the center console, opens the digital album, and hands the phone to her mom.

"What will the menu be?" Charlotte asks as she swipes through the pictures. "Will you get to sample the food?"

"Natalie and I have sampled Tony's food on several occasions." I chuckle. "How about I call him and see if I can arrange to fly him in so you and Stanley can taste it too?"

"You don't have to go through all that trouble for us."

"It's no trouble at all. Once we're settled at home, I'll give him a call and set something up."

"It's charming," Charlotte says, passing the phone back. "But it isn't a church. Will you at least have a minister?"

"We're asking a close friend to be the officiant," Natalie says calmly, leaving no room for argument.

"No church. No minister." Charlotte's voice grows in volume.

"Charlotte. Let's not let the little things put a wedge between Natalie and us again."

"Thank you, Dad." Natalie's voice is quiet. "Would you like to see some of the dresses I'm looking at, Mom?"

Six months ago, this conversation would've turned into a huge fight. But instead, my girl did a great job standing her ground yet staying calm. And now, she successfully changed the subject to something less controversial.

Charlotte passes my phone back to Natalie. "Yes, honey. I'd love to see them."

"I have a bunch saved on Pinterest," she says excitedly.

"What's a Pinterest?"

Natalie laughs. "It's like an online magazine."

She turns in her seat so she can see her mom. "You swipe just like when you're looking at pictures," Natalie explains as she passes her phone to her mom. "Obviously, I'm not paying for the designer price tag." She glances my way with a raised eyebrow. "But I'm hoping we can find something with a similar style to Grandma's dress."

For the remainder of the car ride, Natalie and her mom chat about planning a bridal shower, dress styles, wedding colors, flowers, and cakes.

Each time we make this drive, it feels longer than the one before. I'm thankful when I make the final turn and pull into the Clarke's driveway. I get out first to get the wheelchair. Natalie quickly follows me.

"Thank you for being so patient with mom. I know she can be a lot sometimes."

I reach out and cup her delicate face in my hand. "There's nothing I won't do for you, baby girl." I place a kiss on her forehead. "Let's get your parents inside so I can get you home."

"Yes, Sir." She turns to walk away, but not before I give her ass a quick swat making her giggle.

After I've helped Stanley into the chair, I wheel him up the newly installed ramp.

"This wasn't necessary," Stanley says quietly.

"It's not permanent," I reassure him.

As a man, I understand his reluctance to be dependent on others. It's a defeating feeling.

"You'll be on your feet in no time."

"Yes, I will." Stanley straightens his posture and holds his head high.

"Welcome home, Daddy," Natalie says as she opens the front door.

After months of recovery, her family is back in their home where they belong, and life can begin moving forward again.

Natalie

SPRING IS IN FULL bloom. Mother Nature has done her job of waking the natural world from its winter slumber. The early pink and white tree buds have been replaced with vibrant green leaves. In the wooded area surrounding our lake house, we've had the pleasure of watching newborn fawns, still with their spotted fur, ambling close to their mamas as they learn to navigate their new surroundings.

On the left side of our patio stands a magnificent oak tree that's now adorned with bird feeders. I set them up, hoping to lure in some of the lovely feathered creatures inhabiting the nearby lake. My efforts paid off. A family of bluebirds has taken up residence in the tree's shelter. Over the past weeks, the mother bird diligently brooded over her eggs, guarding and nurturing them until they finally hatched a week ago.

Each day, I watch her as she lovingly cares for her newborn hatchlings. Her vigilant male partner stands watch from afar, safeguarding her and the nest while she tirelessly tends to their young by feeding and nurturing them, prioritizing their well-being over her own. My heart swells with emotion at the sight of her devoted mate, bringing her small tokens of nourishment in the form of insects. As I watch this feathered family, I am startled when Alex quietly comes up behind me, wrapping his arms around my waist.

"Watching the birds again?"

"It's fascinating the way they care for their family."

Alex laughs softly, and I turn in his arms.

"Do you want children?"

We discussed birth control options at great length when we negotiated our contract. But other than one conversation in passing, we've never seriously discussed if or when we'd have children.

"Someday. But not right now." He pauses and searches my face. "Do you want a baby now?"

If someone had asked me that question a few years ago, I would've had an immediate answer. Yes, I want children—a lot of them.

Growing up, especially while Tommy and I were dating, I was surrounded by people who had similar dreams. My girlfriends and I planned to settle down with a boy from town and become mothers. During high school, I babysat as much as possible. I loved caring for newborns and playing with rambunctious toddlers. I figured it would give me the experience I'd need when I had my own children. Even though I dreamt of school and a career, children were always in the picture. Since I've been with Alex, I haven't given much thought to the question of children. Our relationship began as nothing more than a contract between a Dominant and submissive. It was agreed there was no room for children within that arrangement.

Everything is different now. We're still Dominant and submissive, but our relationship has evolved into more. We're in love and will be married. This is something we didn't talk about in our class. I'm not certain where the line begins and ends. We're still very much involved in a lifestyle in which I have no idea how to raise a child.

"I'd like a baby, maybe a few babies. Someday."

"Someday. That's good." He visibly relaxes. "Right now, I have some work I need to catch up on before your parents get here." He pushes a wayward strand of hair behind my ear before leaning in and kissing me.

"I'm going to watch the birds for a while longer. Then I'll be in to start dinner."

"I'll be in my office if you need anything," he says, flashing his sexy smile.

Standing outside, I get lost in a daydream about *someday.*

A day when Alex and I are happily married. He beams with pride and love while holding our newborn baby in his arms. The smile on my face falters when I think about Alex's reaction.

Someday doesn't mean soon.

And with that, I leave my daydream behind and head into the kitchen to prepare dinner.

Babies once again infiltrate my thoughts while I'm chopping vegetables for the salad. How does a couple have a child while they're focused on their Dom/sub relationship? So much of our daily life is wrapped up in the lifestyle. Would we have to hide it or stop it completely? I don't know how we'd adapt if such a big part of our identity as a couple was suddenly gone.

Then I think about how busy my life is right now. Since Dad can't work and Mom has to care for him, I've taken on the responsibility of managing the pharmacy. The first thing I did was close for a week while we updated and rearranged the store's layout. Without Dad, we had no pharmacist, so I hired two recent pharmacy graduates, Donna and Reuben. Mrs. Smith has agreed to stay on and helps oversee a few of the high school students I hired to work part-time after school. Until I can hire someone to manage the store, I have to work a few hours every day.

Alex worked his magic on some simple marketing ideas. We now have a fresh look both inside and out. Despite some initial resistance from my parents, Clarke's Pharmacy also carries souvenirs and other items tourists are always looking for. It's been a big transition, but business is steadily picking up.

My parents are like a full-time job all by themselves. I had hoped things would settle down once they returned home, but that hasn't been the case. In fact, life has become even more chaotic. What used to be weekend trips to Branson has transformed into daily trips to assist Mom with household chores or take Dad to various appointments. I'm grateful to have Alex by my side. He's always more than willing to lend a hand whenever possible.

Dad's a physical therapy rock star. In the month he's been home, he's gone from being totally wheelchair-bound to being able to walk short distances with his walker. Alex and I spoke to his physical therapist, hoping she had a timeline for when she thinks Dad will walk independently. She felt a safe time frame would be about a year. Seeing Dad's accomplishments, I'm confident he'll be ready to walk me down the aisle for our wedding next spring.

Right now, the biggest obstacle Dad has to overcome is himself. He's always been a proud, self-sufficient man who provided for his family. But since the shooting, he's had to rely on Mom, Alex, or me for nearly everything. Dad refuses to go anywhere other than the doctor. His rationale, he doesn't want anyone to see him in *this condition.*

The knife slips, and I nearly cut myself. There's no room in your life for a baby right now, maybe ever. That's a reality I have to face, but not right now. What I need to focus on is dinner. My parents will be here in a few hours. It's taken weeks of begging, but I finally convinced Dad to let Mom bring him over. Neither of them has been here yet. I'm excited to show my father the result of all his sneaking around with Alex.

After dinner, Mom's hoping we can start planning my bridal shower. I wanted it to be in the city, but she begged me to let her host it in Northmeadow. It's a concession I'm willing to make, especially since they aren't giving us a hard time about getting married in the city.

After cutting the salad ingredients, I toss them together in a bowl and stick them in the fridge to chill until later. Then I start assembling the lasagna. It's four-thirty, and the lasagna needs to cook for an hour. Mom and Dad said they'll be here about six, so I have plenty of time to get it in the oven and shower quickly.

After putting on clean clothes and make-up, I head down the hall and poke my head into Alex's office. "Are you almost done?"

Alex doesn't look up from his computer screen. "Mhm."

I walk over and wrap my arms around him. "Is everything okay, Sir?"

"Yeah, I think so," he says and lets out a deep breath. "There are some irregularities in the system I'm trying to figure out."

I rub his shoulders, trying to relieve some of the tension he's holding there.

"Irregularities?"

He grabs my arm and leads me around his body, pulling me onto his lap. Then, pointing at the screen, he says, "I received an alert. There was a failed attempt to access my encrypted folders."

"Do you think it's something to worry about?"

"I don't think so." He continues to stare at his screen. "Probably an employee that tried to access the wrong file." He closes the laptop. "Dinner smells delicious."

"Thank you." His compliment fills me with pride. "My parents will be here any minute."

"What time is it?"

"It's almost six."

"Damn," he says and helps me to my feet. "I didn't intend to be in here so long."

"It's okay. I have everything under control."

The doorbell rings, interrupting our conversation.

"I'll get it. I'm sure Charlotte's going to need help with the wheelchair."

While Alex answers the door, I go back to the kitchen to finish dinner. I'm setting the table when Mom comes into the room. "Natalie," she gushes. "Your home is beautiful."

"Thank you." I stop to hug her. "Alex did a great job with it."

"Don't forget I helped," Dad chimes in.

"Daddy." I throw my arms around him. "I'm so happy you're both here."

"So are we," Dad says. "I hope dinner's ready. I'm starving."

"I'm just about to take it out of the oven."

Grabbing oven mitts, I carefully remove the steaming tray and set it on the stovetop.

"Please, make yourselves at home." Alex holds up a bottle of Merlot. "Can I interest anyone in a glass?"

"I guess it couldn't hurt to have a little taste," Mom says, shocking all of us. "It's a very special occasion, after all."

Alex fills the glasses while I put the food on the table. Then, we sit down and have our first family dinner in our cottage. Looking around the table, I realize how lucky we are to be together. It wasn't that long ago that my parents refused to accept Alex. Then Dad got shot, and Alex and I broke up. This past year has been hell. But thankfully, we've come out the other side and can look forward to what this next year will bring.

"I'm thinking of a late summer bridal shower," Mom says between bites.

"That'd be great. We have a lot of out-of-town guests that'll need time to make travel arrangements."

"My dad and his girlfriend are planning on flying in as well," Alex adds.

I adore Sam Montgomery and his sub, Luna. The week after Dad was released from the hospital, Alex insisted I needed a break. He conspired with my parents and hired an in-home nurse to stay with them. Then he booked plane tickets for us to fly to Seattle to spend a long weekend with Sam and Luna. Even though we'd spoken on video chats,

I was nervous about meeting them in person, especially Luna. She's a free spirit, kind of a hippie. I've never met anyone like her.

Alex and Luna have a friendly relationship. He respects her and her place in his dad's life, but she's not his mom. Luna respects that and has never tried to take her place. Alex doesn't talk about her much, and I assumed they weren't close. So, I wasn't sure where that put me as far as a relationship with her. Was I okay to consider her my future mother-in-law, or would that be disrespectful to Alex's mom? He and I talked a lot about it before we flew out. He gave me his blessing to develop my relationship with her, to let it naturally become whatever it's meant to be.

I was shocked to learn Luna isn't her given name. It's actually Esther. Luna is the name she chose when she was in her early twenties. That's when she decided to leave conventional life behind, trading it for a more bohemian lifestyle. She embraced a vegan lifestyle and studied natural medicine. While we were there, she gave me some supplements to aid my dad's recovery.

Luna and I have similar backgrounds. She also comes from a very conservative, religious family in a small town. That commonality helped us form an instant connection. Being around her, it's hard not to be affected by her peaceful soul. She's become a treasured friend. Since our trip, she and I try to talk at least once a week. Luna understands where I'm coming from and has been a help with balancing both parts of my life. I'm excited knowing they're coming in for our shower.

Alex's phone rings. "I need to take this."

He excuses himself from the table and quickly makes his way to his office, closing the door.

"Let me clean off the table. Then I'll get my notebook so we can go over the guest list."

"Is everything okay?" Dad asks.

"There's a small issue at his office."

"I hope it's nothing serious," Mom adds.

"I don't think so." But, even as I say the words, a small voice inside tells me it's more serious than it appears. "I'm going to grab the notebook. "I'll be right back."

The notebook's in Alex's office. From outside the door, I hear his raised voice. Not wanting to interrupt, I knock and wait for a reply.

"Come in," he calls sharply.

"I'm sorry to interrupt. I just need to grab something."

"Hold on a minute, Viktor." Alex lowers the phone from his ear. "I have to fly out to New York tomorrow."

"Why?"

"Something's going on in the office. I need to be there to get to the bottom of it."

This news shouldn't come as a surprise. We both knew there'd be times he'd have to fly back and forth, but I didn't think it would be this soon.

"I'd prefer if you came with me."

His face is serious, leaving little room for argument, but I proceed anyway.

"I can't leave. I have to oversee the pharmacy, and my parents aren't ready to be alone yet."

"I'll hire an in-home aide."

"You're kidding, right." I cross my arms.

That was okay for the weekend, but going back to New York will be longer than a few days. I know my parents, and they aren't going to be comfortable having a stranger in their home for a longer-term stay.

"Natalie—" Alex issues a warning.

This isn't a topic I plan to give in on. The fact he's exerting himself as my Dominant right now has me frustrated. I swipe my notebook from the desk.

"Can we talk about this later, Sir?" The words leave my lips harsher than I intend.

The look on his face tells me I've overstepped and I'll have consequences later. "I have to finish this call."

There's more I want to say, but I'm already in trouble, so I do the smart thing and walk out of the office. Closing the door, I lean against it, holding the notebook against my chest. Alex is worried about whatever is happening within his company, but that doesn't give him the right to nearly demand I go with him to New York. Or does it? He's my Dominant, and I understand that, but I'd like him to at least listen to my concerns and take them into account before he goes all caveman on me. Now's not the time to worry. My parents don't need to be stressed about it, so after taking a few calming breaths, I put a smile on my face and walk back into the kitchen.

"Got it." I hold up the notebook.

"Oh, good." Mom reaches for it. "Let's get started on the fun stuff."

While Mom flips through a few pages, I make everyone a cup of coffee. Mom and I are squabbling over the guest list when Alex returns to the kitchen.

"Everything okay, son?"

"What did I miss here?" Alex avoids the question, taking his seat next to me.

"Mom just finished showing me her guest list for the shower. I'm trying to tell her there are too many people."

"We can have as many people as she'd like."

Seeing as she's won this battle, Mom smiles proudly.

"Now, let's look at your list." When she turns the page, her eyes grow wide. "Natalie, a bridal shower is for women." She points to the page. "You have men's names on here."

"We're planning a co-ed bridal shower."

"Co-ed?"

My patience is running thin. "Co-ed, as in both men and women."

Mom stares at me. Her mouth hangs open.

"Times are changing, Charlotte." Dad pats her hand.

"I guess so."

"How about we move on to the food." Alex pulls a menu from the back of the notebook, handing it to Mom. "Anthony has graciously offered to cater the bridal shower for us."

"We talked to him about having a tasting," I add. "He and Leo are going to come in for the July Fourth holiday. We'll have a party and tasting all in one."

It's been months since I've seen Leo in person. Of course, we keep in touch through video chats, but it isn't the same.

"Who's Leo?" Mom asks.

I look at Alex knowing this might not go over well.

"Leo is Anthony's partner."

"Oh, Leo's a chef too."

Alex chuckles. "No, not his business partner. Leo's Anthony's fiancé, soon-to-be husband."

The color drains from Mom's face. "He's gay?" Her voice is hushed.

"Yes, Mom. He's gay."

Alex senses my frustration and squeezes my leg under the table, letting me know I need to relax.

"We love them both, so please try to keep an open mind."

"I'm trying." Mom takes the last sip of wine from her glass before raising it. "May I have a refill?"

Her question makes us all laugh, breaking the tension.

"Of course." Alex doesn't miss a beat and pours her another glass of merlot.

We all watch in silence as she takes a big drink. When she realizes we're staring, she sets her glass down and shrugs.

Alex steers the topic away from Tony and Leo's relationship and back to our food choices. Once we decide on the menu, he takes a picture of the list and texts Tony.

"I think it's time we head home." Dad yawns. "It's almost eleven, and I'm pretty tired."

"I'm sorry. I didn't even look at the time."

"Don't apologize, sweetheart. I've enjoyed myself tonight."

Mom gathers their things, including the container of lasagna I made for them to bring home. I try to make extra of all our meals so she doesn't have to worry about cooking. Between the ladies from church and me, they have a freezer full of pre-prepared meals.

"Thank you both for coming," Alex shakes Dad's hand and hugs mom. "Drive safely, Charlotte."

"Thanks for having us."

"Call me when you get home." Now I sound like the parent.

"We will."

Alex steps back and wraps his arm around me as we watch my parents drive away.

Alex

ONCE HER PARENTS' CAR is out of sight, I lead Natalie back into the house. There's an unsettled matter of her coming to New York with me to discuss.

"Viktor booked plane tickets. We leave tomorrow."

"I'm not going to New York right now."

"You aren't staying here alone."

"Tommy's in jail. There's no danger."

"I'm not taking any chances."

"What happened to talking things through?"

I walk over to her and place my hands on her shoulders. "Where your safety is concerned, there's no conversation."

"Can we come to some sort of a compromise, Sir?"

I drop my hands and walk over to the window overlooking the lake. Natalie's right, I know she is, but my overprotective nature doesn't want to compromise. My rational self realizes Tommy isn't a threat, but what if something else happens? I'm not leaving her behind. I refuse to risk losing her again. But if I force this, am I going to do precisely what I'm trying to avoid? So instead of pressing the issue, I relent.

"I shouldn't be more than a few weeks. Viktor will stay with you while I'm gone."

When I bought this cottage, I also purchased the one right next door. Viktor lives there and can monitor our security system while giving us privacy.

Natalie comes up behind me and wraps her slender arms around my waist.

"Thank you, Sir."

I reach my arm around her, bringing her to my front and holding her close.

"Now, there's this little matter of your attitude earlier this evening."

She smiles and bats her eyelashes.

"I don't know what you mean, Sir."

"You have one minute. After that, I expect you to be naked and on the bed, waiting for me."

Giggling, she hurries to our bedroom.

Natalie looks beautiful. She's laid out before me with her arms bound over her head and her legs spread and re-strained to the bed. Since this is our last night together for a few weeks, I plan to make it one she won't forget anytime soon. She watches me as I walk around the bed silently, examining her body from all angles. Her face gives away her curiosity. She's dying to know what her punishment is. But I'm not ready to let her know yet.

Leaving her in the bedroom, I go to the kitchen for a glass of water. The ice cubes will prove useful for what I have in mind. When I return, Natalie lifts her head and bites her lip. I return her stare with a smile, take a drink, and put the glass on the nightstand before sitting beside her. Leaning over with the ice cube between my teeth, I tease her nipple. Natalie gasps from the cold.

I trail the melting cube lightly down the valley between her breasts, over her toned abdomen, and down to her bare pussy. She squirms from the contact, but I hold her waist, steadying her. The ice cube makes contact with her clit, heightening her responsiveness. While the ice melts, I add two fingers, sliding them in and out. She's wet and panting, climbing closer and closer to an orgasm. Then, I pull my fingers out.

"Why did you stop? I was so close."

Bringing my fingers to my mouth, I suck each one, tasting her arousal before answering, "I know."

Without further explanation, I release her wrists and ankles from their bondage.

She sits up. "What are you doing?"

"I'm going to my office. I told Viktor I'd call him after your parents left." I make my way to the bedroom door. "You are not to touch yourself."

Natalie blows out a frustrated breath. Without another word, I leave the bedroom and head to my office. This punishment will remind her to keep her attitude in check when we're having a conversation. What she doesn't know is I don't intend to let the night go by without giving her multiple orgasms.

I call Viktor, who assures me he's checked into the access attempts.

"They all came from an IP address inside the company," he explains.

"I'm glad it's not an outside threat, but I'm going to need to get to the bottom of it when I get to New York."

Taking a few more minutes, I email Brandon, making him aware of the potential in-office issues. He's in the office every day while I'm in Missouri. I want him to investigate this and give me a report when I get there tomorrow. If something is going on, I want to know about it.

It's no surprise that Natalie is sound asleep when I get back to the bedroom. Time to wake up my submissive. After I strip my clothes and climb into bed, I return to my earlier mission of feasting between her legs. My tongue flicks her clit, waking her. The rest of the night is spent giving each other pleasure over and over until we're both exhausted, and she falls asleep in my arms.

Natalie

LEANING AGAINST OUR PARKED car, my heart aches as I watch Alex disappear inside the airport. I know this won't be like last time, but that doesn't stop my tears. Using the back of my hand, I wipe my face.

"Chin up," Viktor nudges my shoulder. "I'm still here."

"Just like old times." I smile sadly at the man who's seen me through so many hard times.

"Come on. Let's grab some lunch."

"Can we stop by the store first? I need to check in."

Mrs. Smith is working today. She has experience, but the majority of the employees are still new. I'm usually there for at least a few hours a day to ensure everyone is properly trained and the store runs the way it should. Once Dad's on his feet, he and Mom can take over. But for now, that responsibility falls on me.

"No problem," Viktor says when we return to the car. "First the store, then food."

"Hungry?" I don't know why I ask. I already know the answer.

"Always." He grins.

While Viktor drives into town, I sulk in the passenger seat. Alex has only been gone for a few minutes, but I already miss him like crazy.

Alex spent all morning reassuring me this would be a short trip, a few weeks at most. That the attempts at accessing the encrypted files were just an employee accidentally trying to get into the wrong file. An innocent mistake. As much as I want to believe him, I saw the stress on his face. There's more to the story that he's not telling me.

"Do you know what's going on with Alex's company?"

Viktor tenses. "Yes."

"Will you tell me?"

"No."

I roll my eyes and look out the window.

"Can you just tell me if it's serious?"

I know I shouldn't push. I should trust Alex instead of trying to extract information from Viktor, but I can't help myself. I don't particularly appreciate being kept in the dark. If there's something serious going on, I want to know.

"What did Alex tell you?"

"Just that an employee tried to access his encrypted files." I shift in my seat to look at Viktor. "But that it was only an accident, possibly from one of the new hires."

"Then that's all you need to know."

"There's more, though, I can tell." I continue to pry.

"Natalie." He shoots a glare in my direction. "If Alex wanted you to know more, he would've told you himself. You need to stop. Now."

"Fine." I cross my arms and return to staring out the window.

We remain silent for the rest of the ride into town, an uncomfortable tension between us. It's my fault. I pushed too hard, again.

Viktor pulls into the pharmacy's parking lot and turns the car off. Neither of us makes a move to get out.

"I'm sorry."

"I forgive you," Viktor says, his features softening. "Alex will tell you what you need to know and when. You need to trust him."

"I know. I'm trying." I open the car door and get out. "Are you coming in with me?"

"I'm right behind you."

Knowing Viktor has my back is a comforting thought. At nearly six and a half feet tall, he's an imposing solid wall of muscle. His build, combined with his shaved head and Russian-sounding accent, tends to intimidate most people. If they only knew what a teddy bear he really is, his status as my bodyguard would be useless. I'll never let that secret out. I quite enjoy seeing people scurry when he comes their way. Viktor takes a step ahead of me so he can grab the door. Always a gentleman.

"Good afternoon, Mrs. Smith," I say with a big smile. "How's everything today?"

"Running smoothly," she answers without looking up.

She finishes with her customer before looking at me. Her body tenses when she notices Viktor behind me. Mrs. Smith has made it perfectly clear she is not a Viktor fan.

"How are the new managers working out?"

"Very well." She looks over my shoulder. "Alex is gone again, I take it?" she asks, her eyebrows pinched.

I pretend I don't hear her prying question or see the disdain on her face and walk away. I didn't come here to engage with Mrs. Smith. Just seeing me with Viktor gives her enough ammunition to start the rumor mill turning.

I've heard it all since we've been here. Whispers about me living with two men. That something's going on between the three of us. Honestly, the stories they come up with make me laugh. The opinions of the people in town no longer matter to me. Let them think what they may.

"I'll never understand these people," Viktor mumbles as we walk to the back of the store.

"I quit trying to figure them out," I reply, shrugging my shoulders.

When we get to the pharmacy area, there's a small line. Reuben, our newest pharmacist, is working the register.

"Good afternoon, Ms. Clarke." He offers me a cheery smile.

"How's everything going? Looks busy today."

"It's been steady all day."

"Do you need help out here?" I have no problem jumping on the other register to give him a hand.

"Nope. I'm enjoying meeting all our customers." He glances at Viktor. "Good afternoon, Mr. V."

Keeping up his tough-guy exterior, Viktor crosses his arms and nods. I bite my lip to keep from laughing.

"I'll catch up with you when you're not as busy."

Using my key, I unlock the door leading to the pharmacy area. Donna's back is to us. She appears to be concentrating on the prescription she's filling.

"Hi." I come up behind her.

She jumps and drops the pill bottle in her hand.

"I'm sorry. I didn't mean to scare you."

"It's okay." She laughs nervously. "I didn't hear the door open." When Donna sees Viktor, her eyes light up. "Hi. I mean, hello, Viktor." She stumbles over her words.

Women are constantly falling all over themselves to get Viktor's attention. But at least when he's with me, he's all business and doesn't indulge their attempts.

"I'm just checking in. How's Reuben doing?"

He looks pretty engaging with the customers. Donna started a few weeks before him, so I'm interested in her opinion.

"He's easy to work with, and as you can see, the customers love him," Donna replies. "I think he's a good fit."

A sense of relief washes over me. Once Reuben's fully trained, he'll be the pharmacist for the night shift. That will ease Donna's schedule and allow us to have the pharmacy counter open for longer hours. It's one step closer to getting the store back to being fully functioning. Aside from Dad getting back on his feet, the store running seamlessly is my biggest concern. My new managers need to be able to handle everything on their own, with minimal help from my parents, before Alex and I can move back to the city.

"How are the new part-timers working out?"

"The kids are doing great," Reuben says, joining the conversation. "Mary really stands out."

"I agree," Donna adds. "She'd make a great assistant manager after she graduates."

A few months back, Billy, Mary's older brother, came into the pharmacy looking for me. He explained that things didn't go well for Mary after she talked to her parents. Something that unfortunately didn't come as a surprise to either of us. Thankfully, Billy and his now-husband, Todd, were prepared. They had a bedroom ready and waiting to welcome Mary into their home. Although her parents' reaction wasn't unexpected, Mary was struggling with it, so Billy sought me out. He wanted to see if I'd be willing to talk with his sister. I knew it'd be walking a fine line, but I agreed.

I invited Mary to spend an afternoon with me at the cottage. She didn't need a therapist as much as she needed a friend. And that I could be. It also allowed me to offer her a part-time job at the store while she finished the last few months of high school.

"I'm not sure what her plans are after graduation, but I'll talk to her about it." I put a reminder in my phone.

She and I have kept in touch, and I know she's considering leaving Northmeadow for a bigger city. That's nothing they need to know about, though. If she decides to stay, I'd love to offer her the promotion.

"Tourist season will start with the Memorial Day holiday in a few weeks." I return to my original plan for this visit. "We've been doing a lot of advertising with the rental companies and other businesses by the lake. I'm hoping it draws more customers into the store. Do you feel prepared for an increase in customers?"

"Yes, we are," Donna answers quickly.

Her confidence inspires me. "I'm glad to hear that."

We take a few minutes to review the inventory order forms, cross-referencing them with our sales figures to ensure accuracy. Though it can be tedious, it's important that Donna and Reuben can confidently perform this task when I'm not present. As we pore over the paperwork, Viktor remains by our side, silently observing. Catching his eye, I signal that I'll wrap up soon. Once we've completed our review, I pass the documents back to Donna. "If you guys don't need anything else, I'm going to head out. Keep up the great work."

Viktor opens the pharmacy door allowing me to exit first. Donna and Reuben stay behind, whispering about the 'scary, but oh so hot man' that's accompanying me.

"We can hear you," I say and laugh as we keep walking.

Donna and Reuben giggle. Both of them have expressed an interest in my bodyguard, but I'm not in the habit of playing matchmaker.

"Ready for lunch?" I ask.

"I thought you'd never ask."

Viktor and I take advantage of the beautiful spring day and walk the few blocks to the diner.

Alex

IT'S BEEN ALMOST THREE weeks since I left Northmeadow and returned to New York City. Part of me missed the constant hustle and bustle the city offers. The other part longs to be back in my quiet cottage, hidden away from everything with Natalie. For the time being, my presence is needed in the office. Brandon's done a great job gathering information for me. Since I've been here, I've been paying attention to the office gossip channels. It's incredible what a person can learn hanging around the break room. It seems there are a few upper-level executives who've taken advantage of my extended absence.

Two of my employees have decided to branch out and start their own business, a move I usually applaud. Instead of going about it in a professional manner, they chose to access my personal files trying to lure my clients to their firm. Unfortunately, they gave their plan away when they tried to access the encrypted files. Now, more than ever, I'm thankful Brandon, and I work together. He had no experience in advertising, but that was easily taught. What was more important to me was having someone I could trust implicitly by my side.

As we went about business as usual, we waited and watched. Our patience paid off because now we have enough evidence to expose the guilty parties. Brandon and I are meeting outside the office tonight to formalize our next step. I plan to send a strong message to the two offenders and the rest of my employees not to fuck with my company or me.

While there seems to be nothing more nefarious going on, I'm not letting my guard down. The information in those files is too important to risk. I contacted Dimitri, the head of Maxim's tech team. He sent an upgrade for the security on my computer system. While I'm waiting for the update to finish, my cell rings. I'm hoping it's Natalie, but when I pick it up, I see it's my father.

"Dad. How are you?"

"I'm doing well. How's Natalie? Is she there so we can say hi?"

Dad and Luna fell in love with Natalie when we visited. Whenever he calls, he always asks to talk to her first.

"What happened to *how are you, Alex?*" I laugh.

Dad joins me in laughing. "Hi, Alex. How are you? Where's Natalie so we can say hi to her?"

"I'm doing okay. Natalie isn't with me right now."

"Where are you?"

"I'm in New York." The update finishes, and I close my laptop. "There's an issue in the office."

Because of his friendship with Maxim, my father is aware of the work we do together. I suspect he's more involved than he lets on and that he at least has his hand in the financials, but some things are better left unsaid.

"What kind of an issue? And why didn't Natalie go with you?"

"A few employees attempted to access my files, trying to poach my clients. I needed to be here to handle it in person. I knew it would take a few weeks, at least. Natalie didn't want to leave an aide with her parents that long so she stayed behind with Viktor."

"Are you sure there's nothing more to this?" The concern in his voice is evident.

"We thoroughly checked it out. The IP addresses were from in the office."

Having that reassurance coupled with the evidence on my desk, I'm confident it's nothing more. I don't want to discuss this topic any longer, so I shift the conversation to wedding planning.

"We have a date for the shower and the wedding."

"Wait a minute. Let me get Luna." Dad covers the phone and calls his submissive into the room with him. "You're on speaker now."

"Hi, Luna. How are you?"

"I'm well. How are you and Natalie?"

"We're doing good. We decided on a date for the bridal shower. August nineteenth, the day after Natalie's birthday."

"That's the hope. And the wedding is set for May seventeenth."

The physical therapist is confident Stanley will be on his feet in plenty of time.

"I wish we could see you before then." Dad sighs. "August seems so far away."

"Tony and Leo are coming in for the July Fourth holiday. We'd love it if you'd come in too."

"I'll book our plane tickets right now." Dad's excitement is palpable even through the phone.

After we hang up, I call Natalie to let her know we're getting more company for the holiday.

It's a balmy June evening as I walk down the sidewalk to the familiar corner bar a few blocks from my apartment. It's Thursday, so there isn't a large crowd. Looking around, I spot Brandon sitting at our usual table in the back corner. I walk across the small, dimly lit room, ignoring the whispers from a group of women standing by the bar.

"Looks like you've attracted some attention." Brandon laughs.

"Lucky me," I answer wryly.

Brandon waves, signaling the bartender, who comes over and drops off two cold beers.

"You look like shit."

"Thanks for the compliment." I take a long drink from the bottle.

"We have everything needed for tomorrow's meeting."

"I can't wait to see the look on those bastard's faces," Brandon says. "They aren't going to know what's hit them."

"That's the plan."

Over the course of the next hour, we have a few more drinks, and I fill him in on my plan for the meeting. I'm not taking the chance of someone figuring out that Brandon and I are on to them, which is why we're meeting at a bar instead of my office.

"We'll have our typical Friday wrap-up. While we're in the meeting, a scheduled email will be sent to my advertising contacts. The guilty parties won't have a chance to undermine us. They'll never find another job in this town—or any other once I'm done."

"Justice will be served." Brandon raises his bottle in a toast. "Lana tells me the wedding plans are moving along nicely."

"They are." With the change of subject, the tension drains from my body. "The bridal shower's in August and the wedding in May."

"Tony told Lana they'll be in Northmeadow for July Fourth." Brandon raises an eyebrow.

"He's coming to do a tasting for Natalie's parents. Kind of a concession for the wedding being here."

"That ought to be interesting."

"Dad and Luna are flying in. You and Lana should come too."

Brandon laughs. "This get-together is something I have to see. We'll be there."

For Natalie's sake, I'm hoping the holiday won't be the circus Brandon's expecting.

It's gotten late. We finish the last of our beers, pay our tab, and walk out together.

"Thanks, Bran." I clasp his shoulder. "I needed a distraction tonight."

His ride pulls up to the curb. "Get a good night's sleep. You're going to need it tomorrow."

I take a slow walk back to my apartment. It's late and, at least in this section of town, quiet.

Tomorrow I'll rectify the situation at work and take the first flight back to Natalie.

Natalie

TODAY MARKS A SIGNIFICANT milestone in Dad's physical therapy journey. He's preparing to overcome a final hurdle - venturing out in public. Despite everyone's relentless efforts, he's been apprehensive about going out in public with his walker. His therapist has decided that the time has come. We've arranged to meet her at a small park in town so he can practice walking outside. This exercise will not only put his physical abilities to the test but will also be a mental challenge for him.

Viktor helps me get Dad into the car. He's unfazed despite my father's constant mumbling and grumbling. Dad's behaving like a toddler who's been denied their coveted lollipop from the store. I try to keep my distance, so I don't make anything worse. After safely stowing away his wheelchair and walker in the trunk, I make my way to the driver's door.

"I'm driving." Viktor tries to get to the door handle before I do.

"Not today." I laugh when I beat him there. "I promised Dad I'd drive. You get to sit in the back."

"You've got to be kidding." Viktor leans down and peeks into the backseat. "I'm not going to fit back there."

"It's a short drive," I say as I get behind the wheel.

Reluctantly, Viktor folds his large frame into the back-seat. Great, now I have two pouty men to contend with. Let them sulk. I plan to have a lovely afternoon at the park.

"Thank you for talking your mother into staying home," Dad says. "Too bad you couldn't get *him* to stay home too." He gestures with his thumb toward Viktor.

"You're welcome." I glance at Viktor in the rearview mirror. What I see makes me laugh.

Viktor's long legs are tightly bent. I'm pretty sure the lump in my back is his knee hitting my seat. I told him to stay home, but no way was that happening. I'm lucky I managed to drive. Returning my focus to my father, I say, "I still think you should've let Mom come."

"Maybe next time." He turns his head to look out the window.

"There's nothing to be ashamed of, Daddy." I place my hand on his shoulder.

"I'm not the man she married," he says quietly. "I can't do anything myself. I'm useless."

"Dad, that's enough." I don't like raising my voice, especially to my father, but something needs to snap him out of this self-pity. "What happened was a tragic accident. Yes, you need some help for now. But you're working hard and getting stronger every day."

He doesn't answer. Instead, he continues staring out the window, ignoring me for the rest of the ride.

The park is situated on the opposite side of town. During the latter part of the summer, local farmers set up an outdoor market. Today, the park is mostly empty except for a man walking his dog. "I'll get your walker."

Viktor beats me to it and has the walker by Dad's door before I'm barely out of the car. Opening Dad's door, I extend my hand.

"Ready?"

"No." But he accepts my help anyway.

After getting him situated with his walker, I look around for his therapist and spot her sitting on a bench a short distance away.

"You coming?" I ask Viktor.

"I'll wait here." He leans back against the car, crossing his arms.

Dad's therapist sees us and starts heading our way. We walk slowly, meeting her on the path.

"Hello there, Stanley," she chirps. "It's a beautiful day for a walk, isn't it?"

"I guess," Dad mumbles.

"Someone's grumpy today." She looks at me over Dad's shoulder.

I shrug, not knowing what to say or do.

"Why don't you hang out here while Stanley and I take a few laps around the park."

"No problem." I smile, glad to let her handle my grumpy parent. "I'll be at the car keeping Viktor company."

It's hard to watch my hero, my father, using a walker to steady himself while he slowly shuffles his feet. He's always been strong and able. Sadness grips my heart like a vice, knowing in one thoughtless, drug-fueled move, Tommy caused this.

"He's a fighter, like you." Viktor appears at my side.

I wave him off, hoping to stave off the tears threatening to fall.

"Dad's so stubborn sometimes."

"Explains where his daughter gets it from," he smirks.

"Shocking, isn't it?" We share a laugh and walk back to the car together. "Have you heard from Alex?" I ask as I pull out my phone. "There was a text when I woke up this morning. But when I tried calling him, it went straight to voicemail."

"Not since last night."

"I hope his meeting goes well today."

"I have no doubt he's handling it," Viktor says matter-of-factly.

Alex is probably busy, and I don't want to interrupt him with a phone call.

(Me) Sorry I missed you earlier. Good luck with your meeting today. i love You.

Alex

MY PHONE VIBRATES WITH a text from Natalie. I texted her early this morning, knowing she'd get it when she woke. I miss hearing her voice. We're both on different schedules and haven't talked since yesterday. She tried calling this morning after reading my text, but I was in a meeting with a new client and had to send her to voicemail.

(Me) I got your voicemail. I'm sorry I couldn't answer. I've been swamped all day. I love you too.

After I hit send, I slide my phone into my pocket. It's almost go time, and I need to keep my head in the game. At precisely four p.m., I send a reminder that the wrap-up meeting is in ten minutes. It's the usual course of events for a Friday, except this meeting will end with fireworks. Once everyone is comfortable in my conference room, my security team will take their place outside. Their task is to escort my soon-to-be-former employees out of the building. Powering off my laptop, I put it in my leather messenger bag and go through the door that leads from my office to the private conference room.

Within minutes, my employees stream in and sit around the expansive glass-topped table. Several employees stop to shake my hand as they pass by. Brandon's the last one in. He closes the door behind him before taking his spot on my right.

"If everyone can take their seats. I want to keep this short, so we can start our weekend early."

My employees settle in and give me their full attention.

"First, I'd like to congratulate Cameron and Morgan on signing two new clients to the agency this week."

A round of applause fills the room.

Once it's quiet again, I continue, "I want to thank Brandon for steering the ship while I was out of town. Everyone's done a great job keeping the day-to-day operations running seamlessly. I appreciate you all. I'll open the floor for any questions or concerns."

A few employees have concerns I'm able to address quickly and easily. "Anyone else?" I look around the room, but no one moves to speak. "I have one more thing, and then you can go." I smile. "It's come to my attention that several of your colleagues are branching out from Montgomery Advertising to start their own company."

It's not the first time I've had employees who possess an entrepreneurial spirit and work to start their own companies. It's a move I typically applaud and even give assistance with, so it's not surprising there are smiles around the table.

"Ben and Michelle, please make your way up here." I motion to the front of the room.

The pair rises from their seats with proud smiles. They've been fooled into thinking their efforts will be praised and offered the standard package I typically give. That makes what's about to happen even sweeter.

"These two employees came to my company fresh out of college. Over the years, they've worked hard and have achieved a remarkable amount of success." I pause, allowing them time to bask in their deceit. "Typically, I support employees taking the next step and opening their own company. But that isn't going to happen."

Their smiles fade as those words leave my lips. A hushed murmur emanates from their colleagues. I can sense that everyone is curious about why I'm unwilling to support Ben and Michelle. I have no intention of letting them off the hook. No one in my company will attempt to undermine me and get away with it. I stride towards the conference room door, yank it open, and summon the security team inside. The room falls silent, and a few employees shift uneasily in their seats.

With measured steps, I return to the head of the table. Brandon takes his place at my side—a united front.

"Ben and Michelle made the mistake of trying to steal my clients." I look at Ben, who refuses to make eye contact with me, and Michelle looks down. "Your personal belongings are waiting at reception. Security will escort you out of the building."

By taking this decisive action, I am confident that nobody else will dare to entertain the idea of undermining me. Scanning the room, it's clear that my employees are taken aback by my bold move. My message has been delivered loud and clear. The room remains quiet as the duo exits. As Ben walks past me, I hear him grumbling under his breath, while Michelle avoids eye contact and trails behind him towards the door. With my security team in tow, I watch as they leave the room and hear the door click shut. Turning to Brandon, I exchange a contented look, knowing that justice has been served.

It takes a minute for what happened to sink in and for the employees to relax. Then, a chorus of *no, sirs* echoes throughout the room.

"In that case, have a great weekend."

With that, everyone gathers their belongings and says their goodbyes on their way out.

"That went well," Brandon says once we're alone.

Sinking into my chair, I put my head back and close my eyes. "I'm just glad it's over."

"Lana's out with the girls tonight." Brandon puts the files in his bag. "I'll drive you to the airport."

"I appreciate that." I reach into my pocket and fish out my cell phone to text Natalie.

(Me) I'm just leaving for the airport. I'll be home in a few hours.

(Natalie) I can't wait to see you.

(Me) You better be well-rested. I don't plan on letting you get much sleep tonight.

(Natalie) I'm going for a nap now.

Viktor's at the terminal waiting for me at the small airport outside Northmeadow. I only had a carry-on bag, ensuring we make quick work of getting back to the car. There's no traffic at this late hour, so we make good time getting back home.

"Everything go okay today, boss?"

"It went exactly as I planned. They're no longer employed and won't work in the advertising world again."

"Dimitri gave me the rundown on the system update," Viktor explains. "I've also applied the same update to the systems at the lake."

Although it was only a pair of foolish individuals who believed they could destroy my business through theft, I find comfort in the fact that our security measures have been upgraded.

"Was Maxim apprised of the situation?"

"There's no need to alert him." My pulse quickens. Viktor knows better than to second-guess me.

"Sorry, boss. I'm just doing my job."

"Lose the *boss*, would you? And it's fine," I quip. "It was an internal issue, and it's been handled."

Viktor makes the final turn onto the narrow gravel road leading to the cottage. My body buzzes, knowing I'm only moments away from being with Natalie. I hate these separations. Next time I go to the city, she'll be by my side—we'll be going home together.

We both get out of the car, the beep signaling the doors are locked.

"Thank you for staying with her."

"My pleasure, *Alex*." He makes a point of stressing my name.

"It better not have been too much of a pleasure." I laugh, trying to ease some of the earlier tension between us.

Viktor's my right-hand man, and I trust him with my life. But, more importantly, I trust him with Natalie's life.

"Night, boss," Viktor says and walks toward his cabin.

I do what I've been waiting all day for. I go to my waiting sub.

Natalie

(**ALEX**) I'LL BE HOME in less than an hour. You're to be wearing something sexy and kneeling by the bed when I get home.

My pulse races with excitement. I don't waste a second taking a shower and fixing my hair. I choose to remain topless, only putting on sexy black lace panties. When I check the clock, I see forty-five minutes have passed. Alex should be here any second.

Right on cue, the sound of gravel crushing under the car's tires reaches my ears. I drop to my knees, placing my palms on my parted thighs, eagerly anticipating the arrival of my Dominant. I hear the front door open and shut, and he takes his time meandering through the house before heading in my direction. The measured and unhurried rhythm of his footsteps draws nearer to our bedroom door. As the doorknob turns, I lower my gaze. Out of the corner of my eye, I catch a glimpse of Alex placing his bag next to the dresser before he sits at the edge of the bed, his movements fluid as he removes his shoes and socks with relaxed ease.

Although he's yet to speak to me, I feel his intense stare taking in every inch of my body, which only heightens my arousal. I glance up and watch as he stands with his back to me and strips his clothes. His muscles flex with each step as he walks to the bathroom and leaves the door open. Alex turns the hot water on and steps into the shower. My nipples harden, and wetness pools between my legs as I watch him lather his body. My hands itch to be rubbing themselves over every inch of his skin. He steps under the hot water letting it rinse away the soap. Alex takes his time drying off before going to the dresser and slipping on a pair of boxers that hang low on his hips. I return my gaze to the floor, hoping he comes to me. The anticipation is driving me crazy.

Alex

I'VE BEEN AWAY FOR three weeks, and even though we've played over video chat, it's never the same as being here, able to run my hands over her soft skin and hear her mewls of pleasure. So, rather than rushing our reunion, as my erection encourages me to, I take my time. Patience is difficult for my submissive, and I know my silence is pushing Natalie's boundaries. But I'm not ready to show my hand yet. Walking past her, I go straight to our closet, where we store our toys. I grab the few things I want and return to the bedroom, where I set a step stool in front of where Natalie kneels.

During the house renovation, I had several suspension hooks strategically installed in our bedroom ceiling. Using the step stool, I carefully secure the swing. When I glance down at Natalie, I notice her biting her lower lip. She's beginning to sense what I have in store for her tonight. With no words exchanged, I retreat to the closet again and emerge with bundles of jute rope in various colors, which I lay on the bed behind her. Then, I pull up the playlist that Master Kiyoshi sent me, featuring soft sounds from a bamboo flute that Natalie would undoubtedly recognize from the night we met.

With sure steps, I move to my place before my sub.

"Remove your panties."

Natalie stands and hooks her fingers in the black lace, sliding them down her legs. I extend my hand, and she places the tiny piece of fabric in my palm. Bringing it to my face, I smell her arousal, a move that nearly forces me to abandon my original plan and sink into her wet heat right now. Tossing the panties onto the dresser, I take a minute to refocus. The past three weeks of separation have been stressful. I don't want to rush tonight. Natalie and I desperately need this time to reconnect. Taking a step closer to her, I trace the seam of her lips with my thumb before kissing her.

"You're so beautiful."

"Thank you, Sir."

"Lie down on the bed."

She spins around and lets out a tiny gasp when she spots the rope. "How do you want me, Sir?"

"On your back, baby girl."

She lies next to the rope, propping herself on her elbows. Then, she spreads her legs just enough so I can see her glistening arousal.

Taking one of her feet in my hands, I begin massaging it.

Her head falls back. "That feels so good."

My hands make their way up her leg as I continue rubbing her muscles. Then I repeat the action on her other leg. Natalie's body relaxes under my touch. "Ready for the rope?"

"Mhm."

Starting with the purple rope, I anchor it around her toe and proceed to wrap it around her foot. At the front of each loop, I create a lark's head knot to add to the beauty of the pattern. Continuing this action, I make an intricate design of wraps and hitches up the length of her leg. Afterward, I tie the rope off on the outside of her thigh and repeat the same pattern on her other leg. Before proceeding any further, I check in with her. "Color?"

"Green."

"I need you to stand." I take her by the hand and help her up.

Taking hold of the black rope, I start tying a chest harness. My ties tonight aren't about restraint. I planned this design to help Natalie unwind and relax into the sensation of the jute material gliding against her skin. Beginning below her breasts, I skillfully wrap the rope around her torso and loop it around the back, gently trailing it along her flesh. Next, I create an intricate crisscross pattern between her breasts before draping it over her shoulders to form a bikini-style harness. Stepping back, I take a moment to assess my handiwork. Despite my best efforts, the ties are not flawless, but that doesn't inhibit me from becoming aroused. Her breasts are held tight, and her nipples beg to be sucked. I adjust the erection, tenting my boxers.

"Come with me." I lead her to the front of the swing.

Placing my hands on her waist, I lift Natalie and help her settle into the reclined position of the swing. Then, I put her feet into the restraints keeping her legs spread and allowing me a view of her beautiful pussy. I drag my finger over her outer lips, teasing her. She whimpers when I take my finger away. Returning to the bed, I grab the last two bundles of pink rope. Setting it next to her, I take her arm, lift it above her head, and run a length of rope up her arm before making a loop and bringing it back to her wrist, tying off the strap on the swing. Then I repeat the process on her other arm. With her fully tied, I check in once more. "Color?"

"Very green, Sir."

Now the fun begins.

I circle the swing coming back to Natalie's spread legs and lick my lips. It's time for a taste. Kissing my way up her leg, I pause and blow gently on her. She tries to squirm, but with her arms and legs restrained, she has nowhere to go. "Hold still, baby girl."

I steady the swing and lick her long and slow before plunging my tongue inside her fucking her slowly while I rub gentle circles around her clit. She moans in response to my ministrations. With a final lick, I stand up, not wanting her to come yet. Leaving her on the swing, I walk back into the closet. This time I come out with the magic wand. I turn it on while I'm still behind her, allowing her to hear it before she sees it. "Do you want me to let you come, baby girl?" I whisper in her ear as I round the swing.

"Yes. Please, Sir."

I press the wand against her swollen clit. It only takes seconds before she's screaming in pleasure. Wave after wave pulses through her body, yet I don't move the wand.

"I can't."

"You can." I turn the wand up to its highest setting.

Natalie's orgasm explodes, and she writhes in pleasure. When I know she's had enough, I remove the wand and set it on the dresser. Then, I make quick work of stripping off my boxers. I'm harder than I think I've ever been as I approach the swing. Natalie lifts her head, watching me fist my erection. My hand rubs up and down. Pre-cum drips from the tip. Without wasting another second, I slide into her inch by slow inch, relishing her tight, wet warmth as it wraps around me. Once I'm fully sheathed, I stop. "I missed you so much." I caress her face. "Promise me that's the last time we'll be separated."

"I promise, Sir."

With her promise given, I begin to move. I alternate between sliding in and out and rolling my hips. Natalie comes two more times before I can no longer hold back.

"Come with me, baby girl." I rub her clit faster and harder, keeping pace with the increased speed of my thrusts. "Now."

Her body rhythmically squeezes my cock as I come inside her. The pleasure of our perfectly-timed orgasms is intense. "You're amazing," I say before I pull out slowly and go into the bathroom to get a warm washcloth to clean her off.

The act of unbinding is done with care. My movements are slow and steady as my hands gently caress her skin. I leave the ropes in the swing and lift Natalie, cradling her in my arms. She rests her head on my chest as I carry her to the bed. With one hand, I pull back the blankets and lay her down. I take her twice more before she's worn out.

Only then, knowing that the most important person in my life is safe in my arms, do I allow myself to drift to sleep

Natalie

"THEY'RE TEN MINUTES AWAY," I call to Alex, who's across the hall in his office, as I finish putting the finishing touches on our guest room for Tony and Leo. The sound of a car beeping sends my heart rate into overdrive—they're here! I put the last pillow on the bed and hurry to greet our guests at the front door. But Alex beats me to it and is already outside when I arrive.

"Pixie." Tony scoops me in a hug, lifting me from my feet.

"I can't believe you guys are here," I squeal.

"You can put my sub down any time now," Alex jokes.

"She's cute." Tony sets me down as Leo sidles up next to him, suitcases in hand. "But I brought my own sub with me."

"Leo." I squeeze him in a hug. "I can't believe you're here."

"I can't believe we're here either." He kisses my cheek and then looks around cautiously. "You really live in the middle of nowhere."

"Wait until nighttime. It gets so dark you can see all the stars," I say dreamily.

"And risk getting eaten by a wild animal." Leo shakes his head. "I'll take a pass."

Leo's a city boy through and through.

"Let's go inside. Natalie will show you to your room so you can get settled in."

I grab Alex's hand, squeezing tightly as we take our guests into our house.

"It's this way." I motion to Leo to follow me to their bedroom while Tony and Alex make their way into the kitchen.

"This place is gorgeous," Leo gushes. "Your pictures don't do it justice, girl."

"Alex has a great eye for design. I'll miss this place when we go back to the city."

We arrive at the door to the guestroom, and I step aside, letting Leo go in first.

"Look at that view," Leo drops the suitcases and heads straight for the windows that overlook the lake.

The azure blue sky is cloudless, and the temperature is mild. A gentle breeze has been blowing from the water, prompting me to leave my windows open to fully enjoy its benefits. It's the perfect summer afternoon.

I make my way to Leo's side.

"I've missed you. But I can see why you've been holed up here. Even I might be able to get used to this."

The idyllic scene mesmerizes us as we watch several boats bobbing on the water, the small waves rippling onto the rocky shore.

"You guys are welcome here anytime." I rest my head on Leo's chest, enjoying the familiarity of his company.

"Natalie. Leopold. We need you both out here," Alex calls.

"Coming."

"That sounds suspicious," Leo grins.

"It sure does. I wonder what's going on?"

"Let's go find out." Leo grabs my hand.

When we enter the living room, I'm surprised to see it's been transformed. The furniture is pushed to the side, and a black fleece blanket is spread out on the floor. Next to the blanket are candles, arranged by color. Alex and Anthony stand beside the candles, arms crossed over their chests—their dominance fills the empty space in the room. The hungry look in Alex's eyes takes my breath away.

"Go change." He hands me a pair of tiny shorts and a bra-like top.

"Yes, Sir."

With the clothes in hand, I hurry to our bedroom. I hear footsteps and look over my shoulder. Leo's right behind me, also carrying a pair of shorts.

"Looks like we're about to have some fun," Leo says before disappearing inside the guest room.

I make quick work of changing and somehow make it back to the living room before Leo. When he enters, he takes his place on his knees beside me.

Alex and I have never done a scene with another couple. Not knowing what he has planned fills me with nervous anticipation.

"Anthony has graciously offered to give us an early wedding present." Alex strokes my hair. "Are you willing to allow him to create a wax design on you?"

I want to squeal in delight but force myself to remain composed. Since the first night I visited Fire and Ice, I've been enthralled with Tony's art. Alex and I have played with wax in a sensual way, but Tony is a master of design. I'm honored he'll be creating a design on me.

"Yes, Sir. I'd love that."

"You and Leo will lie next to one another, and you will remain clothed." Alex raises an eyebrow.

Alex is territorial and possessive. From day one, he made it perfectly clear that he would never allow another man to touch or see me naked. Something I was thankful for.

"Leo, I want you on your stomach," Anthony instructs. "Pixie, lie on your back with your arm and leg against Leo's."

While we get into position, Anthony lights the candles. "Alex tells me you two have played with wax."

"Yes."

"My wax is similar in burn temperature to what you've used," Tony explains. "However, if you're uncomfortable in any way, you are to use your safewords. What are they?"

"Yellow and red."

"First, we're going to prepare your skin. It'll help with removing the wax later."

Alex kneels next to me, a bottle in his hand. He pours some oil into his palm before passing the bottle to Anthony, kneeling beside Leo. While Alex rubs the oil over my abdomen, he lowers his head, whispering what he plans to do with me later. His words, combined with his sensual touch, set my body on fire.

"Ready?" Anthony asks.

Alex brushes his knuckles across my cheek. "I'm ready."

"Let's have some fun." Anthony lifts the first candle, and chills run up and down my body, anticipating what's to come. "Your Dominant is going to be my assistant. I'm going to teach him how to be an artist."

His statement is followed by Alex's laughter. My Dominant might have an eye for design, but an artist, he is not. Anthony hands the dark green candle in his hand to Alex and instructs him where to drip the wax. Alex alternates between Leo and me, drizzling streams of wax across my abdomen. It feels pleasantly warm on my skin. I lift my head, trying to get a peek at the design they're creating.

"Head down," Alex instructs. "You'll see it when it's time."

"May I have a hint?"

"No." Both men say in unison. I blow out a frustrated breath.

"Patience, little pixie. Relax and enjoy this."

Following my instructions, I shut my eyes and surrender myself to the various sensations. The initial warmth of the wax as it touches my skin, followed by its swift cooling and solidifying. Lost in this dreamlike state, I don't know how much time has passed until Anthony's voice jolts me back to reality. "It's done." My eyelids are heavy. I have to blink a few times before they cooperate and remain open. Turning my head, I see Leo having the same struggle. "Alex, can you grab the black light from my bag?"

Alex rummages through the duffle while Tony pulls the black-out curtains closed. The room is bathed in darkness. I lift my head slightly, hoping to get a glimpse of the design. I gasp when I see the wax glowing.

"Shh," Anthony admonishes me.

I feel a twinge of guilt for disobeying and trying to peek—again. Tonight, Anthony's gifting Alex and me something extraordinary, and I don't want my impatience to spoil the grand gesture. As a submissive, I know that cultivating patience is essential, and I need to work on it.

As Leo and I lie covered in the luminous wax, Alex reaches for his camera and starts snapping pictures from different perspectives, the sound of the shutter clicking filling the air.

"I think I got enough," Alex says as he scrolls through the pictures.

"It's time to lift the wax. Hopefully, we can get it off in one piece."

Our Dominants return to our sides on the floor.

"You look gorgeous covered in so many colors, baby girl." Lust swirls in Alex's blue eyes.

The men work together to remove the design. The oil underneath helps their efforts, and they remove the wax with minimal cracking. Then, they set it carefully on our dining table. Alex offers his hand and helps me to a seated position. My body is a little stiff from lying still so long. He notices right away and gently rubs my arms and legs before helping me to stand.

"Ready to see it?"

"I'm so ready." The double meaning behind my words isn't lost on Alex.

He places his hand on the small of my back and leads me to the table. What I see there is beyond anything I imagined. Together the men created a colorful meadow of flowers. The design flows until it turns into the shimmering turquoise water of the lake. It's all set to the backdrop of a purple and pink sky depicting the sunset over the lake.

"Is that glitter?" I ask and run my finger gently over the wax that makes up the water.

"It is. Do you like it?" Tony asks.

"Like it? It's the most beautiful thing I've ever seen." I kiss his cheek. "Thank you so much. I'll treasure this always."

"I have a custom frame for it in the car. Leo and I will arrange it in the frame for you before we leave."

Alex clasps Tony's shoulder. "Thank you. This means a lot to both Natalie and me."

"It's my pleasure," he says before turning to Leo and me. "You two go get cleaned up so we can eat."

Leo and I make our way back to the bedrooms. He follows me into my room so I can wash the oil from his back before he goes to his room to get dressed.

I'm in the bathroom with the water running when I hear the door open again.

"Did you forget something?" I call over my shoulder, but there's no answer.

Maybe I'm hearing things? I return to washing the oil from my skin when strong arms wrap around my naked body, hands teasing my pebbled nipples.

"I didn't forget a thing," Alex says in between kisses on my neck. "Bend over."

I lean over, resting my arms on the marble counter. Looking over my shoulder, I watch as Alex lowers his zipper.

"I've wanted to do this since I rubbed that oil on you." He lets his pants and boxer briefs fall to the floor. "I'm going to fuck you hard and fast. Hold on and do not make a sound."

In one swift motion, he's inside me. I swallow a moan and grip the counter bracing myself against his punishing pace. My head drops, and I close my eyes.

"Pick your head up," Alex demands. "I want you watching as I come inside you."

I lift my head and meet his piercing gaze in the mirror. He's focused on his task as he continues his pounding rhythm. The first waves of my orgasm catch me off guard, and I struggle to keep my eyes focused. My whole body shakes from the intensity of the pleasure rocketing through me. Alex's eyes remain locked on mine as he ruts wildly before coming with a deep groan. His expression is one of complete ecstasy. When the last waves of his orgasm subside, he folds his body over mine, placing kisses along my back.

"Don't move," he instructs.

He gently washes between my legs and then tosses the washcloth into the sink. When he finishes, I turn to face him. Alex pins me to the counter, caging me in with his arms.

"You're amazing, baby girl," he says before leaning down and kissing me slowly and seductively. A direct contrast to the way he just fucked me. Despite having just had an orgasm, my body is ready for more. But he ends the kiss. "Go get dressed. We have company waiting."

"Something tells me our company may be preoccupied as well."

"Possibly. But I did promise them dinner."

After I get dressed, Alex and I go back to the living room. I grab a bag and start cleaning up the bits of leftover wax. Anthony and Leo join us a few minutes later.

"Here, let me help." Leo takes over the task, and I pick up the blanket from the floor.

"Shall I put this in the washer, Tony?"

"That would be great."

While I go to the laundry room, the three men work together, putting the furniture back into its rightful places.

Instead of cooking, Tony and Alex decide to order take-out. The four of us share our meal outside on the patio, watching the last few minutes of the sunset transition to a star-filled sky. Fireflies dance in the grassy area while bullfrogs croak by the water's edge.

I already know this weekend will be one I'll never forget.

Alex

THE FOLLOWING DAY, I wake up early to pick up my father and Luna from the local airport. Brandon and Svetlana arrived in Branson last night and are en route to our location. Stanley and Charlotte are expected to arrive later in the afternoon. I hope they will get along with our eclectic mix of family and friends.

Careful not to disturb Natalie, I slip out of bed and throw on a pair of shorts. Natalie rarely sleeps in, so I want to give her the luxury of doing so today. When I walk into the kitchen, I find Anthony and Leo well into their preparations for tonight's meal.

"Good morning," Tony says while stirring a pot on the stove.

"Can I make you a cup of coffee?" Leo asks.

"Thanks. That'd be great."

"Have a seat, and I'll get your breakfast."

"I wasn't expecting this, but okay."

I sit at the table, and Leo brings me a steaming mug. A second later, he places the sugar and creamer in front of me. Then he fills my plate with French toast and bacon. After serving me, Leo returns to Tony's side, and I scroll through the morning's news stories on my phone while eating.

I'm taking my last bite when Viktor strolls into the kitchen. "Ready to go, boss?"

"I am." I stand and move to clean up my plate.

"I've got it." Leo rushes over, taking it from me.

"Thank you, Leo." Anthony has his sub trained impeccably. "When Natalie gets up, will you tell her I've left for the airport?"

"Will do," Anthony replies. "Drive safe."

Viktor has the car already started. I get in, and we drive down the bumpy gravel driveway. "Remind me to get some estimates to get this paved."

"Gladly." Viktor laughs.

We discuss the rest of the day's events on our drive. With some of the strong personalities that'll be in attendance, there's a good chance things might blow up in our faces before the night's over.

"Everything will be fine," Viktor reassures me.

"That's what I'm hoping."

My phone chimes, alerting me to a message. "Natalie must be awake." I pull the phone out of my pocket. When I see the screen, I freeze.

"What's wrong? Is Natalie okay?"

"There was another attempt on Maxim's files."

Dread fills my entire being while I process what this might mean. It has to be Ben and Michelle. That's what I tell myself because I can't accept the alternative.

"Alex," Viktor says, glancing my way. "I think it's time to call Maxim."

I want to argue with him, to deny that it's anything more than the actions of vindictive ex-employees. But I know there's no possible way for Ben and Michelle to access my system. "Call the security team," I relent. "But this stays between us for now. I don't want to upset Natalie."

"Yes, boss."

There's a palpable silence between us. I can sense that Viktor's just as lost in thought as I am, contemplating all the potential outcomes of the situation. Unfortunately, my mind can't imagine any positive scenarios, and I'm left with a growing sense of unease.

Viktor pulls the car up to the sidewalk in front of the airport's only terminal. "I'll make the call while you're inside." His tone is calm. The only sign of nerves is his white-knuckle grip on the steering wheel.

"Their plane is scheduled to land any minute. I shouldn't be long."

The small airport is bustling with last-minute travelers for the summer holiday.

"Alex." I hear a familiar voice call my name.

Turning around, I spot Dad and Luna hurrying toward me.

"Did I have the wrong flight time?" I hug my father.

"We had a tailwind and landed early."

"It's so good to see you." I hug Luna before grabbing her bag. "Come on, Viktor's outside with the car."

"Where's Natalie? I thought she'd be with you," Luna asks.

"I didn't want to wake her." We get outside, and I search the parking lot for Viktor. It takes a few minutes, but finally, I spot him leaning against the car, talking on his cell phone.

When he sees us coming, he ends the call and rushes over to take the bag from my father. "Mr. Montgomery. Luna. It's a pleasure to see you both."

"Good to see you again." Dad shakes Viktor's free hand.

We get their luggage situated in the trunk and pile into the car. I send a text to Natalie, hoping she's awake.

(Me) Plane landed early. We're on our way home. There's French toast waiting for you in the kitchen.

She texts back immediately.

(Natalie) Thank you for letting me sleep in, Sir. French toast, yum! Be careful, and I'll see you soon.

Natalie

I ROLL OVER AND reach out to Alex, but he's not there. When I open my eyes, I find a note on his pillow.

baby girl,
I didn't want to wake you. I've gone to pick up Dad and Luna. See you soon.

Sir

Swinging my legs over the bed, a surge of excitement mixed with fear courses through my body. It's the first time my parents are meeting our friends and Alex's family. I'm worried my parents won't find anything in common with anyone. There's a very real chance today might end in disaster. I quickly push that thought aside and try to focus on the positives—everyone I love will be here today.

As I push open the bedroom door, a mouthwatering aroma wafts through the air and fills my nostrils, pulling me toward the kitchen. Walking down the hallway, I step lightly, my bare feet soundless on the hardwood floor. I stand quietly in the kitchen archway and watch Leo wash the dishes. Anthony stands closely behind, nuzzling his neck. Witnessing such an intimate moment feels almost intrusive, but I can't help being drawn in. The obstacles they've faced and conquered make their love all the more potent and inspiring.

"Good morning," I chirp. Feeling like I need to make my presence known. "It smells so good in here."

"Good morning, pixie. Hungry?"

"Very," I grin. "Alex mentioned something about French toast."

"Have a seat," Leo says. "I'll make your plate."

"I can get it. You guys look pretty busy." I motion at the food in various steps of preparation all over the kitchen.

"Sit." Anthony points to the chair. "Today, Leo waits on you."

"Yes, sir," I chuckle and sit at the table.

Leo serves me a plate of French toast dripping with fresh maple syrup, crispy bacon strips, and a cup of coffee. He kisses the top of my head before returning to his task of washing dishes. I start eating, thoroughly enjoying my breakfast. Why does food always taste better when someone else cooks?

While I eat, I can't help but be captivated by the perfectly choreographed routine of Anthony and his staff. Their movements are precisely timed, ensuring their work doesn't stop.

"Do you have a lot more to cook?" I ask in between bites.

"We're just about done with all the prep work. Later, we'll put the finishing touches on the dishes."

"You're amazing."

"You're too kind, baby girl." Alex's arms wrap around me, startling me. I drop my fork on the floor. "I didn't mean to scare you." Leo quickly picks it up and replaces it with a clean one.

"Where's Sam and Luna?"

"Viktor's showing them to their room. They'll be along in a few minutes. You should go get dressed."

I take my final bite. "Give me a few minutes, and I'll be ready."

I hurry to our bedroom and look through the closet pulling out several different outfits before settling on a pair of jean shorts and a black tank top. I pull my hair into a half ponytail and put on mascara and lip gloss.

"You going to be in there all day?" A familiar female voice calls from the other side of the door.

Opening the door, I find Lana with a massive smile on her face. I squeal and wrap my arms around my best friend.

"I can't believe you're here!"

"I wouldn't miss this for anything in the world." She squeezes me back. "Your parents were just pulling up when we walked into the house."

"Lana, I'm so nervous. What if they hate everyone?"

"Not even Charlotte could hate Leo."

We both laugh.

"I hope you're right." I grab her hand. "Come on, let's go say hi."

Everyone's seated at our outdoor table, enjoying the delicious food the guys prepared for us. Lana was right. I had nothing to worry about. Tony and Leo charmed my parents in a matter of minutes. And what's not to love about Sam and Luna?

"Anthony, dear," Mom says. "Your food is exquisite."

"Thank you, ma'am."

"Our wedding guests will be getting a real treat."

Tony smiles proudly.

Sam stands. "I'd like to propose a toast to the future Mr. and Mrs. Montgomery."

A round of cheers and the clinking of glasses sound around us. I sip of my champagne and grab Alex's hand under the table. I'm overwhelmed at the realization of how incredibly lucky I am—every one of my dreams is coming true.

Alex

THE AFTERNOON COULDN'T HAVE gone any smoother. Despite the various personalities around the table today, everyone's getting along. Tony's culinary creations impressed all. Our guests are currently indulging in a selection of delectable desserts. Meanwhile, nature puts on a show in the sky with a beautiful sunset preceding tonight's fireworks. Viktor catches my eye from the back door and signals for me to come inside. He must have heard from Maxim.

"I got a text from Dimitri."

"And?"

"At first glance, it looked like another internal issue. But that didn't make any sense, especially with the updated security. Alex, it didn't come from inside the office."

Shit. My stomach turns.

"Dimitri went back to compare the attacks. The IP address appears to match your internal system—an innocent mistake like we first thought. It was when he attempted to trace it back to a specific computer that he found the anomaly. This is a professional job. Someone outside the company made it look like an accident, and we missed it."

"Fuck." I run my hand through my hair. "Max is going to kill me for not calling him sooner."

"Alex." In a rare display of emotion, Viktor puts his hand on my shoulder. "It's a highly constructed attack. They got lucky with their timing because of the issues with the employees. Even Dimitri missed it."

I pace back and forth, wondering what will happen next. It only takes a minute for my phone to ring. I know who it is even before I look.

"Maxim."

"I just got all the information. I do not want to discuss it over the phone. My jet is enroute to JFK. I want everyone here immediately."

"Max. I'm sorry."

"There is no need to apologize. But until we know who is behind this, everyone needs to be at the compound."

"Everyone's at my house for the holiday."

"I will speak to Svetlana. She and Brandon will need to change their plans and stay at yours or Viktor's home tonight," Maxim instructs. "There is no need to ruin your gathering tonight. You will need to leave first thing in the morning, though."

"We'll see you soon."

"*Do Svidaniya.*" Maxim ends the call.

I slip the phone back into my pocket and look outside at my family and friends. Everyone's enjoying a relaxing evening. Little do they know the potential danger in store for us.

"Natalie is so happy right now. I don't want to spoil any of this for her," I say softly.

"You heard Maxim. Go back out and enjoy the evening."

"I can't. I need to arrange for Charlotte and Stanley to have an in-home a—"

"I'll make the arrangements. All you need to do tonight is enjoy your family. Let me worry about everything else."

"Thank you." I school my features and walk back outside.

As soon as I take my seat, the fireworks light up the sky. Natalie's emerald eyes are filled with questions as she looks at me. I grasp her hand and pull her onto my lap, hoping my pounding heart doesn't betray my nerves.

Lana pulls out her phone and reads a message. Her expression gives nothing away. She's been down this road before and knows how to handle it. Lana looks my way and gives me a nod of understanding before turning her attention back to the fireworks.

The thought of breaking Natalie's heart by delaying our wedding planning and forcing her to travel to Russia weighs heavily on me. This won't be an easy conversation to have, but I'm left with no other choice.

After the fireworks show, Natalie's parents leave, bidding us farewell before driving out of sight. We return to the gathering, where our other guests are gathered around the fire, chatting quietly. I sit, hoping to put off what needs to be done for a while longer, but Natalie stands before me with her arms folded. She's clearly upset.

"Are you going to tell me what's going on now?"

"No," I say calmly. "Sit down. We have guests."

She ignores my quiet warning. "I saw the look between you and Lana earlier. What's going on?"

Anthony stretches and forces a yawn. "I think it's time we turn in."

"You don't have to." My anger builds. "Don't let my wayward sub chase you away." I narrow my gaze at her, warning her to stop.

"It's really okay," he says and motions to Leo, who's kneeling at his feet. "It's time for us to turn in anyway."

Lana pulls Natalie aside, whispering in her ear. I'm sure she's letting her know she stepped out of bounds. Natalie doesn't take her eyes off me as she shrugs.

"Lana, we should go too," Brandon adds.

"No, you two need to stay."

"Oh?" Brandon looks at me, searching for a hint, but I give him none.

"Dad, I need you to stay too."

He gets the hint by what I haven't said. "Luna, go to bed. I'll be in shortly."

Although Luna looks concerned, she doesn't question her Dominant. She says goodnight and makes a quick exit. I wish my submissive was as obedient.

"Let's move this inside," I say, standing. "I have to get Viktor. I'll meet you in the living room."

I need to take a step away to get myself under control. When I get into the office, Viktor's sitting behind my desk.

"Have you made any progress?"

"I hired the same aide the Clarkes had when you went to Seattle. She'll arrive tomorrow afternoon. I've also arranged for a discreet security team."

"Are you ready to share the good news?" I ask sarcastically.

"Can't wait."

Viktor follows me back to the living room, where everyone's gathered. Natalie's standing by the window, looking out into the darkness. I sit opposite Brandon and Lana on the sofa to keep an eye on Natalie while I talk.

"There was another attempt at accessing the encrypted files earlier today." I take a deep breath. "I was wrong from the beginning. The files weren't being accessed from within the company."

"It wasn't the employees you fired?" Dad asks.

"No. The timing of everything was purely coincidental."

"Is Max aware?" Dad looks concerned.

"Yes. He called earlier. His jet is enroute to JFK. We're leaving in the morning for an extended stay in Russia."

"We're what?" Natalie spins around. "We can't do that. My parents. Our bridal shower." She's nearing hysterics.

I hurry over and grab her shoulders. "We don't have a choice."

She pulls from my hold. "I'm not going to Russia."

I'm usually very patient, but my blood's boiling right now. I don't want to have this argument in front of everyone. "Come with me." Taking her by the arm, I lead her outside.

Once we're out of the house, she pulls out of my hold. "I can't just leave. I have to oversee the store and my dad's therapy—"

"Do you think I want to drop everything and go?"

She turns away from me. I knew she wasn't going to take this news well. But between her arguing with me in front of our company and her complete disrespect for me now, it's too much. As her Dominant, it's my responsibility to find the balance between discipline and caring for her emotional state.

"baby girl." I wrap my arms around her waist, but instead of relaxing into my touch, she stiffens in my arms. "I know this is a shock and not what either of us wants. Whoever's behind this could pose a great danger to us. We need to be at Maxim's until we have more information."

"What about my parents?"

"I don't believe they're in danger." I turn her to face me. "But Viktor arranged for a security team, just in case. They'll remain out of sight so we don't alarm your parents. Viktor also rehired the same aide. She'll be there tomorrow."

"I don't like this."

"Neither do I." I tuck a stray curl behind her ear. "But we have to go."

"Yes, Sir."

I'm thankful she's accepted the inevitable, but I can't let her attitude slide. "We need to address your earlier behavior. Not only did you disrespect me. You were also rude to our guests." Natalie lowers her head. "I'll administer your punishment when we're alone." Taking her by the hand, I lead her back into our now-empty living room. Everyone must've gone next door with Viktor. Since we're alone now, I continue walking to our bedroom. "Take your clothes off and kneel."

While she strips, I go to the closet to retrieve the paddle. Our current guests won't be concerned if they hear the punishment that's about to happen. I prefer privacy which is why I had the bedrooms soundproofed.

Returning to the main bedroom, I stop and take in the sight. Natalie's naked on her knees with her head bowed and her palms resting on her slightly spread legs. The view makes me rock hard, but I push those thoughts aside.

Although I dislike administering punishments, it's an important part of our Dom/sub dynamic.

"Do you know why I'm punishing you?"

"Because I disrespected you and our guests, Sir."

"Stand and bend over the bed," I instruct. "You will receive ten strikes."

Natalie rises from her position on the floor, averting her eyes from my face. She leans over the bed, resting her cheek on her arms.

"Count aloud." I don't give any warning before landing the first strike.

She gasps. "One."

I don't care to draw this out any longer than necessary. Each strike comes in quick succession, but Natalie keeps the count. By the end, her ass is bright red. She'll be uncomfortable on the flight in the morning. However, I'm confident she's learned a lesson and will grow in her submission from this experience. "Stay here."

"Yes, Sir." Her words come out quietly between sobs.

Once I put the paddle back in its place, I pick up the soothing balm. Even though this was a punishment, I'm responsible for properly caring for my sub. I squeeze some of the lotion onto my hand and apply it gently to her skin. Natalie flinches. "I understand it stings, but it will help." When I finish, I toss the tube onto the dresser and lift Natalie into my arms. She buries her head into my chest, and tears continue to fall.

"I'm sorry for my behavior. I'm so scared, Alex."

"I know, baby girl." I wipe the tears from her face. "I won't let anything happen to you, I promise."

Natalie

"WE'RE ON THE WAY to the airport now." It's no surprise my mom isn't taking the news of our sudden departure well. "I know this isn't ideal."

"Why such a hurry? Couldn't you at least wait until after your bridal shower to take a trip?"

"Maxim surprised us at the last minute." I don't want her to think this is more than a spur-of-the-moment vacation.

"But why do you have to go right now?" Mom persists.

I repeat the story Alex and I came up with last night. "Maxim and Irina aren't able to make it to the shower. You know they're like family to Alex. They want to celebrate our upcoming wedding with us. This is their way of doing so."

I look to Alex for support. He nods in approval.

"That Maxim is always trying to outshine everyone," Mom complains.

Her comment makes me laugh. "Please try to understand. We'll be home in a few days. There'll be plenty of time for anything that comes up last minute."

"Okay, dear."

I spend the remainder of the drive explaining that Dad's aide will arrive this afternoon. I also remind her that Sam and Luna will leave tomorrow, but Tony and Leo will be staying for the rest of the week. "We just pulled into the airport. I have to go."

"Have a safe trip," she says reluctantly.

"We will. Give Daddy a hug and kiss for me."

When I get out of the car, my stomach turns, and a wave of dizziness washes over me. I grab Alex's arm for support.

"Are you okay?"

"I'm really nervous."

"Relax, baby girl. Everything will be okay."

I can only hope Alex is right because, at the moment, nothing feels okay.

The men grab our bags and walk into the airport ahead of Lana and me.

"What's wrong?" Lana asks.

"This is all very sudden."

"It's part of the territory." She waves her hand as if having to drop everything and go to Russia is entirely normal. "Dad will find out where the threat is coming from and stop it. Then, we can all return to life as usual."

"Doesn't this bother you at all?"

"I grew up in this life, remember? Consider it a vacation before the wedding planning really starts." She skips ahead to catch up with Brandon.

Lana may have grown up amidst danger, but I didn't. When I learned about Alex's involvement with Maxim, I didn't stop to think about the possible repercussions. Now that I'm getting a first-hand taste, I don't like it. I know what he and Maxim do is important, but does Alex have to be involved? That's ridiculous. I can't ask Alex to walk away.

After an uneventful two-hour flight, we land at JFK where we're met by Max's security team. They whisk us away to a private hangar where Maxim's jet waits. One of the men reaches out to take my bag, and his jacket shifts, revealing the gun strapped to his waist. Another wave of dizziness washes over me, and I stumble.

Alex grabs me by the waist, steadying me. "I'm texting Maxim. I want a doctor waiting to examine you when we land."

"I'm fine. I didn't eat before we left, and all this"—I motion to Viktor and the rest of the security team, who are hurrying to get everything ready for what I'm sure will be an imminent take-off—"is a lot."

"I want you to get checked out anyway." I resist rolling my eyes at my overprotective Dominant.

Hand in hand, Alex and I ascend the steps into the luxurious airplane, and he guides me to a plush leather sofa. Across from us, Brandon and Lana are seated. Lana offers me a reassuring smile. Viktor and another gentleman are engrossed in something displayed on the laptop screen before them.

"Who's he?" I whisper to Alex.

"Dimitri. He's the head of the tech security team." I've heard his name mentioned several times over the past twenty-four hours, but I wasn't expecting him to be on the flight with us.

The pilot announces we're ready for take-off as the jet engines roar to life, and we start our taxi down the runway. The plane's wheels leave the ground in one of the smoothest takeoffs I've ever felt. Before I know it, we're high above the clouds flying over the ocean on our way to Russia.

A pretty blonde flight attendant, who only speaks Russian, emerges from the back of the plane. I don't miss how she bats her eyes at Alex trying to get his attention. His body tenses before he entwines his fingers with mine.

After a short conversation with Lana, she momentarily disappears. When she returns, she's pushing a cart full of food. We're each served appetizers of fresh figs and a selection of cheeses, followed by the main course of Chicken Kyiv. My stomach growls from kipping breakfast, and I quickly finish everything on my plate.

After the dishes have been cleared, Alex stands and takes my hand. "Come with me."

"Where are we going?"

"To the bedroom. You barely slept last night."

"I'm fine." I wave him off.

"It's a long flight. I want you to get some rest."

I've been on this plane before but have never been in the bedroom. I'm surprised at how big it is. There's even a king-size bed.

"The bathroom's over there." Alex points to another door.

"This is incredible."

"Maxim's a very wealthy man who prefers to travel in comfort."

"I guess so." I move closer to Alex and reach for the button on his pants, but he grabs my hands.

"Sleep." He points to the bed.

"Can't blame a girl for trying."

Alex pulls the blankets back, and I crawl into bed, appreciating the feel of the bamboo sheets caressing my skin. He climbs in and lays next to me, pulling me close. It doesn't

take more than a few minutes for my eyes to close and my
body to give way to sleep.

Natalie

I STARTLE AWAKE, MY heart beating furiously from the terrible nightmare I was having. I'm momentarily disoriented and push up on my elbows to take in my surroundings—I'm on Maxim's plane. We're in the bedroom, which is mostly dark except for the sliver of light coming from the bathroom door that's cracked open. Alex lies next to me, his breathing soft and even. Gently, I run my fingers along the dark stubble on his jaw.

"Did you sleep well, baby girl?"

"I did," I answer before crawling over him, straddling his body, and rocking my hips gently.

Grabbing the hem of my sundress, I pull it over my head and toss it to the side. Alex groans in response. Reaching between us, I open his pants, freeing his erection. This time instead of stopping me, he lifts his hips, allowing me to slide his pants down his muscular legs.

He reaches behind me to unclasp my bra. The straps slide down my arms, exposing my breasts to him. He removes the lace fabric from my arms and drops it off the side of the bed. Alex stares at me, his eyes full of lust, before leaning in and taking a nipple in his mouth. My head falls back, and I moan in pleasure. He releases it with a pop and lavishes the same attention on my other breast.

"You're so beautiful," Alex's voice is deep and seductive. "Can you be quiet?"

"Yes, Sir." He slips his fingers into the thin fabric of my panties and pulls, tearing them. "They were one of my favorite pairs." I pretend to pout.

"I'll buy you more."

Placing his hands on my hips, he lifts me, and I position myself over him. Then, I lower my body slowly, allowing it time to stretch and take every inch of his long, hard length. His face tightens in concentration. Alex is used to being in control, but right now, he's allowing me to set the pace. I lean close, my breasts pushing against his chest as I roll my hips, teasing him. He grabs my ass in frustration.

"Is there something wrong, Sir?" I ask coyly.

He lifts his hips encouraging me to move. Pushing on his chest, I lean back onto my knees before quickly sinking onto his cock. He palms my breasts as I continue the rhythmic motion. Without warning, he flips us, and I'm underneath him.

Alex sets a pounding rhythm, an unspoken message of need and want being exchanged between our bodies. Wrapping my legs around him, I pull him even deeper. Encouraging him to let go and lose control. To consume every part of me.

"Come for me," he growls.

And I do. He kisses me deeply, muffling my cries of pleasure as his body trembles with the force of his orgasm—our bodies pulsing as one.

"You're amazing. Let's hope we didn't wake the whole plane."

Although I laugh at his comment, I'd be mortified if they heard us.

Alex rolls off me and grabs his cell phone to check the time. Turning on the light, he says, "We should be landing soon. Get dressed so we can get back to our seats."

I collect my clothes from where they landed on the floor. "What do I do with this?" I hold up the torn lace.

"I'll take that." He swipes the shredded panties from my hand and balls them in his fist.

"I'll be out in a few minutes."

I take my time washing up before I get dressed and run my fingers through my hair. Opening the door, I peek my head around, "Alex?"

"What is it?"

"Do you think they heard us?"

His laugh fills the room. "No, I don't think they heard us. Let's go."

We make our way back out into the main seating area just as everyone is getting settled. Alex and I retake our seats on the sofa. He reaches across my lap and fastens my safety belt, pulling it tight. This time when the pilot's voice comes across the speakers, he's announcing our landing.

The plane descends from the sky, landing in the dark at the Pulkovo Airport in St. Petersburg. When the plane's door opens, we're met by a group of large and very intimidating men standing in front of a lineup of black SUVs. Alex walks ahead and shakes hands with one of the men.

"What is all this?" I ask Viktor, who remains at my side.

"Part of Maxim's army." There's no trace of humor in his voice.

"Are we in that much danger?"

"Maxim's ensured our safety. There's no need for concern."

"A small army of your clones has met us, but I shouldn't be concerned?"

"Exactly. Come on, let's go."

Viktor escorts me to one of the waiting vehicles and opens the door. I slide onto the back seat, and Alex gets in after me. Viktor rounds the car and sits on my other side.

One by one, each vehicle in the convoy starts to move. We're officially on our way to the Soloniks' home.

Alex

I SETTLE IN FOR the two-hour drive to Maxim's compound. Natalie pulls out her cell phone.

"Don't turn that on." I grab the device from her hand.

"Why not? I texted my parents after we landed. I wanted to see if they texted back."

Shit. I toss the phone to Viktor, who quickly powers it off and puts it in his pocket. Natalie looks between us, silently questioning our actions.

"What's going on?"

I'm not ready to disclose how serious the problem is.

I reiterate the only version of the story I'm willing to tell her. "There were attempts to access Maxim's files from outside my company. Maxim wants us here as a precaution until he discovers who's behind this cyberattack."

"And as a *precaution*, Maxim sends his army of Viktor-look-alikes to escort us to his home. As what, a welcoming committee?"

Viktor bursts out laughing, and I follow, which only frustrates Natalie more.

"I'm glad you two think this is funny." She crosses her arms, trying to protest, but even she can't keep a straight face.

"You know Maxim. He likes to go over and above."

"Why can't I use my phone?"

"Until we know who's behind this," Viktor explains. "We'll only use burner phones or the secure line at Maxim's—something that can't be traced."

"So, I can call them when we get to the house?"

"Yes."

Viktor throws a disapproving look over Natalies's shoulder, but I can't bring myself to tell her we're not going to Maxim's house. Instead, I wrap my arm around her and draw her close as we ride silently until we arrive at the heavily fortified gates of the Soloniks' compound.

Natalie lifts her head and looks out the window. "Where are we?"

"Maxim's compound."

"Maxim's what? I thought we were going to their house?"

"No, baby girl." I grab her hand and rub circles on it with my thumb. "Because of the security threat, we'll be staying here."

"Behind gates and walls?" She pulls her hand from my grasp before returning her gaze out the window, watching as the SUV makes its way up the long drive. "With guards and guns?"

"Yes."

"Alex—"

"No more questions. Right now, you need to trust me."

I hate silencing her. The lack of communication is already putting distance between us. But until we know more of what's happening, there's nothing else I can tell her.

Our vehicle comes to a stop in front of the expansive mansion. I've been through this before, so I understand at least some of the thoughts going through Natalie's head. My previous stay was a false alarm, and we were able to resume our normal lives within a few days. I only hope this time is the same.

I open the car door, and we step out. The smell of seawater wafts in the air. We round the car and are greeted by Maxim and Irina, who are waiting at the front door. Lana runs up and is wrapped in the arms of her parents. Brandon's right behind her and shakes Max's hand before being pulled in for a hug by Irina.

"I've missed you both so much," Irina gushes over her daughter and Brandon. "Go, get settled in your room."

"Thanks, Mama."

"Food will be served in a half-hour in the dining room," Irina calls after the couple. "Don't be late."

Natalie and I approach next. Irina reaches out to hug Natalie while I shake Max's hand.

"We're so glad you made it." Irina looks at Natalie. "Alex told us you were ill?"

"I didn't sleep well and skipped breakfast," Natalie answers.

"Come, I'll show you to your room."

Natalie looks over her shoulder to me for permission. "Go ahead. I need to speak with Max. I'll see you in the dining room."

Natalie follows Irina into the house.

"Let us go to my office," Maxim says.

He leads the way down the cavernous hallway. Unlike his residential home, which is traditional and full of history, the compound has clean lines and a modern design. Its sole purpose is for the maximum protection of its inhabitants.

Timur, one of Maxim's guards, stands outside the large double doors that lead to his office. When we approach, he steps aside.

Maxim sits behind his desk. "Have a seat." He motions to the tufted armchairs opposite him. Resting his elbows on the desk with his fingers steepled, he studies his computer monitor before he speaks. "My men have been working non-stop since Viktor called yesterday." The stress and exhaustion of the past twenty-four hours is evident on his face. It's not like Max to reveal his emotions like this. That fact alone has me concerned. "Whoever is behind this attack is using an intricate network of proxy servers to conceal their identity."

"This is all my fault. I'm sorry. I thought it was just my wayward employees. If I'd had any idea—"

"Alexander." Maxim interrupts. "I am not angry with you. This is a high-level attack made to look like an innocent attempt from within your office. The fact that it happened simultaneously with your actual internal issues is purely coincidental. Whoever it is got lucky."

"I let you down." Insecurity and fear eat away at me.

"You did no such thing." Maxim pushes from his chair and walks around his desk to stand before me. "You are a good steward of this information. Do not doubt your integrity or ability."

"Yes, sir."

Maxim flips his computer screen around so we can all see. On the monitor is a map marked with dozens of red flags. I lean forward, trying to make sense of it all, but I'm not a tech genius. I don't know what any of it means. I look to Dimitri for an explanation.

"These." Dimitri points to the screen. "Are the locations the hacker's IP address has pinged off. My team is still trying to determine the actual origin of the attack, but each time it looks like we're reaching the end of the trail, a new group pops up."

I turn to look at Viktor, who's sitting back in his chair, arms crossed and an impassive expression on his face.

"So, what now?" I ask.

"We stay here and keep working until we find out who is behind this," Maxim says.

"That's my cue." Dimitri stands. "If you don't need me here, I'm going to head back to the tech room."

"Where do you want me, sir?" Viktor asks.

"Your priority is Natalie. If Alexander cannot be with her, you will be. When you are not with her, you are to be in the tech room."

"Understood. Text me when you need me, boss." He clasps my shoulder on his way out of the office.

Once we're alone, I ask, "Do you have any idea who's behind this?"

"Not yet."

My stomach sinks at his revelation.

Maxim points to the monitor as we discuss the next steps in the plan. In addition to Dimitri and the tech team here, Maxim has his contacts around the globe working on this. Until the threat is neutralized, the compound is on code red—complete lockdown.

"We are safe here. Everyone is free to come and go within the compound's walls." Maxim concludes the briefing. "Now, let us move to the dining room and eat."

It's after midnight, and although I'm not hungry, I'm wide awake. Maxim and I make our way through the halls to rejoin the group.

Natalie

"HERE'S YOUR ROOM. YOUR bags will be brought up shortly," Irina says as she opens the door to a suite that's the size of an apartment. "I hope you will be comfortable here." Irina's warm and welcoming despite the less-than-desirable circumstances. Walking into the room, the first thing I notice is the wall of windows. In the center is a set of open glass doors. I'm drawn to the balcony, where I can hear the sound of ocean waves in the distance. Looking out into the night, I see nothing but blackness. Even the moon is hiding behind the thick cloud cover.

Irina steps out next to me. "The compound sits on cliffs overlooking the Baltic Sea. In the daylight, you will have an extraordinary view."

I give her a sad smile before returning inside to look around the room. This place, although magnificent in design, feels uninviting and cold. It's a direct contrast to the welcoming feel of the Soloniks' home.

"I don't mean to sound ungrateful. I'm still trying to process all of this."

"I understand, honey. I felt the same way the first time I had to go to a safe house. This life can be a lot to handle sometimes. But you must trust Maxim and his men to handle the situation and keep us safe."

"Safe from what?" I desperately want to understand.

"We don't need to know the details."

But I want to know the details. I need to understand why we had to drop everything and get on a plane.

"Alex was very concerned about you when he texted Max." Irina quickly changes the subject.

"I told him he was overreacting. Once things settled down, and I had some food on the plane, I was fine."

"In any case, the doctor will be here in the morning. Why don't you take a few minutes to settle in." She walks to the door, her high heels muffled by the plush carpet. "I'll return shortly to show you to the dining room." Irina closes the door gently behind her.

Now that I'm alone, I take the time to look around the room, which really is more like an apartment. There's a sitting area complete with a marble-tiled fireplace and a kitchen. When I open the fridge, I find it fully stocked with our preferred foods and drinks. Somehow, even with very short notice, every detail has been taken care of.

As I scan the room, I noticed two doors, and I immediately decide one is a closet and the other must lead to the bathroom. After careful consideration, I try the door on the right. Upon opening it, I discover a spacious walk-in closet with glossy white wardrobes and drawers lining the walls on both sides. At the far end of the room, I spot floor-to-ceiling shelves designed to house a vast shoe collection.

After exploring the closet, I head towards the remaining door, which leads me into the en suite bathroom. The room mirrors the luxurious decor of the bedroom, with an entire wall of windows. One side of the bathroom features

a massive walk-in shower with two rain heads suspend-
ed from the ceiling and strategically positioned body
jets. While admiring the shower, I notice a touchpad
mounted on the wall, indicating that it controlled the
various functions.

On the other side of the room, a white vanity houses
double sinks. A purple orchid sits on the counter between the sinks adding a touch of nature to the otherwise sterile space.

I feel like I'm intruding on someone's private space,
but I open the drawers anyway. What I find makes it look
like we're staying in a fancy hotel. There are brand-new
toothbrushes, hairbrushes, and all the toiletries one
might need for an extended stay. If they're here, I may as
well use them to freshen up. While I'm in the bathroom,
I hear a knock on the bedroom door.

"Come in."

"It's just me. Are you ready to go to the dining room?"
As Irina and I stroll through the compound, she points
down various hallways telling me where everyone's
rooms are. "Don't worry. After a few days, you'll know
your way around. Until then, Alex will get you where you
need to go. He's stayed here before."

"I'm hoping we're only here for a few days." I don't
want to be hidden behind the compound walls any
longer than that.

It doesn't go unnoticed that Irina fails to respond to my
comment. I'm filled with a sense of dread that we may
be here much longer than I hope. As we approach what I
assume is the dining room, I hear familiar voices laughing

and chatting like we're here for a vacation. Am I the only one who sees the abnormality of this situation?

When Alex notices me, he stands and pulls out the chair next to him. "I've missed you."

"Me too."

"Make yourself a plate, Natalia."

Despite my reservations, Maxim's Russian use of my name always makes me smile. The food laid out looks and smells fantastic. It's been hours since I ate last, and my stomach growls in response. I fill my plate and start eating. Alex places his hand on my thigh under the table and makes lazy circles with his thumb. I allow myself to relax and join the conversation and laughter, pretending that everything is okay, at least for now. But I fully intend to interrogate Alex when we're alone.

I don't know how long we've been talking or even what time it is when I find myself yawning.

"Are you tired, baby girl?" Alex whispers in my ear.

"I am."

"It's time for Natalie and me to get to bed." Alex stands, offering me his hand. "We'll see everyone in the morning."

Irina was correct. Alex is sure of his steps as we walk hand-in-hand back to our room. I wonder how many times he's been here. I'm just about to ask when he opens the door to our room, but I get distracted. "Our bed's turned down?"

"Maxim's staff is nothing if not efficient."

When I peek in the closet, I find that not only has our luggage been delivered, but our clothes have been put away as well.

"I'm going to get changed for bed." I grab a pair of my satin pajamas and spin around, finding myself in Alex's arms.

"I know this isn't ideal, but please try to relax and enjoy yourself."

"Relax?" My frustration level rises, and I pull out of his arms. "We're in a mansion. No, a walled compound with heavily armed guards because of a threat to our safety. And what I'm gathering, from what's not being said, is that we may be here for an extended stay. But you're asking me to relax?"

Alex places his hands on my arms. "I know this is hard, but you'll see it's not so bad. We have everything we could possibly want at our disposal. Tomorrow, I'll take you for a walk around the grounds. It's beautiful. I know you'll love it."

"I don't know about love it."

"Please try to keep an open mind," Alex pleads. "As soon as the threat is dealt with, we'll be on the first flight home."

"Promise?"

"I promise." Alex leans in and kisses me.

Despite the nagging feeling that it won't be that simple, I promise to keep an open mind about our impromptu *vacation.*

Natalie

MY MIND AND BODY drift in the blissful place between sleep and awake—where the lines separating dreaming and reality are blurred.

Sensation.

Pleasure.

Wetness.

My eyes flutter open, and I find Alex's head between my legs, his tongue circling my clit. I run my hands through his dark hair, and he looks up at me, his blue eyes full of sensuous longing.

"Good morning, baby girl." He smiles, his sexy dimple giving him a mischievous look.

"Good morning." I barely manage to get out before he's back to licking and sucking, working me quickly toward an orgasm.

I fist the sheets and arch my back as I come undone. Alex doesn't stop until he's sucked every last bit of pleasure from me. Then he crawls up my body and kisses me. Tasting my arousal on his tongue only turns me on more.

"I need You." Three words that hold so much meaning. I need more than just a connection with his body. My soul needs to connect with his. I need his strength to quell the fear that's plaguing me.

Slowly, he slides inside. I raise my hips, trying to make him go faster, but he stills.

"Patience." He nips at my lower lip.

When I relax, he moves again, still achingly slow.

"Please. I need more."

"You need more, do you?" He pulls out, and I blow out a frustrated breath.

"Always so impatient."

Then, he grabs my hands, putting them up over my head. I hear one click and then another. When I try to move, I find they've been restrained to the headboard. Knowing I'm at his mercy, fully dependent on him for my pleasure and safety, allows me to relax. I need the freedom to still my thoughts and focus only on Alex and this moment.

After he's given me more orgasms than I can count, we take a shower and dress. We're on our way out of our room when we bump into Lana and Brandon in the hall.

"Good afternoon, sleepyheads," Lana says, linking her arm with mine. "Planning on joining us for lunch?"

"I wouldn't miss it. I'm starving."

"Did you sleep well?"

"Surprisingly, yes."

"Good, I'm glad to hear it. I know how nervous you were yesterday."

"Alexander. Natalia." Maxim's booming voice fills the hall startling me. "I was just coming to get you."

Maxim's heading in our direction with a well-dressed woman at his side.

"Natalia, this is Dr. Turova. She is one of the physicians that volunteers her time at Jelena's Hope."

"You didn't have to go through all this trouble." I can only imagine what it costs to have a doctor do a house call on a weekend.

"It'll give me peace of mind if you let her look you over. Then we'll eat and go for a walk."

I look back and forth between Alex and the doctor, who smiles warmly at me.

"It'll only take a few minutes," she says.

"Natalia, do you know the way back to your room?"

"I'm pretty sure I can get us there."

"I'll see you shortly." Alex kisses my cheek.

"I don't know how to get to the dining room, though." I know Irina showed me last night, but this place is huge. I lost track of where we were and how we got there.

"It's okay. I do," Dr. Turova answers.

Alex and the others continue to the dining room while Dr. Turova and I make our way back to the bedroom.

"I'm really okay, doctor. Yesterday was just very stressful."

"Please call me Karina." She motions to the sofa. "How about we just sit and talk?"

I take a minute to study her. She's wearing a dark blue dress and high heels. Her hair and makeup are done like she's dressed for a night, not a medical visit. I nod in agreement and take a seat on the sofa. Karina chooses to sit on the chair across from me.

"Sorry, I don't know why I'm so nervous. As I said, this trip was very sudden, and I'm feeling a bit out of sorts."

"That's understandable, given the circumstances. Would you be willing to tell me what happened yesterday that caused Alex concern?" Her demeanor is calm and serene, putting me at ease.

"Well, I've had my hands full running my parent's store and helping my mom care for my dad as he recovers. We're also planning my bridal shower and wedding. I've been working on very little sleep. Then there was the news that we had to drop everything and fly to Russia. I was nervous and didn't eat breakfast. Then, I had a dizzy spell. I don't know. Maybe I had a panic attack or something."

"I see. It sounds like you have a lot going on right now."

"I do."

"Since I'm here, do you mind if I give you a quick exam? It will save me a lot of explaining to Maxim if you'd agree."

I don't want Maxim to think I'm ungrateful for his help, and I certainly don't want to get Karina in trouble with him.

"I guess it wouldn't hurt."

While she examines me, she asks the typical doctor questions. Whether I have any health problems or take any medications.

"The only thing I take is a birth control pill." That's when panic sets in. "I run out next week and didn't have time to fill my prescription."

"I'll fill it and have it delivered." After Karina finishes her exam, she asks, "Are you ready to head down to the dining room?"

My hands are still shaking, and I can only manage a nod.

I follow her back through the hallways, my head a chaotic mess of thoughts and emotions.

Alex

IT SEEMS TO TAKE forever before Natalie returns to the dining room with Karina at her side. As soon as I see her, my stomach drops. She's white as a ghost and trembling.

"What's wrong?" I hurry to her and grab her arm.

"Nothing."

I look at Dr. Turova, who offers a reassuring smile. "Other than being a bit worn out from all the stress she's been under, Natalie's completely healthy. All she needs is some rest and proper nutrition."

"Thank you, doctor." I turn to Natalie. "Are you sure you're up for a walk?"

"Absolutely. You promised me a tour, remember?"

"You have my number, Natalie. I'll be in touch," Dr. Turova says. "I'll see myself out."

"Where is everyone?"

"They've all eaten and gone their separate ways. You don't mind a quiet lunch with just me, do you?"

"Never."

"Let's go then."

"I thought we were eating?" she asks, confused.

"We are."

I lead her outside to start our tour. It isn't until we walk along a trail that overlooks the sea that Natalie begins to relax. I knew the fresh air and sheer amount of outdoor space would help her feel less confined.

"What's this?" she asks when we come to a laid-out blanket with a basket in the center.

"It's our lunch."

While she was with the doctor, I arranged for a picnic to be set up. Natalie loves being outside, especially by the water. I'm hoping this will provide a bit of normalcy. We sit together, and I unpack the basket. The cook prepared some American sandwiches and Natalie's favorite, Olivier salad, along with a variety of snacks.

"It's beautiful here," Natalie says as she looks out over the cerulean water.

"I know you weren't happy about coming, but I need you to understand there was no other choice."

"I'm sorry about the way I reacted." She reaches out to cup my cheek in her tiny hand. "I do understand."

We eat our lunch quietly. Natalie may be physically present, but her thoughts are a million miles away. I let her go for a while, hoping she'll tell me what's on her mind without my having to ask. When she finishes her sandwich, she walks to the lookout spot, her gaze fixed on the water. I follow and stand next to her.

"Alex," she says quietly. "I have something I need to tell you."

"What is it, baby girl?" She looks up at me, tears in her eyes. "I'm afraid to say it. I don't know—"

"You don't have to be afraid to tell me anything."

"I'm pregnant."

My world stops.

Alex

"I'M SORRY." THERE'S A desperate plea in her voice. "I took all my pills. I don't know how it happened. Karina said sometimes—"

I lift her chin with my finger. "You're pregnant?"

She nods.

I place my hand on her belly. "You have a child, our child, growing inside you right now."

"I do." She covers my hand with hers. "Are you mad?"

"Is that what you thought? That I'd be mad?" I wipe the tears from her cheeks with my thumbs.

"I wasn't sure. I didn't know."

"Shh." I place my finger over her lips.

This baby wasn't planned. It wasn't something I even knew I wanted, but the second she blurted out the words *I'm pregnant*, my heart filled with an all-consuming love for this little life growing inside her.

"We didn't plan this." Tears are now streaming down her face.

"No, we didn't. But I don't care. I love you, and I love our baby."

"You do?"

"How could I not love something you and I created to-gether? I wrap my arms around her, never wanting to let her go. "Dr. Turova checked you and the baby? You're both healthy?" Thinking about the stress of the past few days fills me with worry.

"Yes."

"How far along are you?"

"I haven't gotten my period in months from being on the pill, so I'm not exactly sure." Natalie pulls her cell phone from her pocket. "Karina felt my uterus and estimates I'm about probably about twelve weeks pregnant." She opens a recorded video on her phone. "Listen."

Swoosh. Swoosh. Swoosh.

"Is that our baby's heartbeat?" I ask, swallowing over the lump in my throat.

"It is."

I drop to my knees, humbled by the knowledge we created a new life. My head lowers as my tears fall like rain. Natalie drops down next to me.

"Alex." Her voice is small and unsure. "What's wrong? Are you ok?"

The feeling in my chest is unlike anything I've ever experienced. I'm going to be a father. A new life is going to come into this world, entirely dependent on Natalie and me. No longer will life be just about us. We'll have a child, a mix of the best of us to protect and love.

It's even more critical now that we find out who's behind the cyber-attack.

"This is the best gift you could ever give me." I smile through my tears at this amazing woman.

Natalie

WE WALK BACK TO the compound, each with puffy red eyes from our happy tears. My heart is so much lighter knowing Alex is happy about this baby. His face is alight with a smile. He has a secret he's bursting to tell, and he won't have to wait long. We're heading straight to Maxim's office to discuss my visit with Dr. Turova.

Everything's quiet when we get back inside. Alex leads me down a hallway I haven't seen yet.

"The security rooms are down there." Alex points to the end of the hall. "And this is Max's office."

A guard is stationed outside of the double doors. He looks up when he sees us approaching.

"*Kak vy segodnya?*"

"*U menya vse khorosho a u tebya?*"

"I'm doing well. Timur, this is my fiancé, Natalie."

"Pleasure to meet you, ma'am," Timur answers in perfect English.

I smile in return, suddenly too nauseous to speak. The elation I was feeling has given way to nerves. My pregnancy is going to complicate an already difficult situation. I know Maxim will be happy about the baby. What I don't know is what his reaction will be when we ask to leave the compound.

"Is Maxim available?"

"He's finishing up a phone call. Is he expecting you, Mr. Montgomery?"

"He isn't. But something's come up, and it's imperative I speak with him right away."

The guard nods in acknowledgment before opening the doors and disappearing inside. My stomach is doing tumble saults. I've known Lana's family for many years. But things feel very different here—less like a family and more like a business. Instead of Max being the kind, approachable man I know him to be, he's distant, almost cold. His eyes don't hold their usual warmth. In its place is a dark ruthlessness that, if I'm honest, scares me. I'm just about to ask Alex if we can wait to tell him when the doors open.

"He'll see you both now." Timur steps aside, allowing us to enter the office.

Max's office is ultra-modern. The huge room is sparsely furnished, with only the shiny black desk Maxim is currently sitting behind and several grey leather chairs opposite him. Like most of the other rooms, there's a wall of windows allowing in the natural light and scenic views outside. Yesterday, Irina assured me all of the glass is bulletproof, and each window is equipped with steel shields that activate by the press of a button in the case of an emergency. I don't know whether that knowledge helped or made me more afraid of what sort of threat requires that much of a response.

"It is a pleasure to see you both. What brings you by this afternoon?" Concern appears on his face. "Did everything go well with the doctor?"

I sit next to Alex with my hands folded tightly in my lap. I'm hoping to hide how badly they're shaking.

"That's what we came to talk to you about," Alex says.

The room is silent for what feels like hours. My heart's beating so fast and loud I'm sure Maxim can hear it.

"We have good news to share with you." Alex takes my hand. "Natalie and I are going to have a baby."

Maxim's face lights up. "I am going to be a *dedushka*!" he exclaims as he jumps from his seat and rounds the desk.

Alex stands and extends his hand, but Maxim ignores it and pulls him in for a hug instead. Then, he leans down, grabbing my face in his strong hands, kissing both cheeks before wrapping me in a Maxim-style bear hug.

"This is indeed wonderful news, my sweet girl. We must celebrate tonight."

"I have something I need to ask," I interrupt.

"What is it?"

This lighthearted version of Maxim is the one I'm used to and comfortable with. It helps dissipate some of my nerves, although I'm still unsure of his answer.

"Karina wants to do an ultrasound to determine how far along the pregnancy is and to check on the baby's health. But we need to leave the compound to do it."

Maxim leans back on the edge of his desk with his arms crossed over his chest. Alex returns to his seat next to me. We sit in silence, watching Maxim deliberate his answer.

"We wouldn't ask if Karina didn't think it was necessary."

"I know, and I will not stand in the way of Natalia and *moya vnuchka* getting the medical care they need," Maxim says thoughtfully.

"Granddaughter?" Alex asks, raising an eyebrow.

"*Da.*"

"What if it's a grandson?" I ask.

""I will love this baby either way. But you will see, this baby is a girl." The love he already has for our child fills me with warmth. "When is your appointment?"

"Karina told me to call after we spoke to you."

"I'm assuming Viktor will accompany us?" Alex asks.

"No. Viktor is not familiar enough with the area. Timur will escort you."

"Your guard?" I ask, surprised.

"Yes. You and your child will have only the best protection." Maxim returns to his seat behind his desk. "Set up the appointment, and I will arrange to get you there and back safely."

"Thank you, Max."

"Thank you, Natalia. You have brought much-needed joy to my life."

Alex and I leave his office together. With that hurdle crossed, a weight lifts off my shoulders.

"How are you feeling?"

"It was a long day yesterday. With the time change, I'm kinda tired. I was thinking about going to lie down for a bit."

"You go ahead. I'll be along shortly. I have to check in with Viktor." Alex kisses my forehead, and we part ways.

Once I'm back in our room, I take the card Karina left with her contact information from my pocket and lift the receiver to place the call.

"Hello, Ms. Clarke," a man's voice answers. "Can I help you?"

I wasn't expecting to get a live person. "Yes. I need to make a phone call."

"Who do you need to reach?"

I give the information to the unknown man on the other end, and the line rings.

"Hello?" Dr. Turova answers.

"Hi. It's Natalie Clarke."

"How are you?"

"Tired, but well."

"How did Alex take the news?"

I recount our afternoon, telling her how delighted Alex is. "We got the okay to leave the compound for the ultrasound."

"I'm glad to hear that." Karina goes silent, and I hear the click of keys on a keyboard. "Let's do Monday at seven p.m. The clinic will be closed then. I think that will be best."

"Okay, I'll let Maxim know."

"See you then."

With that taken care of, I hang up the phone, crawl into bed, and fall asleep.

Alex

AFTER SEEING NATALIE OFF, I go directly to the security room. When I get there, the door's open.

"What brings you this way, boss?" Viktor asks.

"I'm just checking on the progress. Any updates?"

Viktor motions for me to take a seat next to him. He's sitting with one of the men on the tech team, someone I'm unfamiliar with. They're looking at several computer screens, each with an image similar to the one Maxim showed us when we first arrived. Red flags, more than we saw yesterday, dot locations on a map that's now spread across the globe.

"Whoever it is clearly doesn't want to be found," Viktor says.

"How do you even make sense of that?"

"It's a slow process." Viktor sits back in his chair. "It's taking more time than we'd hoped, but we won't stop until we uncover who's responsible for this."

"Alexander, I was hoping to find you here." Maxim walks into the room.

"Did we forget something?"

"*Nyet*. I did not want to say anything that might upset Natalia."

I appreciate his thoughtfulness. Natalie doesn't need to worry about anything more than necessary, especially now.

"I was on the phone with Nicholai when you came to the office. Unfortunately, his computer system sustained a series of attempted cyberattacks overnight. They were unsuccessful, but this raises my level of concern. Whoever is behind this is serious about getting our information."

His words are like a punch to my stomach, knocking the wind out of me. "We aren't going home anytime soon, are we?"

"I am afraid not."

I close my eyes, absorbing the information and making a quick plan to tell Natalie.

"I spoke to my staff," Maxim adds. "Everything is set for tonight."

Viktor looks at me curiously. "Did I miss something?"

"All will be revealed later." Maxim turns to leave the room. "I will be in my office."

I shrug, pretending not to know what he's talking about. "I'm going to go talk to Natalie. Keep me updated."

When I get to our room, I find Natalie sound asleep. Quietly, I pull a chair next to the bed to watch over her while she rests. My girl looks so peaceful sleeping—she's radiant. Her arms draped across her still-flat belly. In a few weeks, her body will begin changing, growing round as our unborn child grows. The image makes my pulse accelerate with excitement.

She begins to stir as if she can sense me staring at her.

"Hi," she says, her voice quiet.

"I hope I didn't wake you."

"You didn't. Come lay with me?"

I slip my shoes off and get in bed, pulling her into my arms. She lays her head on my chest. I've never felt as emotional as I do right now, holding my whole world, the two people I love most, in my arms. My heart aches, knowing I'm going to spoil the moment with the news I'm about to deliver.

"Viktor briefed me on the tech team's progress."

"Have they found whoever is responsible?" Natalie pulls back to look at me. Hope fills her eyes.

"No." Watching disappointment wash over her is hard. "Nicholai called." I force myself not to look away as I tell her the rest of the update. "His systems are being attacked as well."

"What does that mean?"

"This attack is more sophisticated than we first thought. We're going to be here longer than we planned."

"What about the bridal shower?"

"We need to call your parents. It's going to have to be postponed."

Natalie doesn't answer. She lays her head back on my chest and begins to cry. All I can do is hold her and tell her everything will be okay. I don't know how or when, but I have to trust it will.

"Can't we have dinner in our room?" Natalie sits on the edge of the bed. "I want to be alone."

"We can't do that to Maxim. He's excited to tell everyone our news." I look at her through the mirror while I finish straightening my tie. Maxim requested formal dress for tonight's dinner. "It would be disrespectful if we didn't show up."

"I know." She shrugs. "I just don't feel much like celebrating."

I walk over and stoop down before her. "I know you're disappointed, and so am I. But we're together, and we have this." I place my hand on her belly. "The news of your pregnancy is exactly what everyone needs to hear right now."

"I can't believe we're having a baby."

"You're going to be a wonderful mother." My heart overflows with so many emotions.

Elation.

Awe.

Fear.

Fear is the biggest one. The one I'm trying to hide from Natalie.

I don't know how long we'll have to stay in Russia. Although we're safe at the compound, I want to get Natalie home as soon as possible so we can move up our wedding date. Then our focus will be on preparing for our little one's arrival.

"Should we call your parents before dinner?"

"Can you tell them, please?"

"Of course, baby girl. I'll take care of everything."

I'm connected to her parent's line, and after we get past the formalities, I break the bad news.

"Postpone the shower?" Charlotte screeches so loud I have to pull the phone away from my ear.

"I'm afraid so," I reply calmly. "I've had some important business matters come up that require my attention. I need to see them through before we fly home." Charlotte knows I do business internationally, so this story won't raise any red flags.

"Can't Natalie fly home on her own?"

"We discussed that option and decided against it."

"How am I going to cancel everything?"

"We aren't canceling, just postponing." I grab Natalie's hand. "We don't have good cell service here. If you can make the calls for us and let everyone know, we'll get back to them with a new date as soon as we're home. That would be a big help."

"Where's Natalie? I want to speak to her." Charlotte's tone is clipped.

"She and Lana are out in town shopping. Doing girl things."

"I'll give her a call."

"Unfortunately, she left her cell phone here." I don't like being dishonest with her, but my priority will always be to protect Natalie. And right now, the less her parents know, the better. "I'll have her call you when they get back."

"I don't like this one bit, Alexander."

"We're disappointed too. But Natalie and I discussed it and agreed that since we're already here, we should stay and get this handled now. Otherwise, this will be hanging over our heads, and we won't get to enjoy planning our wedding."

"I don't understand all this business stuff." Charlotte blows a frustrated breath into the phone. "Just have Natalie call me."

"I will. Have a good afternoon." Natalie lays her head on my shoulder. She's under too much stress. It can't be good for her or the baby. "I know that was hard. I'm sorry for all this."

She doesn't respond.

I close my eyes and, for the first time, wonder if getting involved with Maxim was a mistake. At the time, I had no one to think about other than myself. Now I have Natalie and a baby on the way. If I could go back, would I change anything? My thoughts are interrupted when there's a knock on the door.

"You guys in there?" Lana calls.

Natalie answers the door. "We're here."

"What's wrong?"

"Just disappointed about having to postpone my bridal shower."

Lana wraps Natalie in a hug. "I'm so sorry. But, on the bright side, you get to spend more time hanging out with me."

I check the time on my watch. "Ladies, we need to get to the dining room. If we're late, Maxim will have our heads."

"What's up with him tonight anyway?" Lana spins around, showing off her evening dress.

"I guess we need to get to dinner and find out." I take Natalie's hand in mine. "Let's go."

Natalie

BRANDON JOINS OUR TRIO as we make our way through the labyrinth of hallways. While we walk, Lana chatters away about how lucky we are to get this extended vacation. I smile and nod in agreement. She doesn't seem to notice my lack of enthusiasm as she prattles on about spending afternoons swimming and exploring the many paths on the property

I love my best friend, but I'm relieved when we arrive at the dining room, and she takes her seat across the large table next to Brandon.

Alex leans over and whispers, "Lana's used to coming here. Growing up, Maxim would periodically bring her and Irina here to make it seem normal."

I meet his gaze. Looking back at me are eyes filled with so much love and devotion.

"I'll be okay. Everything will work out the way it's supposed to." Alex offers me a reassuring smile.

I'm surprised when Viktor and Timur join us at the table. Viktor takes the empty seat next to me, and Timur sits across from him. Looking around the table at this unexpected mix of people that's become my second family takes away some of my sadness. Maxim signals to a member of his staff standing near the kitchen entrance. She disappears behind the door. Seconds later, several staff members enter the room, carrying plates of mouthwatering food they set before us.

"Are you going to tell us why we had to get all dressed up tonight?" Lana asks.

"All in due time, *moya babochka*." Maxim grins.

Lana huffs a loud sigh and rolls her eyes, to which Brandon gives a warning glare. I'm amused watching their dynamic silently play out.

Despite the circumstances of our being here, the conversation is light and easy throughout the remainder of the meal. I don't think I could ever get used to this or consider it *normal,* but even I can't help myself from enjoying the company of my friends. It isn't until drinks and dessert have been served that Maxim winks at me and stands.

"I know you are wondering why I have called for formal attire at this evening's meal."

I look across the table at Lana, who sits silently with her hands folded in her lap.

"We have had little to celebrate the past few days, but that all changed with some news I received today." Maxim motions for his wife to stand next to him. "Irina and I are going to be grandparents," Maxim announces proudly.

Brandon's eyes grow huge as he looks between Maxim and Lana. "What?"

"I have no idea what he's talking about," Lana says, her face going pale.

Maxim chuckles. He's enjoying the confusion around the table. Irina gives him a subtle look imploring him to finish the story.

"Alexander and Natalia, although neither of you is our child by birth, Irina and I have come to love you as family. We are so excited that you will be adding to your own family."

His sentiment brings tears to my eyes.

"You're pregnant?" Lana squeals as she jumps from her seat and rounds the table. "I'm going to be an aunt?" She grabs me from my seat and pulls me into a tight hug.

"You're not going to get to be an aunt if you squeeze the life out of her." Alex jokes.

Lana lets go. "Oh my God. I'm so sorry. Did I hurt you?"

"You didn't hurt me."

Brandon walks around the table. Alex extends his hand to shake, but Brandon pulls him in for a bro hug. Then he turns and hugs me. Timur is the last to congratulate me before I sit and resume eating dessert. Viktor mindlessly drags his fork through his *Ptichye Moloko* cake. It surprises me that he didn't offer his congratulations. Instead, he remains sitting, a serious look on his face.

"What's wrong?" I ask quietly, putting my hand on his shoulder.

"Nothing."

"That's not true. Please, tell me."

"I'm happy for you. But you know me, always thinking about safety and logistics." He offers me a strained smile.

I put my hand on my stomach. "I've got it covered for now."

"I'm going to take my cake with me and get back to work," Viktor says quietly and kisses my cheek. "Congratulations."

"Where are you going to so soon?" Maxim asks.

"I told Dimitri I wouldn't be gone long. I need to get back to work."

Maxim nods, not at all bothered by my bodyguard's sudden exit. But I can't shake the feeling that there's more to Viktor's mood than he's letting on. Maxim must notice my concern.

"Do not worry, Natalia. He has a lot on his mind right now."

"Yes, he does." Although I'm not convinced, that's the whole story.

Lana moves to Viktor's vacated seat and dives right into planning everything we need to do before the baby's born. She's only known for a few minutes, and already she has a list a mile long. I'm forced to put my concerns about Viktor aside. As the evening progresses, Maxim and Irina entertain us with parenting stories—they had their hands full with Lana as a young child.

It's very late when we finally return to our room. Despite my initial reservations about tonight, I'm glad Alex forced me to have dinner with everyone. It ended up being a fantastic evening that filled me with joy. .

Natalie

ONCE AGAIN, I'VE SLEPT well into the afternoon, a luxury I haven't been afforded in months. The sheets on Alex's side of the bed are cold. He must've been up for hours. I'm sure he and Maxim are planning out each and every detail for our appointment with Karina this evening. I swing my legs over the edge of the bed and sit up slowly, hoping to avoid the nausea I've been experiencing if I get up too fast. Once I'm sure my stomach will remain calm, I shower quickly before heading out of our bedroom, searching for food and Alex—in that order.

The dining room is empty, which doesn't surprise me since I slept through breakfast and lunch. Carefully, I open the kitchen door. I've never been in here before. I'm not certain if I'm even allowed in here. I stand just inside the doorway and watch the chefs busy at work preparing what I'm assume will be tonight's dinner.

"Excuse me," I say, hoping to get someone's attention.

An older woman looks up from her task.

"I know I missed mealtime, but is it possible I can make myself a quick bite to eat?"

"*Nyet*." The woman leaves her stool where she's cutting vegetables and ushers me out of the kitchen.

My stomach growls in protest. "I'll stay out of your way. I just need to make—"

She takes my arm. "Sit," she says with a heavy accent. "I will feed you."

"You don't have to go to any trouble."

She puts her finger to her lips, silencing me. "Stay."

With that, she turns and disappears into the kitchen. A few minutes later, she comes out carrying a bowl of *Okroshka*, a cold soup with potatoes, eggs, and cucumbers. I thank her and begin eating, savoring the fresh ingredients. She returns carrying a Charcuterie Board filled with cheeses, meats, crackers, and fruits. I laugh at the vast amount of food she's laid out.

"I hope you plan to stay to help me eat all this."

"Eat." She points to my tummy. "For *malysh*."

"*Spasibo*." I thank her in Russian, bringing a big smile to her face.

Then, I do my best to put a dent in the food that's been prepared for me. While I'm eating, Alex comes into the room.

"There you are," he says, kissing me before sitting down. "I've been looking all over for you."

"I was going to come find you after I got something to eat." I gesture to the food. "Want some?"

He plucks a few grapes from the tray and pops one in his mouth.

"I assumed you'd be busy with Maxim. I didn't want to interrupt you."

"You're never an interruption, baby girl. Maxim's taken care of every detail. We'll go, get our baby's first picture, and return for a late dinner. Unfortunately," Alex says as he stands up. "I have some work to do before we leave."

"That's okay. I'm going to find Lana and see if she wants to spend the rest of the afternoon at the pool."

When it's time to leave for the clinic, Viktor walks us outside, where Timur waits in one of the black SUVs we arrived in.

"Natalie, give Viktor your engagement ring to hold until we return," Alex instructs.

"Why?" I haven't taken the ring off since we got back together.

"We're going into a section of town where the ring could draw unwanted attention. It'll be safer for us if you leave it here."

I slide the ring off my finger and place it in Viktor's palm.

"I'll keep it safe until you get back."

I feel naked without my ring. But I have no doubt Viktor will take care of it until we get back.

We get in the car and slowly start to pull away. I wave goodbye to Viktor. Surprisingly, he returns it with a wave and an unexpected smile.

I didn't realize how far away from everything we actually are at the compound. It took almost three hours for us to get to the clinic. Finally, Timur pulls around the back of a nondescript building into a private parking lot.

"Wait here," Timur instructs before taking his gun from the seat next to him. He steps out of the car and scans the area.

I grab Alex's hand. "I'm scared."

"Maxim took care of everything. Timur's just being extra cautious."

We wait while Timur makes a call on his cell. As soon as he slides the phone into his pocket, the back door of the clinic opens. Karina stands in the doorway, smiling as she motions for us to come in.

Timur turns and opens the car door. "Everything's all clear." He offers his hand to help me while Alex gets out on his side. Together we make our way inside the clinic.

"I'll wait here, sir," Timur says, closing the door.

"It's so good to see you again, Natalie." Karina kisses me on both cheeks. "How are you feeling?"

"Other than tired and a bit nervous, I'm okay."

"There's nothing to be nervous about. The clinic is a secure location."

"How are you this evening, Alex?"

"Doing well, thank you for asking."

She escorts us into a small, dimly lit room. Inside is a twin bed covered in a beautiful bedspread with several fluffy pillows arranged at the top. Sitting next to the bed is a plush armchair. On the opposite side, the ultrasound equipment is set up. Despite the room's purpose being for a medical procedure, it has a comfortable, homey feel.

"If you could lie down, we'll get started."

I get on the bed and lay back, finding a comfortable spot on the pillows. Alex sits on the chair next to me.

Karina turns a large TV-like screen in our direction.

"I'm going to put some gel on your tummy, and we'll get started." She places the wand on my stomach and starts moving it around.

The screen comes to life with a fuzzy, grey-and-white picture that doesn't look like much of anything to me.

"I'm just doing some measurements," she explains as she pauses the screen and clicks some buttons.

I strain my eyes, trying to find something that looks like a baby, but I can't decipher the grainy image on the screen. "Now we get to the fun part." Suddenly, the room is filled with the rapid swooshing of our baby's heartbeat. Then, with the click of a button, the image on the screen changes to a very clear picture.

"Is that?" Alex's voice cracks.

"Yes. That's your baby." She explains the 4D images we see on the screen. "From my measurements, I'd say you're about thirteen weeks pregnant. As you can see, the baby still looks a bit like an alien at this stage." We all laugh at her comment.

She continues moving the wand around, giving us different views of our little one. I'm amazed at how active the baby is as it kicks its little feet and moves its hands close to its face.

"Is the baby sucking its thumb?"

"Yes, it is." Karina freezes the screen on the image.

I turn and look at Alex. Tears are streaming down his face, his gaze fixed on the screen. Seeing my Dominant so humbled by our unborn child leaves an indelible imprint on my heart.

"How is this even possible, though? I was on the pill. I never missed a day."

"Did you make sure to take it at the same time every day?"

"Yes."

"Except for the weekend we visited my father. I got you, um—" Alex clears his throat. "Sidetracked. And you forgot your pill that night, remember?"

My cheeks blush. "Yes, but I took two the next night."

"That could do it," Karina says.

"And that was about thirteen weeks ago." Alex smiles.

Karina gives us a pregnancy book to read about the changes my body will be going through. She also provides us with a bottle of prenatal vitamins. We finish our appointment and are about to walk out the back door when Karina rushes over. "Don't forget these." She hands me a small stack of black and white photos. "Baby's first pictures."

"Thank you so much."

"Please let me know if you need anything else while you're here."

Alex

TIMUR'S STANDING GUARD OUTSIDE. When he sees us, he grabs the door and holds it as Natalie and I walk through. "All set, sir?"

"Yes. We're ready to go."

Natalie shows him the ultrasound pictures as we walk to the parked car. He nods and smiles, pretending to be looking, but his eyes never stop scanning our surroundings. I'm feeling lighter than air as I help Natalie into the car. I figured we might have a child, eventually. *Someday*. But when I saw my unborn child on the screen, nothing else mattered other than the unconditional and all-consuming love I felt for our child. I can't imagine my life any different.

Timur starts the car and pulls onto the main road to begin the drive back to the safety of Maxim's compound. Natalie and I are immersed in our child's photos and looking through the thick paperback book Dr. Turova gave us.

"What the fuck?" Timur's voice startles me.

"What's wrong?"

"It's the police. They're pulling us over."

I hadn't even realized they were behind us, let alone that they had their lights on.

"What's going on?" Natalie asks, panic filling her voice.

"Don't worry, baby girl." I grab her hand. "I'm sure it's nothing more than a routine stop."

I meet Timur's worried eyes in the mirror. He puts his gun under his leg before signaling and pulling to the side of the poorly lit road. A million scenarios run through my head. This shouldn't be happening. Maxim called his contact in the police department. We were cleared for travel without interference. "Don't worry. Timur will handle this, and we'll be on our way."

An officer dressed in a black uniform walks up to Timur's rolled-down window.

"Can I help you, officer?" he asks in Russian.

"Turn the car off and step out of the vehicle."

"Did I do something wrong?"

"Turn it off and step out of the vehicle," the officer repeats.

Timur slides the gun between the seats before opening the door and stepping outside the car.

"Alex, I'm scared," Natalie whispers.

Another car drives by and pulls in front of us, blocking us in. That's all the confirmation I need to know that this isn't a routine stop. Something's wrong. I lean forward to grab the gun at the same time the backdoors of our car are pulled open.

"Get out of the car," a masked man orders.

"Alex," Natalie yells as a second masked man pulls her from my grasp.

I jump out of the car. "Get your fucking hands off her."

I find myself forcefully dragged toward the rear of our car, where I'm placed next to Timur and held at gunpoint by our captors. The officer in charge is currently occupied with a cellphone conversation. I take a quick look around to assess the situation. Natalie is at the front of the car, but I can't see who is holding her or if they are armed. Despite having some knowledge of hand-to-hand combat, I am not as skilled as Timur. However, we exchange a meaningful glance and decide to make a move against the men standing in front of us.

Timur nods, and in a sudden motion, one of the men falls to the ground. I quickly take advantage of the opportunity to pin him down while delivering a powerful right hook to his face, causing him to drop his weapon. I kick the gun out of his reach. However, he regains his strength and overpowers me, causing me to fall to the ground. Meanwhile, I hear the sounds of a struggle between Timur and the officer next to me.

A gunshot rings out.

Time stands still.

Timur's body falls to the ground next to me—lifeless.

Somewhere in the distance, Natalie's screams fill the night.

I scramble to my feet. "Let her go."

Momentarily I forget about the man I'm fighting, my only goal is to get to Natalie, but it's dark. I know she's near the front of the car, but I can't see her. My feet struggle to find purchase when the sound of a gun's safety being removed stops me in my tracks.

"If you continue to fight, we'll shoot the girl." A gun digs into my temple.

"Alex," Natalie whimpers.

The police vehicle's lights are turned on. That's when I see the man holding Natalie with one arm around her waist. In his other hand is a gun pointed at her head.

I stop struggling, paralyzed by fear. "Don't hurt her. I'll do whatever you say."

The officer barks out instructions in Russian. The man holding Natalie grabs her arm, pulling her to the car in the front.

"Where's he taking her?"

Natalie struggles, trying to grab anything to keep from being taken. She loses the fight when the man grabs her hair and drags her toward the waiting car.

"Get your fucking hands off her."

Crack.

My world goes black.

Natalie

THE DOOR IS YANKED open, and I am forcefully pulled from the car by a pair of gloved hands. During my struggle to break free from the grip of the masked assailant, my unborn baby's ultrasound photograph tumble to the ground.

The police car no longer has its lights on, rendering the area pitch black. I'm unable to locate Alex and Timur, but their grunts are audible. Alex yells for the masked man to release me.

A gunshot echoes into the stillness of the night, startling birds that take flight from a nearby tree.

"No." My world moves in slow motion.

The police car's blazing lights create a surreal world around me. A pool of blood surrounds Timur lying on the ground. My eyes shift to Alex, who's being held at gunpoint. His eyes widen in terror, and he freezes in place.

Suddenly, I feel the chill of metal pressed against my temple, and I silently beg Alex to rescue me. The officer barks orders in Russian, and the man holding me yanks my hair, throwing me off balance as he drags me towards their car.

Alex struggles again, fighting to reach me. The police officer coolly approaches him and slams the butt of his gun into Alex's head. He falls motionless beside Timur. Panic grips me, and I attempt to scream, but no sound comes out.

I'm no match against the man's force, and he drags me toward the second vehicle while the other men toss Alex's lifeless body into the police car. Seeing them taking Alex rather than leaving him dead beside Timur gives me a flicker of hope he may still be alive.

I'm shoved into the backseat of the second car. "Alex," I call, tears pouring down my face as the masked man takes his place beside me. The door barely shuts before the driver squeals the tires, tearing away from the scene.

"If you don't shut up. You'll meet the same fate as your boyfriend," the driver says in perfect English.

I don't listen and fight with every ounce of my strength, yanking at the door handles, doing everything in my power to break free and escape.

"Do it," the driver orders.

The man beside me pulls a syringe from his pocket. Before I can react, he jabs it into my neck.

My baby.

Darkness creeps into my vision, and I fall into the black abyss.

My thoughts are jumbled, and confusion engulfs me. Where am I? Why does it feel like I'm in motion? My eyes flicker open for a fleeting moment, and a flood of memories rushes back. I force myself to shut them once more and remain motionless. The reality hits me hard - Timur is dead, Alex's fate is unknown, and I have been taken.

With deliberate slowness, I reach for my pocket, hoping my phone is still there, but I find nothing. It must have fallen during the struggle. Panic rises within me, knowing the phone was my only link to the people who could save us.

"I know you're awake. You may as well open your eyes."

It takes a few moments for my eyes to adjust and focus. We're no longer on the desolate highway. Instead, bright lights surround us, forcing me to squint. The presence of other cars suggests we're in a city of some sort. When we arrived, we landed in St. Petersburg. That's at least a two-hour drive from the compound and in the opposite direction of the clinic. How long was I knocked out? Could we really be in St. Petersburg?

Suddenly, the sound of a low-flying airplane catches my attention, and I sit up to look out of the window. My heart races as I see the familiar airport. My mind races as I try to make sense of the situation. The driver takes us to a small building far from the main terminals and opens my door without turning off the engine. But I stay rooted in place, making no move to follow.

"Get out." I refuse to move. The man forcibly pulls me out of the car.

A tall man with bronzed skin steps out from the shadows. He's well-dressed in an expensive tailored suit. His hair is dark, sprinkled with strands of grey. Soulless black eyes stare at me. "She's lovely. She'll command a handsome price."

Oh my God, they plan to sell me.

In a panic, I scan the surroundings for a means of escape. The entrance we drove through is now closed, and the only other exit is blocked by this new man standing in front of me. It's an impossible task for me to make it past him. I can't think clearly. My head is still fuzzy from the drugs they administered. Did they harm my unborn child? I push the thought aside for now. I have to remain level-headed, prioritize the safety of my baby, and preserve my strength until a real opportunity to flee arises.

The well-dressed man reaches into his suit jacket, pulls out an envelope, and hands it to the driver, who tears it open. Inside is a large stack of cash. I gasp as I watch the man quickly count the money. When he's done, he nods and gets in the car. The garage door opens, allowing him to speed away before it slams closed.

My body trembles as I stand face to face with this stranger.

"Who are you? What do you want with me?"

"Tsk, tsk," the man sneers. "A trained submissive should know her place, which is silent unless spoken to. It seems we'll have to do some more training with you."

How does he know I'm a submissive?

"Alex is going to come after you. You won't get away with this."

"Silence. It's time to go." He grabs my arm.

I struggle to match his long strides as we exit the building through a black door. Before us sits a large, unmarked jet. My feet anchor to their spot as I resist his pull. For a fleeting moment, his grip loosens. Boarding that jet is not an option. If I let them take me, I'll vanish without a trace, and I refuse to become a statistic. I quickly scan my surroundings and spot the main terminal in the distance. It's a long shot, but it's my only chance. I have no choice but to take it.

The night air is filled with the man's menacing laugh. "What do you think you're doing?"

Without wasting another second, I sprint toward the terminal, hoping to put as much distance between myself and the plane as possible.

"Fuck," he yells.

I have a split-second head start, but the man's heavy footsteps catch up quickly. I will my feet to move faster. My lungs burn, but I don't give up. I have to get away. Then, a heavy weight tackles me from behind. My body crashes to the ground, and I'm rolled onto my back. The man straddles me. With a burst of adrenaline, I fight back, using all the strength I have left. I claw at his face, and he grunts in pain, but his grip only tightens. My heart races as I struggle to break free. I refuse to give up, even as he overpowers me.

"Your fight only turns me on."

His erection pressed against my stomach makes me nauseous. My stomach churns, and I can't stop the urge to vomit. I turn my head to the side and empty my stomach onto the ground.

The man's laughter echoes in my ears. I feel his hand on my shoulder, pulling me back to my feet. He retrieves a white handkerchief from his suit pocket and holds it out to me. "Clean yourself up," he says with a twisted smirk.

Reluctantly, I take it and wipe the vomit from my face before dropping the white fabric to the ground.

"You will be punished for that." Then, without wasting any time, he lifts me and tosses me over his shoulder.

"Put me down." I kick and scream, trying to get out of his hold.

He slaps me hard—the impact reverberates through my body.

"Hold still," he orders. "If you fight, your punishment will be worse."

As much as I want to keep fighting, I must think about the baby. Protecting him or her is my number one goal. I can't take any more foolish chances.

With that in mind, I stop fighting, surrendering to the man who easily carries me up the jet's stairs, taking me away from Alex and everyone who can save me.

Viktor

ANXIETY GNAWS AT ME as I pace outside the front door of the compound, my eyes glued to the driveway. If I concentrate hard enough, maybe I can make the SUV appear.

Alex texted me over three hours ago, saying they were on their way back, but they're nowhere in sight. They should've been here by now. I've tried calling and texting them, but there's been no response. My calls go straight to voicemail.

Frustrated, I pull out my phone to check the SUV's GPS, and my heart sinks. "What the hell?" I punch the side of the house in frustration. Shoving my phone into my picket, I burst through the front door and storm into Maxim's office without bothering to knock. The doors slam against the walls, echoing through the quiet halls.

Maxim's face flushes with anger from my rude intrusion into his office. "What's the meaning of this?" he demands.

"There's a problem."

Alex

MY HEAD POUNDS FROM the most wicked headache I've ever had. Men's voices echo around me, the sound so loud I have to fight the urge to vomit. I force myself to wade through the fog and concentrate on my surroundings. That's when I feel the unmistakable rumble of the engine beneath me. I'm on a plane, and we're in the air. Staying quiet and keeping my breathing even, I continue to assess the situation. The feeling is just beginning to return to my limbs. I attempt to wiggle my fingers but realize my wrists are secured to the armrests. Testing my feet, I find they are also restrained with chains. I'm completely immobilized.

The sound of men's voices gradually comes into focus, drawing my attention to the two figures sitting across from me. Though they speak English, their elongated vowels and rapid speech suggest Mexican heritage. My heart races when I hear them mention a *guera*. They must be referring to Natalie, but I don't hear her voice. If they've hurt her in any way, I'll make sure every one of them suffers a slow and painful death.

"You're finally awake," one of the men says, kicking my leg.

I slowly open my eyes and survey my surroundings. The sun is just beginning to peek over the horizon, revealing a seemingly endless expanse of water—we're flying over an ocean. Inside the jet, I'm seated on a plush caramel-colored chair. The two men facing me wear chino pants and dingy button-down shirts that hang open, revealing their white undershirts. The tattoo on their necks, a dagger piercing a rose with a drop of red blood, strikes fear in my soul. Suddenly, everything falls into place: the attempts to hack into encrypted files, the complex network of IP addresses, and my abduction. The tattoo branding the men's skin is the infamous mark of *El Tomador*, a notorious figure in the world of human trafficking. I also don't have to question where we're going. We're headed to Mexico.

"Where's the girl?" I ask.

"The pretty blonde? She's in good hands." They elbow one another and laugh.

"Where the fuck is she?" I struggle, but it's a futile effort. I can't get free.

"If you're a good boy, maybe you'll get to see her before the boss sells her." The man gets up and moves closer so we're face to face. His breath smells rancid when he speaks. "Give us any trouble, and we make a call that ends her life now. It's up to you." He shrugs casually and walks past me.

I clench my jaw, forcing myself to stay silent and not make any more demands. It's a struggle, but the thought of Natalie and the baby's safety gives me the strength to hold back.

The remainder of the flight passes in relative quiet. The men alternate between napping and texting. When they do speak, it's in Spanish, a language I only have a basic understanding of.

When the plane begins its descent, I strain to catch a glimpse of anything outside the window that could give me a clue to our exact whereabouts. But all I see are nondescript buildings and an unremarkable landscape passing by.

Finally, the wheels touch the ground, and I straighten in my seat, eager to get a better view. We come to a halt in a small airport. The engines power down, and the men rise from their seats.

The taller of the two, who also has a shaved head, pulls out his gun, pointing it at my head. "Don't do anything stupid."

I nod, showing I'll cooperate—for now.

The second man, who's very thin and has greasy hair that hangs over his face, pulls out a pocketknife and approaches my seat. He cuts one zip tie and slaps a handcuff on that wrist before cutting the other free. Then, he pushes me forward, cuffing my hands together behind my back.

"Let's go." The bald man waves the gun.

Standing is difficult, and walking with the short chain around my ankles is clumsy. Greasy hair man grabs my arm and drags me as I stumble to keep up. We're met on the tarmac by what looks like an older model tan military vehicle. The bald man opens the door, and I'm pushed in. I fall on the seat and try to right myself. A difficult task without the use of my hands. Greasy hair guy gets in after me, shutting the door. We start moving. He pulls me to a sitting position and puts a black hood over my head.

I'm restrained, helpless, and at the mercy of dangerous criminals.

Natalie, please be okay. Just hang on, baby girl. I will find you.

Natalie

DESPITE MY CURRENT SITUATION and the adrenaline running through my system, I'm exhausted. The last thing I wanted to do was fall asleep on the plane, flying to who knows where with a madman sitting next to me. My body has other plans and screams for rest. My eyes close of their own accord. I'm lost to sleep.

"Wake up, beautiful. We've landed." I feel the light caress of knuckles against my cheek and the warm whisper of his breath against my ear. The words are gentle, but the voice is all wrong.

It's not Alex.

I startle awake. Plucked from the sweetest dream and dropped into the nightmare that's become my reality. Leaning in closer, the man tries to kiss me, but I turn my head and pull away before his lips meet mine.

"Don't touch me," I snarl.

"*Mi pequeña mascota*," he says smoothly. "Soon, you'll be begging me to touch you."

"Never."

"You are not to speak unless given permission." He grabs my hand. "Come, *mascota*. We don't want to be late."

I pull against him refusing to stand. "Where's Alex?"

He spins around to face me. "I warned you about speaking out of turn. I'm going to enjoy punishing you very much." His black eyes twinkle with eerie delight. I open my mouth to let this guy know exactly what I think about him, but his warning glare makes me think twice, and I remain silent.

"Good girl."

His words send shivers down my spine. This time when he pulls my hand, I follow him out of the plane. We walk to a black stretch Escalade where a man holding a large gun across his chest waits.

"I hope you had a good flight, sir." The man opens the door.

"It was a very smooth flight," my captor responds. "Get in, pet."

I slide across the black leather seat, moving as far away as possible.

The man gets in and laughs when he sees me. "Sit closer. I won't bite—yet."

I inch closer, still leaving distance between us. He pulls me the rest of the way until our legs are touching.

"When I give instructions, you will reply *yes, Master*. Is that clear?"

He expects me to call him Master?

"Answer me." His raised voice bounces off the walls of the car.

"Yes, Master." The disgusting words slip from my mouth.

"That's a good girl." He pulls out his cell phone. "Now, sit quietly. I have work to do."

He spends the rest of the drive on the phone while he strokes my thigh with his free hand. I try to distract myself from his touch by watching out the window, seeking any clue about our location. Because I fell asleep, I lost track of how long the flight was, but wherever we are, the sun is still well above the horizon. It won't set for at least a few hours. It isn't until we've been driving on a highway for quite some time that I finally see a sign. Although the words are in Spanish, I recognize the town's name, Juarez.

Oh my God, we're in Mexico.

The driver takes an unmarked exit, and the surroundings begin to change. The city's buildings disappear. All signs of civilization are now behind us as we drive down a single-lane road through the desert.

Alex, where are you?

I haven't seen or heard mention of him since I watched those men toss his lifeless body into the back of the police car. Is he still in Russia, or did they bring him here too? Our drive comes to a stop when we pull up to a tall chain-link fence with razor wire on top. Heavily armed guards nod at the driver and then slide the gate open, allowing us to pass through. The driver takes us on a series of roads that weave in and out of warehouse-like buildings. Outside of each building are several armed guards patrolling the perimeter. Is this place some sort of prison?

We wind our way up a gentle slope until we stop in front of a sprawling estate. The building looks as though it's been standing for centuries, made of a combination of crème-colored stone and stucco. Multiple archways grace the front of the structure, and the red Spanish-style roof boasts a terrace with intricately adorned white railings. The property is surrounded by lush gardens that lend it an almost magical quality as if it were plucked straight from a fairy tale. Except in this fairy tale, this is where the villain resides.

"Welcome to my home." I look between him and the estate, my mind reeling with unasked questions. "You may speak."

"What is this place? Where am I?" The questions are rapid-fire. "Who are you?"

"My name is Silverio Moreno."

"What is this place?"

He gets out of the car, pulling me along with him. "This." He motions around us. "Is my headquarters."

"Excuse me?"

"I specialize in the delivery of human commodities."

I can't believe what I've just heard. Looking around at the rusty corrugated metal buildings, the gravity of the situation threatens to drown me. The highly guarded buildings are filled with people—people being trafficked.

"You, *mascota*, are fortunate." He strokes my arm. "You will be staying with me as my special guest."

"Where's Alex?"

"He'll be along shortly." Silverio's menacing laugh fills the otherwise quiet space. "Come, let's go inside."

The last thing I want to do is go inside, but I have no choice but to play with his sick little game until I can find Alex.

Viktor

"THE GPS WAS TRACKING their location—everything was fine." I shove my phone in his face. "But then we lost the signal."

Maxim calls Dimitri and orders him to figure out what's happening.

"I can't stay here. I'm going to look for them." It's not a question, and I'm not seeking his approval.

"Take one of the guards with you. I'm trusting you to find them."

On my way to the weapons room, I call the guardhouse, letting them know I need their best man weaponed up and ready to go in five minutes. I grab enough ammo to take out a small town before going to the garage to get a vehicle. Misha, another one of the guards, is waiting there, keys in hand.

I exceed every speed limit on the way to the GPS's final destination. Legal repercussions can wait. All that matters now is ensuring the safety of my boss and his fiancée.

"Over there." Misha points out the SUV that was carrying Natalie and Alex. It's been abandoned on the side of the road.

II swerve across the grassy divider that separates the two directions of travel. This route was chosen because it's not a highly traveled road. My tires screech to a stop behind the SUV, and I jump out.

The scene I find confirms my worst suspicions. The car's empty. To anyone driving by, they'd assume the unfortunate motorists had mechanical issues and abandoned their vehicle to get help. I know that's not the case, and I inspect the scene closer. There are several tiny drops of dried blood on the ground outside the driver's door.

"Get Maxim on the phone, now," I yell over my shoulder to Misha, who's just getting out of the car.

My feet stop dead in their tracks when I get to the back passenger door. Scattered on the ground are pictures from Natalie's ultrasound. My hands tremble as I pick one up. The image of their unborn child is crystal clear. I gather all the discarded pictures and carefully put them in my pocket. The same pocket that holds her engagement ring.

Misha hands me the phone.

"They're gone." I slam the side of the SUV. "Where the fuck are they?"

"I have all my men on it. We will find them."

I disconnect the call to search for more clues.

"Viktor, over here," Misha calls from where he's crouched in the high grass.

I rush over and find Timur lying in a puddle of blood. "Is he alive?"

"His pulse is weak, but he's still with us."

I drop down next to his motionless body. "Timur, can you hear me?"

Misha rips open his shirt to locate the source of the blood and finds a gunshot wound in his chest. He tears his own shirt off and uses it to apply pressure to the injury. Timur groans in response but doesn't open his eyes.

"Hang in there. You're going to be okay," I reassure him.

He has to be okay. He's the only person who can tell us what happened—our best chance of finding Alex and Natalie.

Alex

THE HOOD IS RIPPED off, and after a quick look around, I know exactly where we are—The Chihuahuan Desert. If I had any doubt, our current location, combined with the tattoos, confirms Silverio Moreno, one of the most prominent and dangerous men in the trafficking world, is behind all of this. We're in deep shit. My first priority is finding Natalie and making sure she's unharmed. Then I must figure out how to get us out of this highly guarded fortress alive.

I'm sickened as we drive past warehouse-like buildings, most with no windows, knowing that countless numbers of men, women, and children are being held against their will. Innocent people were swiped from the streets, plucked from their families, never to be seen again. We don't stop at any of them. Instead, we head straight for the sprawling hacienda atop the hill.

"Get out," greasy hair man orders and pushes me out of the car door.

My feet hit the ground, and my head spins. I'm sure I have a concussion from the hit I sustained. "Where's Natalie?" I growl.

"She's busy with the boss." The men elbow each other.

Murderous rage boils through me. If anyone touches her, I'll kill them. I'll kill them all.

I'm pushed through the front door of the house, my legs tangle around the chain, and I fall to my knees. A pair of leather boots appear in front of me. When I look up, I recognize their owner. Silverio Moreno, better known to his associates as *el Tomador* or *The Taker*. He stands in his tailored suit, arms crossed over his chest, and a sinister smile on his face.

"It's nice of you to join us, Alejandro," he drawls. "Your beautiful girlfriend has been asking about you."

"Where is she?"

He lowers his hands to his sides and smiles. "She's a little tied up at the moment. We've been waiting for your arrival to get started."

"If you touch her—"

Moreno fists the top of my shirt, pulling me to my feet. His face only inches from mine. "I suggest you consider your next words very carefully. Your girlfriend will pay for every threat you make. Do you understand?"

"Yes." The single word comes out with a snarl.

"Uncuff our guest," Moreno orders before dismissing the men who dragged me in here. They're replaced by Moreno's guards. "Now, if you'll join me in the courtyard, I have a little something waiting for us."

One of the guards shoves his gun between my shoulder blades. A little encouragement to follow their boss. We walk down an open-air hallway with tall arched ceilings. It would be beautiful if evil didn't permeate every inch of the place. Moreno approaches an archway and stops walking. When I look into the center courtyard, my stomach turns.

Natalie is naked. She's been positioned on her hands and knees and restrained to a bench.

"Your submissive is a stunning woman." His eyes never leave what's mine.

"What the fuck?" I roar.

"Alex?" Natalie pulls against her restraints, trying to look behind her.

"It's me. I'm here." My heart feels like as though it's being ripped from my chest.

Moreno strolls over to Natalie and runs his fingers up her spine. "Sit him down. Struggle, and her punishment will be worse."

The guards firmly grasp each of my arms and force me onto a hard wooden bench, positioning me to face Natalie from behind. Dread fills me as I realize I'm about to witness whatever evil intentions Moreno has in store for her. Moreno positions himself in front of Natalie and begins stroking her hair. She flinches and attempts to avoid his touch. Rage builds within me. Suddenly, Moreno bends down to pick up an object. I can't see what it is until it's flying through the air, producing a deafening crack that echoes throughout the courtyard.

"No," I yell and jump from my seat. The guards grab me, shoving me back down.

"You've just added another lash," he says with a maniacal laugh.

Natalie's never experienced a whip. She doesn't like pain. Yes, she's received punishments, but never at the hands of an animal. I can't let him do this. She's pregnant. "Punish me instead of her."

"That would be too easy. My *mascota* earned her punishment and will accept every lash. Won't you?" He leans close to her neck and nips at her ear.

"Yes, Master." Natalie's voice is small.

Hearing her call him *Master* makes my body shudder violently.

Without further delay, he flicks his wrist, and the tail of the whip soars through the air. It lands with a crack across Natalie's upper back. The impact reverberates through her body.

"One," she says through tears.

Again, he wields his whip. A second lash marks Natalie's perfect skin.

"Two," she chokes out.

Moreno doesn't stop until he reaches ten strikes, each delivered with the same intensity as the last. Natalie's back, upper thighs, and ass are now crisscrossed with angry welts. Thankfully, he hasn't drawn blood, but that does little to stop her cries that echo throughout the courtyard. I can barely contain my own tears as I witness her pain. I can't let my feelings get the best of me. I have to stay focused and keep a clear head, no matter how difficult it may be.

He removes the restraints from Natalie's wrists and ankles. "Kneel," he commands.

Gingerly, Natalie slides off the bench. Each move looks like agony. She turns in my direction, only sparing me a quick glance, but it's enough time for me to see the tears pouring down her face. Then, like a dutiful submissive, she lowers to her knees.

Moreno stands beside her while he addresses me. "*Mascota* did not understand her place when we first became acquainted." He strokes her hair. "However, she appears to be a quick learner and has since pleased her new Master."

"You will never be her master," I growl through clenched teeth.

He fists Natalie's hair forcing her to look at him.

"Who is your Master?"

"You are, Master." Natalie's voice shakes.

He pushes her head back down before looking at me with a cocky smile.

"As I was saying. You're probably wondering why you're here." He walks over to me. His leather cowboy boots click on the stone walkway. "You have information I want."

"What information could I possibly have that you want?"

The guard to my right lands a fist on my jaw, snapping my head to the side.

Natalie gasps.

"Let's try that again. You have information that I want, and you're going to get it for me."

"I'm listening." I meet his stare, not showing any of the fear threatening to suffocate me.

"I want Solonik and Federov's files." He turns his back on me, returning to Natalie. "He and his minions have been getting in the way of business and making my life difficult lately. You are going to help me take them down."

"And why would I help you?"

Once again, he grabs Natalie's hair, pulling her to her feet. "Because if you don't. She'll disappear, and you'll never see her again."

Natalie's terrified green eyes meet mine. I want to run to her. Console her. Promise her everything will be okay, but I can't. I need to play this carefully, or we're fucked for sure.

"If you expect me to cooperate, I need your word that she'll remain untouched."

Moreno drags his finger between her breasts and down her abdomen. Natalie tenses and I give her a slight shake of my head, trying to warn her not to flinch. Not to give him any reason to deliver punishment to her abdomen. She can't let on that she's trying to protect her stomach and the life growing inside. My brave girl fights through her fear and remains still despite having Moreno's hands on her. My eyes zero in on where his hand hovers. If he touches her, I'll cut his hands off myself.

"As much as I'm dying to taste her." He licks his lips. "I will guarantee she remains untouched as long as you get me what I want."

I don't trust Moreno or his word, but it's the only assurance I have right now.

"We have a deal. I'll get you whatever you want."

Natalie

Knowing Alex was behind me, watching me stripped naked and whipped by this monster, split my heart in two. I didn't want to give this bastard my tears, but the pain was unbearable, and I couldn't stop them from falling.

I hate being naked in front of all these men. Silverio's hands on me as he drags his perfectly manicured finger down the front of my body, lower and lower, make me sick. Alex shakes his head, a subtle warning for me not to move.

The baby.

Pulling from a strength hidden deep within, I force myself to remain poised, never breaking the connection of my Dominant's determined stare.

I don't want Alex to work with Silverio, even if it's just a means to buy us some time. I understand his reasoning, but I hate the proud look on Silverio's face. Now, I can only hope that he'll hold up his end of the bargain. But those hopes are quickly dashed when he pulls something from his pocket.

"*Every mascota* needs a collar so they don't get lost." Silverio wraps the piece of leather around my neck and fastens it with a click. Reaching into his pocket again, he pulls out a thin chain that he attaches to the collar. He tests the leash, giving it a light tug. With Silverio in front of me, I can't see Alex. But I can hear his growl from where he sits. "Come, *mascota*. Time to eat."

Silverio pulls the leash like I'm an animal, leading me away from Alex. I catch one last glance at him over my shoulder until we turn a corner, and he's out of sight. We keep walking through the estate, most of which appears to be open-air, a feature that would be appealing if we weren't in the middle of hell. Finally, we turn into what appears to be a small dining room. In the center is a table set for one. My captor sits in the chair and pulls my leash, forcing me to kneel on the floor next to him.

Within seconds, a young girl wearing a tiny white lace dress carries out a plate of food which she sets on the table in front of Silverio. She's so young, she can't be more than fourteen or fifteen. It appears she's been here a while. She's already trained to keep her head down, her body almost folded in on itself. The girl rounds the table and gasps when she spots me on the floor. I meet her eyes, offering a small smile, hoping in some way to comfort her. Silverio clears his throat loudly, startling the child, who scurries away.

Without a word, he picks up the fork and knife, cuts into the juicy steak on his plate, and takes a bite. He takes his time before cutting a second piece and bringing the fork to my mouth. My stubbornness says to resist, that I'm not some animal to be fed on the floor. But I have to think of my baby first. He or she needs nourishment, so despite my reservations, I open my mouth and take the offered food.

"Good girl," he croons and then offers me another bite. This time its vegetables.

After I swallow, he holds a glass of water to my lips. I hate how much I enjoy the cool liquid that slides down my throat. The remainder of the meal continues in the same fashion. Silverio takes a few bites, and when he chooses, he offers some to me. It's degrading to be treated like an animal, but each time I open my mouth to accept the food, I remind myself I'm doing this for my baby.

As soon as he finishes, the young girl returns, clearing his empty plate.

"Get up."

I struggle to get to my feet. My legs are numb from kneeling for so long. Silverio doesn't allow me to work out the pins and needles. He's already on the move, pulling me along behind him.

We retrace our steps until we come to a grand staircase. Silverio takes the steps quickly, and I struggle to keep up. Then, we walk down a long hallway lined with doors on both sides until we stop at the last entrance. He doesn't have to open it for me to know where we're going—his bedroom.

Inside, the room is dark and soulless, just like its inhabitant. Being alone with a madman makes my heart pound. I fight the fear that threatens to paralyze me. Looking around, I quickly search for anything that can be used as a weapon. For any possible means of escape. Of course, it comes as no surprise there's nothing. Silverio wastes no time stripping his clothes before walking over to me and nuzzling his face in my neck.

"All evening, I've imagined how delicious you'll taste. Pity I gave Alejandro my word that I wouldn't touch you, for now." He snickers before grabbing the end of the leash.

I follow him around the bed, where I see a pillow and blanket on the floor. He leans down and attaches the leash to a lock.

"I can't risk my *mascota* getting away overnight."

As though this scenario is normal, he crawls into bed and, using a remote control, turns off the lights leaving the room in complete darkness. I feel around on the floor until I find the blanket. It may be thin, but it covers my nakedness—a small amount of comfort. Lying down, the silence of the night is suffocating. When I close my eyes, images of the past few days play like a movie.

Timur being shot. His dead body was left lying in a ditch.

Alex being knocked unconscious. His lifeless body dragged away. Not knowing if he was dead or alive. My relief at seeing Alex alive and my heartache when I saw him restrained. Knowing he had to watch Moreno whip me and hear me call him master.

And the worst horror of all, being injected with an unknown drug, not knowing if it harmed my baby. If their life ended before he or she even had a chance to live.

I wrap my arms around my stomach and cry until sleep pulls me under.

Alex

WE'VE BEEN AT MORENO'S compound for two weeks. I haven't laid eyes on Natalie since the first night we got here. My new routine is ingrained in my being, my existence reduced to that of a prisoner held in a metal box. Holes have been drilled along the top of the walls. They serve as both ventilation and lighting. It's almost a relief each day when the guards come for me and shackle my ankles. Although the desert heat is scorching, I relish the minutes I'm outside walking from my cell to the concrete building that I've figured out is their tech headquarters.

Once inside, I'm deposited in a tiny room with nothing more than a metal table and a chair. My shackles are locked on the chair's legs, ensuring I don't challenge the guards or attempt an escape. Like all the other buildings, there are no windows. The light source is a lone bulb dangling from a frayed wire on the ceiling. In direct contrast is a state-of-the-art laptop that sits on the table. I've spent hours trying to access Maxim and Nicholai's files. Unfortunately, nothing I'm doing is working. The security codes have all been changed again.

"Fuck," I yell and slam my fists on the table.

The guard throws the door open. "What's going on in here?"

I run my fingers through my filthy, matted hair. "Where's your boss?"

"Do you have the files?"

"I want to see him."

I'm certain Moreno's patience is running thin. I need to see Natalie. I have to know he's holding to our agreement. That she's unharmed.

"Until I see him, I stop working."

"*El Tomador* doesn't take well to demands."

"I don't take well to not seeing Natalie."

He leaves the room without another word—the lock clicks into place. I drop my head into my hands. I've been trying to keep it together, trying to stay level-headed, but who am I kidding? Natalie's in the hands of a madman who's threatened to sell her to the highest bidder. I'm locked out of the encrypted files and unable to deliver the promised information. My plan of accessing the files and leaving a message for Dimitri has proved futile. Timur was the only one who knew what happened, and now he's dead.

No one knows where we are or who's holding us captive—no rescue is coming.

I'm Natalie's Dominant, the one responsible for her safety. But look at me. Look at what I've been reduced to. A chained-up prisoner helpless to do anything. It's my fault we're in this situation and may never get out. I'm slipping into a familiar black hole of depression.

After I finish berating myself, I do the only thing I can. I get back on the laptop and keep trying to access the files. The one thing I know is that Dimitri can see all the attempts I'm making. Although I don't know whether my continued failures will help their efforts to locate the source or if it's wasting their time, sending them on yet another wild goose chase. It doesn't matter. I have to keep trying. I'm hanging on by a thread to the only hope I have left.

Not having a window, I don't know how much time has passed before the door is wrenched open. Like every day, I'm released from the chair and brought outside. The sun hangs low along the horizon, giving a much-needed break from the brutal desert heat. I'm ready for the daily trading of one cell for another. But instead of heading the usual way, the guards lead me in the opposite direction. Today we stop at a building on the outskirts of the property.

The door opens with a creak, and I find myself standing in a room that resembles nightclub. The walls are dark charcoal, and the lights are set low. My skin prickles from the evil permeating the space. Like all the other buildings, there are no windows, yet the air is crisp and cool from the air conditioning vents in the ceiling.

At the far end of the room is a large stage that's currently empty. The reality of what happens in this room sickens me. This place is where men, women, and children are sold to the highest bidder. On auction nights, each attendee has a private booth with a door and walls high enough to ensure they remain anonymous. But anonymity isn't mandatory. If the guests are comfortable, they are free to leave their booths to socialize with one another. This place is exactly how Moreno's undercover buyers described it.

As we walk toward the stage, I notice the doors on the booths are open, and I glance inside. There's a leather armchair with a small table next to it. Hanging on the wall is a flat-screen monitor. Each booth we pass has the same setup. At the end of the rows, I see Moreno sitting in his black leather chair. He acts like a king sitting on his throne overlooking my submissive, who's kneeling at his feet, The collar still around her neck and the leash clipped to the wall.

"Alejandro." He drags out each syllable. "Come join me."

Each time he utters my name in his native tongue, it fuels my desire to tear his heart from his chest. A heart that I'm not convinced exists. My hands, which the guards have left out of cuffs, ball into fists. The only thing that stops me is knowing that even if I could get my hands on Moreno, the guards will kill Natalie before I could get the job done. I can't take my eyes off Natalie, scanning her body to ensure she's unharmed and willing her to look up at me. But she remains still. Her eyes never leave the floor in front of her.

"Glad you could join us today. Please have a seat." He motions to a chair across from him.

I sit, my eyes remaining fixed on Natalie.

"Why is she naked?"

"My *mascota* is training for when you fail, and she's sold." Moreno stares at me. His black eyes are empty of all humanness. "It's a pity she's already used. She would've brought in top dollar. However, she'll still command a high price with her body and excellent obedience skills."

Rage burns hot, and despite the consequences, I lunge at him. I don't even make it to my feet before his guards push me back down. The click of guns being readied to shoot fills the otherwise silent room.

"Please don't hurt him," Natalie screams.

"And what are you willing to do to keep him safe?"

"Do not answer him," I warn, but she ignores me.

"I'll do whatever you demand, Master. Just please don't hurt him."

"Come closer to your Master, *mascota.*" Natalie crawls to him, and he pets her hair, making my stomach turn. "Have you made any progress with your task?"

"Not yet. Their security's been upgraded. It locked me out. Let me send them a message. We both know they'll never pinpoint the source. I'll demand they give me the files." As hard as I try, I can't hide the desperation in my voice.

Moreno laughs. "Do you think I'm stupid? Even if I allowed you to contact them, I have no reason to believe they'd hand over that information. Tomorrow, this room will be filled with men who wish to sample my merchandise. By the end of the weekend, they'll be ready to pay whatever price I demand for the opportunity to own one of my products."

"And what does that have to do with us?" I don't know why I asked. I already know the intention of his thinly veiled threat.

"I plan to show off my latest acquisition. A beautiful slave who'll be available to purchase by the end of the weekend."

"I'm doing everything I said I would. You agreed not to lay a finger on her."

Moreno stands, rising to his full height before me. "This is my kingdom. I'm the only one who makes the demands here." He taps the gold watch on his wrist. "Your time is just about up, Alejandro. My little *mascota* will be the star of the show. By the end of the weekend, men will be willing to do anything I ask to have a chance at owning her."

Grabbing Natalie's hair, he pulls her to her feet. That's when I see how thin and pale she is.

"Feed her. She'll be useless to you if she's not nourished and able to perform in your little show. Nobody wants to buy a sick slave."

Natalie doesn't look up, doesn't react to my words. It's as if she's given up. Don't quit on me. Keep fighting, baby girl.

"This is my kingdom," he reminds me. "And *mascota's* part of it now. She'll eat when and if I choose."

Motioning to one of the guards, he hands Natalie's leash off, instructing him to return her to his room. His eyes never leave Natalie's body as she walks away. When he turns back to me, the sick bastard adjusts his erection. We don't scene in public for this reason. I won't tolerate anyone looking at or getting off on what's mine. But right now, I'm forced to tamp down my rage. Forced to offer something I never thought I'd do, but this is for our survival. It's bad enough that men will look at her and lust for her, but I'll be damned if I allow anyone other than me to touch her. If sceneing in public is part of his twisted plan, I will be the Master of it. Natalie may hate me for it. But right now, I don't see any other option.

"I'll do the scene." I'm not asking for permission. "I know her body better than anyone. If I'm her Master, her body will respond to me. Your clients will get a show they'll never forget."

Several long minutes pass while he paces back and forth, considering my proposition.

"Fine," he concedes. "You will do it, but it will be a scene of my design." He stops in front of me. "And if you don't follow it exactly, I will step in and finish the job for you."

Without any further conversation, he turns and strides to the exit.

I'm escorted back to my cell and left to worry about what he'll require of me tomorrow.

Viktor

I'M IN THE TECH room pouring through the data with Dimitri and his team. We're looking for any clue, any weakness in the IP encryption, when I get the text I've been waiting for. Pushing my chair out, I get to my feet quickly. "Timur's awake."

The men look up from their screens, knowing this could be the break we've all been waiting for.

"Does he have any intel?"

"I'll let you know as soon as I find out."

I'm more hopeful than I've been in weeks. I pray Timur has the information we need and that we're not too late. As soon as I get out of the room, I break into a sprint and don't stop until I get to the medical wing of the compound. The door to Timur's room is open. Maxim's sitting at his bedside, where the two men talk quietly.

Timur looks up as I walk into the room. "I'm sorry, Viktor. I did everything I could to stop them."

"I know." I take the seat next to Maxim. "Can you tell me what happened?"

Although Timur's weak, he recounts the events from the night they were ambushed. He explains about being pulled over by *politseyskiy*.

"I found it odd," he struggles to speak. "We were cleared to travel undeterred." Timur stops to catch his breath.

Maxim continues for him. "We got the description of the officer. I have already dispatched a team to extract information from him. And after we get it, he will be made an example of."

"When the second car pulled up, I knew we were in trouble," Timur adds.

I can see how taxing this is on him, but I need him to tell me every detail he remembers.

"The officer made me get out of the car. I slid the gun back, hoping Alex had enough time to get it, but we were outnumbered. They grabbed him and Natalie so fast." He closes his eyes as if he's reliving that night. "I fought hard, boss." He looks between Maxim and me. "Then they shot me. I was coming in and out of consciousness but didn't open my eyes or move. I let them believe I was dead. Then, I heard them threatening to kill Natalie." Timur's voice is pained.

My blood pressure spikes. Natalie is my responsibility to protect. If we don't get them back, I'll never forgive myself for not fighting harder to accompany them.

"Do you remember anything else?"

"I don't know if it was real or a dream. But I thought I heard them mention *El Tomador.*"

I freeze. Silverio Moreno. If Timur heard them correctly, we have a clusterfuck of epic proportions on our hands.

"You did well." Maxim lays his hand over Timur's, reassuring him. "You did real good."

"They were so happy talking about their baby." He closes his eyes again. "Natalie was showing me pictures—" Timur's voice trails off as he drifts to sleep

"I'm going to find them and bring them home." I'll move heaven and hell to bring them back.

Pulling my cell phone out, I shoot a text to Dimitri.

(Me) I need you to get all the recent intel on Moreno's operations.

(Dimitri) Fuck. We're on it now.

Maxim and I leave Timur's room, quietly closing the door.

"Boss—"

"Do not say anything more." Maxim knows as well as I do the danger Alex and Natalie are in. "I have some calls to make," he says as he walks away.

Natalie

I WASN'T SURE HOW much time had passed since I last saw Alex. It wasn't until he was brought into the auction room the other day that I had confirmation he was still alive. I was so relieved to see him, although he looked awful. He's still wearing the pants and polo shirt he wore the day of the ultrasound, but now his clothes are torn and dirty. And he's so thin and pale. Dark circles weigh down his blue eyes, which have lost their usual sparkle. Seeing him in that condition was heartbreaking, but I'm holding onto the knowledge he's still alive.

Thankfully, Silverio was generous today and chose to feed me. I don't know how much longer I could've gone without food. This forced starvation can't be good for my baby, if he or she is still alive. Stop, Natalie. If I let myself go down that rabbit hole, I'm not sure I'll make it back out.

I've spent most of the day in my capture's office. Silverio's been busy taking phone calls and doing things on his computer. He's made sure my back is to the desk while I kneel at his feet, so I've been unable to see anything. A knock on the door breaks the silence.

"Enter."

I hear footsteps but don't see who's come in.

"Get up." He jerks my leash, forcing me to stand.

I lose my balance from moving so quickly and stumble. Before I hit the floor, Moreno catches me, pulling me onto his lap. My body stiffens as he brushes my hair aside and licks my neck.

"You smell so good, *moscata*. I should forget the deal I made and fuck you right now. But you're in luck. I have more important things to do." He shoves me off his lap.

A guard is waiting in front of his desk, and next to him is the same girl that serves Moreno's meals.

"Take these two back to my room," he orders the guard before turning to me. "You will prepare your body for your debut tonight. *esclava*, you will help."

"Yes, Master." Her voice is no more than a whisper.

"Behave, *mascota,* or you will suffer." He unlocks my leash from his desk and hands it to the guard. "When they are ready. Escort them to the club."

"Yes, sir."

We trail behind the guard as he leads us back to Silverio's bedroom. Once we're inside, he faces me and tugs the leash tight. His eyes take in every inch of my body.

"I'd like to fuck every hole you have. Too bad the boss said you're off-limits."

I'm relieved when he leaves the room and locks the door. For the first time since I was brought here, I'm alone in a room without Silverio. It's just the girl and me.

"What's your name?" Her stormy blue-grey eyes dart around the room, stopping on each camera mounted from the ceiling. "It's okay. You can talk to me. I won't hurt you." I smile, trying to reassure her.

"Amelia," she whispers.

"That's a pretty name. My name's Natalie."

She looks at me briefly before returning her gaze to the floor.

"I'll draw you a bath, miss. We mustn't waste time." She hurries into the bathroom, where she begins to run the water.

Although she hasn't spoken much, I hear a distinct accent. "Are you from Australia?"

She nods.

"Do you have family looking for you?"

She shakes her head.

"Get in, please."

I step into the coconut and vanilla-scented water. For a moment, I'm distracted from our conversation as I allow my stressed body to slide into the warm water. Relaxing, if only for a few minutes, is a luxury.

I don't know how long we'll be alone to talk. And although I hate throwing so many questions at her, I want to get as many answers as possible. "How old are you?"

"Fifteen," Amelia whispers as she dunks me under the water to wet my hair.

My heart shatters. She's the same age Jelena was when she was taken. Where is this girl's family? How did this happen to her? What horrors has she endured while being held captive by this monster?

She helps me wash and rinse my hair before giving me a razor and instructing me to prepare my body.

"Prepare my body? For what?"

Ignoring my question, she instructs, "When you're done with the razor, I'll give it back to the guard." Amelia looks up at the camera as if to warn me not to do anything stupid.

I finish my task and step out of the tub. Amelia offers me a fluffy towel, which I gladly accept. Besides the blanket at bedtime, this is the only time I've had something to cover my naked body.

"Do you have a family?"

"My parents were killed in a car accident. I didn't have any other family, so I was put in a foster home. The family I lived with, their son—I hated it there and ran away. For a while, I lived on the streets." Tears fill her eyes. "One night, a man grabbed me. I should've stayed in the foster home." Her voice catches on a sob.

I reach out to embrace her, but she jumps away from my touch. "Everything's going to be okay. We're going to get out of here. My fiancé will make sure of that."

"We shouldn't be talking." She puts her walls back up and turns away from me.

Realizing I've pushed her enough, for now, I grab the comb that's on the counter and carefully work to untangle the knots in my hair.

"We're almost out of time," Amelia says, grabbing the razor and taking it out of the bathroom.

I follow her back into the bedroom and watch as she knocks on the door. It opens a crack just enough for her to hand the razor over to the guard. Then she hurries across the room and disappears into Silverio's closet. When she reemerges, she has a white silk robe draped over her arm and a pair of silver heels in her hand.

"Put this on." She holds out the robe for me to slide my arms into.

The sensation of the silk against my skin feels foreign. It takes me a few minutes to become reacquainted with the feel of clothing before I'm able to tie it closed. Amelia helps me fasten the straps on the silver heels.

"It's time to go." She returns to the door and knocks.

A few seconds later, the door opens wide, and Amelia scurries down the hall. It's only now that I'm alone with the guard that I allow fear to creep into my consciousness. What have I just readied my body for?

The guard reattaches my leash and escorts me out of the house to a waiting car.

"Where are we going?"

"You'd be smart to shut up. Unless you wish to meet *Tomador's* whip."

I shut my mouth, holding back my next question. I never want to feel the sting of a whip again.

The sun is setting over the horizon as we drive past all the warehouse buildings and stop outside Moreno's club.

"Let's go." The guard grabs my arm. Without a center console, he easily pulls me across the seat.

Music and men's voices drift from inside the building when he opens the backdoor. Fear, as I've never experienced, hits me. We're out of time. Moreno's going to sell me. My legs threaten to give out.

The guard sees my hesitation and tugs on my leash, forcing me through the backdoor and into a new level of hell.

Alex

LAST NIGHT WAS A nightmare. The heat in my room was oppressive, and coupled with my fears about our fate, I couldn't sleep. Every time I closed my eyes and tried to drift off, the horrors of what might happen tonight jolted me back to reality. I'm awake and sitting up against one of the concrete walls when a guard brings a breakfast tray. Today's meal is slightly more substantial than usual. I devour the oatmeal, almost licking the bowl clean before drinking the water. I need all the strength I can muster to get Natalie and me through the night.

When the guard returns to collect me, I'm prepared. I anticipate being led on the usual walk to the tech building. Instead, we veer off and enter one of the warehouse buildings. As we walk down the hall, I hear the cries of innocent victims coming from behind the closed doors. The depravity of this place only strengthens my resolve to get us out of here alive and then burn this hellhole to the ground.

We stop in an open shower room where the guard unchains my hands and feet. With the stakes so high, Moreno and his minions must feel confident that I won't attempt an escape.

"Shower and put those on." He points to a pile of black clothes folded off to the side.

The water is cool, but I don't care. It's been weeks since I last took a shower. Being able to wash the grime from my body is a relief. After my shower, I find a thin, tattered towel that I use to dry myself. Then, I dress in black pants, a black button-down shirt, and the black boots left for me.

I expect to be restrained, so it comes as a surprise when my guard motions for me to walk without them. Even with the sun setting, it's still a long walk across the facility's grounds in the scorching heat. As we get closer to the club building, I see there's already a line of cars, all with tinted windows lined up. Inside the high-end vehicles are men who'll be in attendance tonight. From reading Maxim's files, I know that some of the world's wealthiest men, from both the private and government sectors, attend these functions. One at a time, the cars are brought around the side of the building to a special entrance ensuring each man retains their anonymity. We go in the back door and walk down a deserted hallway until we come to an office.

"*El Tomador* is expecting you."

I enter the office with my shoulders back and head held high. I've already been apprised of what's expected of me tonight. And as hard as it's going to be, I refuse to cower in fear in front of Moreno. Tonight the tables will turn, even just a bit. Moreno may think he's in control because he gave orders. But on that stage, I'm Natalie's Dominant. It's me that's in control of the scene and her safety. That puts me in a power position.

"Sit, Alejandro."

His voice makes my skin crawl, but I keep my composure. Taking a seat, I spread my legs and cross my arms over my chest. I'm in full Dom mode and am prepared to beat Moreno at his own game.

"I take it you're ready to entertain my guests this evening?"

The only response he gets is a slight shrug.

"Let's get right to this then." He closes his laptop, giving me his full attention. "There are a few things we didn't discuss at our last meeting. You are to remain silent during tonight's scene, and you will wear this." He reaches into his drawer and tosses something at me. I hold up the black hood with cutouts for my eyes and mouth. "We don't want your identity to spoil things, do we?"

I ball the hood in my fist. I'd hoped Natalie would at least be reassured that I was behind the torture. This disguise and the order to stay silent are going to change my plan. Think Alex. I have to find another way to let her know it's me. It's the only way it'll be bearable for her.

Moreno picks up his phone and makes a call. "Bring it in now."

A guard appears carrying a black lacquered box. Almost reverently, he sets it on the desk in front of Moreno before leaving the room.

On the top of the box is an intricate etching of a pewter dagger spearing a red crown. Carved into the crown is the name *Moreno*. What's inside the still-closed box is something that many tell tales about, but few have ever seen.

"It's time for a history lesson, Alejandro." Moreno places his hands on the lid. "This box has been passed down in my family for many generations, each having carved their initials inside." Then, he opens the top and lifts out the infamous dagger.

My eyes land on the metal as it glints in the light. Seeing it before me gives credibility to everything I've been told.

"I see you've heard the stories." His laugh is sinister. "You will be one of the few outside the Moreno family to have the privilege of using this."

Moreno continues schooling me on the history and features of his implement of torture. The knife has a contoured, hand-carved walnut hilt with bronzed edging. The hand-forged blade boasts an intricate carving of two ravens perched on a castle's turret—the Moreno family crest.

"For many generations, my family has enjoyed carving the skin of our slaves. Tonight, you will give my guests what they desire. The tears and screams of a slave. And if you do not perform to my liking, I will replace you as *mascota's* Master tonight."

I won't allow that to happen. I'll give Moreno the show he's demanding and deal with the repercussions when we make it out alive.

I'm locked in a holding room backstage. Knowing men are gathering in the audience ready to purchase a sex slave, someone they will maim and torture until they finally take their life, makes me sick. I've always supported Maxim's efforts to take down trafficking rings and rescue the victims. But being here and experiencing this personally has given me a different perspective. When we get out of here, I need to do more than provide a network to transfer information. I plan to step up and take an active role in wiping these animals from the face of the earth.

The monitor on the wall of my holding room comes to life. Moreno sits on his throne in the front as a man steps onto the stage.

"Before tonight's auction, our host has a special performance. So please, sit back and enjoy the show."

The lights dim, and the curtains open. A masked man dressed in all black holds the end of Natalie's leash. He leads her onto the stage, where a large Saint Andrew's cross is set up. He comes to a stop in front of it. Despite the circumstances, I can't help but admire how beautiful Natalie is wearing a white silk robe and high-heeled shoes. Her long blonde curls hang loose down her back. My girl is so brave. She doesn't cringe at her surroundings. Instead, she stands proud and unafraid, even though, unbeknownst to her, she's the innocent lamb being prepared for slaughter.

"Strip," the man commands.

Despite the terror I know she must feel, she doesn't hesitate. Pulling at the knot, her robe opens, revealing her naked body. My stomach turns when I hear the catcalls and whistles from the sick bastards hiding in their booths. But I refuse to take my eyes off Natalie. The only outward sign of her nerves is the slight tremble of her hands. A second man steps onto the stage and takes the robe before quickly exiting. Then, the hooded man unclips her collar and sets the leash on a table next to the apparatus. He pushes her from behind, forcing her to step up to the cross.

The camera view switches, allowing me to see Natalie as she's bound, facing the cross. I can only imagine what she's thinking, knowing this position is typically associated with being whipped. She'd be right, but she doesn't know that tonight will be much worse. After she's fully restrained, the man steps up to her. In a move that makes my pulse spike, he presses his body against hers.

"Open," he commands.

Natalie opens her mouth, and a ball gag is shoved in and fastened behind her head. One of her hard limits is being gagged. I know she's going to hate it, and she may hate me for it. But it was my one demand for tonight. What's about to happen is going to be torture. The gag will give her something to bite down on. To absorb her screams—something to help us both get through this. Before he steps away, he secures a blindfold over her eyes.

With a loud squeal of metal, the door to my room is wrenched open.

"Let's go."

I'm led onto the stage and am standing behind my sub. Natalie's body is now shaking—she's terrified. I want to reach out and caress her, tell her it's me and she's going to get through this, but I can't. Doing so will give Moreno the excuse he's looking for to step in and take my place. If I don't approach this with a cold, heartless exterior, I'll never make it—the consequences of which I won't be able to live with.

The hooded man returns with the black box in his hands. He removes the lid in front of me, and I take the dagger out.

In my hand, I hold a weapon, a symbol of power passed down through generations of traffickers. It's been used to mutilate the bodies of countless people for nothing more than the pleasure of the sadistic man wielding it. It's a symbol of the worst humanity has to offer.

Tonight, I'm being forced to use it. Not to torture or kill but to mar the flesh of my submissive. It sickens me, but I have no choice. This is buying us a little more time for me to continue searching for any weakness, any chink in the armor. Anything to get us out of here.

The room is deadly silent. Straining to see through the darkness of the club, the only thing I can make out is the silhouette of Moreno sitting in his chair. I don't need to see his face to know he's waiting for me to screw up so he can take my place on this stage. But the joke's on him. I won't be making any mistakes.

I turn back to face Natalie and lift the dagger holding it flat. She doesn't move as I drag the cold blade down her back. Turning it, I press the sharp edge against her perfect skin. It's her first hint at what's to come. Without putting too much pressure, I make my first cut—her body tenses. I continue my task, making shallow cuts that, once they heal, won't scar. It does little to lessen the pain she's suffering each time I drag the knife's edge down her back. Time loses all meaning as I continue making cuts.

Moreno's voice pierces the silence, "I want to see blood. Hear her scream."

His comment is followed by the whistles of the cowards hiding behind the walls.

"Cut her deeper, or I'll be forced to show you how it's done."

Natalie shakes her head back and forth violently. The words she's trying to say are garbled by the gag. I lift the dagger to the area by her shoulder blade and press, slicing her skin open. Her blood-curdling scream fills the room, and cheers erupt from the audience. This is the show they came to see.

Movement from the side of the stage catches my eye. Once again, the hooded man is walking toward me. This time with a white cloth over his hands. It's my cue. One more cut, baby girl. This torture's almost over. Parallel to the deep slice I made, I drag the dagger down her body. Rivulets of blood follow its path. Her screams fill the room again, shattering the remaining pieces of my heart. Turning, I place the dagger in the man's hands. The white fabric soaks up the blood, turning it red. My stomach turns, and I nearly vomit. The guard sees my disgust and snickers exiting the stage.

Natalie's out of energy. Out of endurance. But we aren't done yet. The biggest challenge is still ahead of us. I have to fuck her on stage, knowing Moreno and his buyers are watching. This disgusts me. It's a part of our relationship we never wanted on public display. When she finds out it was me behind all this—taking her in front of an audience. It might be the very thing that causes her to walk away from us. Losing her will ruin me, but it's a chance I have to take. It's the only way I can keep her alive.

Stepping closer, my body brushes against her mangled back, and she hisses in pain. I bring my hands up and release the restraints from her wrists and then her ankles. Taking her hands, I place them on the center of the cross and push on her back, bending her over. Then I open the button and unzip my pants, leaving them hanging low on my hips. When she hears the zipper, she tries to stand—she knows what's about to happen. But I force her back down. Even with the gag in place, I hear her crying as she shakes her head back and forth. She thinks she's about to be raped by an unknown evil man. baby girl, please forgive me.

Fisting my erection, I take the final steps forward and impale her in one hard thrust. She cries out from the violent intrusion. I close my eyes and put all thoughts of where we are and who's watching out of my head. I need to fuck her hard and fast to end this charade.

"Take the gag off. I want to hear her scream," Moreno calls from the audience.

Leaning over her back, I grab the strap of the gag. "I'm so sorry, baby girl," I whisper. She freezes. "Keep fighting and screaming. Do not let on you know it's me."

I hope she understands the seriousness of our current situation. Our lives depend on her continued fight. After discarding the gag on the floor, I pull out and thrust in hard. I don't stop the punishing pace as Natalie screams and thrashes about, forcing me to hold her in place.

No longer is she fighting against me. Instead, she's fighting with me.

Tonight isn't about her pleasure. The men in the room don't care if she's allowed to orgasm. Giving her a release is the least I can do. Reaching around her waist, I find her clit. She shakes her head back and forth, yelling for me to stop, but I don't. I know her body and how to make it respond to me, even against her will. I rub fast, hard circles while I pump in and out of her. Regardless of our circumstances,

I'm right there with her. She's fighting it, but her body is tensing, readying itself for an orgasm. I pinch her clit hard. Natalie screams as her body jolts with the force of her orgasm. Her inner walls squeeze my cock tight, and I let go, spilling inside her.

Natalie falls limp in my arms. Applause fills the room.

Fuck, what did I just do?

I pull my pants up with my free hand and then lift her into my arms, cradling her against my chest. Then, I hurry off the stage. "Where can I bring her?" I ask the guard standing there, but he doesn't answer. I look around, panicked, but there's nowhere to go.

"Alejandro, very well done." Moreno appears backstage. "My guests are already asking how much she'll cost."

"Fuck you," I spit. "I need to take her somewhere for aftercare."

"I don't engage in aftercare with my pets."

"As long as I'm breathing, she's still mine." My eyes lock on his. "Where can I take her?"

"I will give you this only because you followed my instructions with your performance. Take them to a room," Moreno orders. "You have one hour."

We're led down a dark hallway. Natalie hasn't opened her eyes or moved. The guard pulls the door open, and I brush past him to go inside. The room is dark and dingy. A single lightbulb overhead offers a small amount of illumination. Across the room is a bed with a metal frame. Cuffs hang from both the headboard and footboard. I can't stop to think of the atrocities that occur in this room.

Using one hand, I pull back the blanket and lay Natalie down before ripping the hood off and looking around.

There's a doorway without a door that leads to a small bathroom. Inside I find a towel and washcloth, presumably Moreno's attempt at hospitality for his *guests*. Grabbing the cloth, I let the water in the tap run, hoping it gets warm, but it doesn't. I settle for cool.

When I return to bed, I find Natalie still passed out. I roll her onto her side and gently clean off her back, wiping away as much blood as possible. Then, I spread the towel on the mattress and carefully place her on her back. Leaving her once again, I rinse off the cloth. When I return, I wipe between her legs. When I pull the cloth away, it's covered in blood.

No. Oh my God. No.

I drop the washcloth onto the floor and crawl on the bed, pulling Natalie into my lap.

"baby girl," I say softly. "It's time to wake up." I rock her back and forth. "Please wake up."

It feels like an eternity before she begins to stir in my arms.

"I'm here, baby girl." I kiss her forehead. "Everything's okay. I'm here."

"Alex? Is it really you?"

She cries in my arms as I stroke her hair gently.

"I'm here. You're safe," I whisper.

Unable to hold back any longer, my tears silently fall. I'm holding my whole world in my arms. But my heart is heavy knowing I've ended our unborn child's life tonight.

Several men burst into the room. "Time's up."

"It hasn't been an hour," I yell.

"And I care?" He reaches for Natalie.

"Get the hell away from her."

Natalie grabs onto me. "Please, Alex. Don't let them take me."

"Shut up, bitch," the hooded man snarls and reaches out to refasten the leash onto her collar.

"Get away from me." She slaps his hand.

"That was a mistake." He goes to grab her hair.

"Keep your fucking hands off her," I yell and shift my body, trying to keep her away from him.

The sound of the safety being taken off a gun rings in my ear. The cold metal presses against my head.

"I said time's up."

This time I have no choice but to let her go.

She struggles with all her might.

"Natalie," I yell, getting her attention. "Stop fighting and go with them."

She looks at me, tears streaming down her face as she's dragged away. My eyes go to the blood dripping down her legs.

Then, with a final look over her shoulder, she whispers, "i love You."

I'm frozen on the edge of the bed, unable to move or speak as I watch her disappear.

Natalie

THE SKY IS DARK and cloudy. The only illumination comes from lights that line the driveway leading back to Silverio's estate. My body is in agony, so I don't resist when the guard pulls my arm, forcing me out of the car. My torn flesh rips from the leather seats, causing another wave of pain to roll through me.

"You made quite an impression tonight, *mascota*," Silverio's slimy voice startles me.

I look up and find him leaning against a tree outside the entrance to his home. He's still wearing the suit he had on at the club, only now his tie is loosened, and the first few buttons of his shirt are undone. The guard transfers ownership of the leash back to Silverio.

"*Gracias por devolver mi mascotita.*"

The guard nods before returning to the car and pulling away.

"I've received many lucrative offers to purchase you this evening. Seems you're in high demand." He runs his knuckles down my cheek."

"I'm not for sale."

"I'll let that indiscretion pass this time." He pulls my leash. My bare feet scrape on the pavement as I struggle to keep up with him. "On your knees, *mascota*," he commands once we're inside.

I'm sore and tired. My muscles scream in pain each time I miss a step as I crawl behind him on the way back to the bedroom. The scene tonight was grueling—unlike anything I've ever experienced.

All the while the man was cutting me, I silently cursed him. Wished he'd die for unleashing his violence on my body. Then, I heard him open his pants, and I knew I was about to be raped by one of Moreno's depraved men. Instead of wishing for my death, I imagined the many ways I could end his life.

But then the man leaned in close and whispered to me.

Natalie

IT TOOK A SECOND for my mind to accept it was really him. He insisted I keep fighting. That I wasn't to let on I knew his identity. Which wasn't hard to do because even though it was my Dominant, I didn't want to be fucked in a roomful of sick men. Men I knew were getting off on what was happening on that stage. The fear and regret I heard in Alex's voice hurt so much more than the physical wounds. What he was doing was beyond his control. Alex is a puppet in Moreno's sick and twisted world. What he did was necessary to keep us alive.

Afterward, as Alex held me, he tried to hide that he was crying. His tears fell on my skin, betraying his secret. But then the men came too soon. They dragged me away from Alex before I got to talk to him. To tell him I knew none of it was his fault. That I didn't blame him. I only hope my silent declaration of love was enough.

Silverio drags me through his bedroom into his bathroom. The collar pulls tight around my neck as Silverio unclips the leash. Then, turning the shower on, he opens the glass door and pushes me in.

"Wash him off you. I don't want to smell another man on what's mine," he growls in disgust before storming out of the bathroom.

Reluctantly, I step under the water, knowing it'll sting the cuts on my back. And it does. Red-tinged water sluices down my body from the cuts on my back. From the amount of blood coming off my body, I can only imagine what my back must look like. I find a bottle of shower gel. It turns my stomach because it smells like Silverio. But it's all that's in here, and I don't want to waste the opportunity to clean up, so I squirt some into my hand and begin to wash. I wipe my hand between my legs, but when I pull it away, it's covered in fresh blood. I do it again and find more. This blood isn't from the cuts on my back. My hand flies out to the wall steadying myself.

My baby. Oh my God, there's so much blood.

I'm losing my baby.

As I watch the steady stream of red wash down the drain, a part of me dies along with the life inside me.

"I didn't think he had it in him," Silverio's eerie laugh startles me.

I look up at him and hope he sees the hate in my eyes. He's the monster responsible for this.

"He made you bleed. Maybe I'll keep him on after I sell you. Alejandro might prove useful in breaking in new acquisitions."

Silverio's words, coupled with the knowledge of what I'm losing, are too much. I vomit in the shower. My body retches until my stomach is empty, and I'm on my knees.

This is too much to handle, and my world goes black again.

Natalie

I DON'T KNOW HOW long I've been out, but when I wake, I'm chained to my *bed* on the floor of Silverio's suite. Sunlight streams in from the open window, letting me know a new day has dawned. Grief overcomes me. I wish I didn't wake up. Lowering my hand to my abdomen, I feel something unfamiliar—fabric. I'm wearing underwear.

"I cleaned and dressed you." Amelia kneels next to me. "I think you were injured in the scene last night. But when it didn't stop, Master believed it was your time of the month, and he doesn't like when a woman bleeds from *that.* You were also given a birth control shot last night, so Master isn't inconvenienced again."

My eyes fill with tears as I grab her hands. This time she doesn't pull away.

"I'll get the guard to unlock you so you can go to the bathroom and change your—" She motions to the underwear.

As usual, the guard takes his time answering. "What do you want?"

Amelia's reply is so quiet I can't make out her words. The man pushes her out of the way and heads straight to me, unlocking the leash.

"Hurry up," he says gruffly.

I'm only given privacy in the bathroom because there's one door and nowhere to run. I use the toilet and change the pad, thankful for the little bit of humanness I've been allotted. After washing my hands, I work up the courage to look at my back. Turning slightly to see my reflection in the mirror, I examine the marred flesh. Most of the small, shallow cuts have stopped bleeding and should heal without scarring. However, the two deeper wounds on my shoulder blade are red and angry. They look like they need stitches, but I don't think properly caring for my wounds is on Silverio's agenda.

The door flies open. "You've had enough time. Let's go."

He grabs my leash and returns me to my place on the floor, where I wait for a plate with food and a bottle of water. I look around for Amelia, but she's no longer in the room. My heart drops. I was hoping to have her company for a bit longer.

"*El Tomador* expects you to eat the lunch he's left," the man says as he reattaches my leash to the lock on the floor.

I nod, grateful for the food and for being allowed to feed myself.

Days pass without seeing Silverio. The only person I see is the guard who unlocks me twice daily to use the bathroom. The solitude is a welcome relief. The only person I wish was here is Alex. I need his arms to hold me. To grieve the loss of our baby together. This routine continues for the next week until the bleeding finally stops.

"Wake up, *mascota*." I'm kicked in the side.

Instead of opening my eyes to escape a nightmare, I wake to find I've been thrust back into the same one. Silverio stands above me, my leash in his hand.

"I'm told the inconvenience of your *condition* is finally over." He wears an evil smile.

As far as he's concerned, the bleeding was from an injury during the scene. I'll never tell him. Never allow him the opportunity to claim the victory that would come with knowing he killed my baby.

"Get up. We have work to do."

I don't give him the satisfaction of a reaction as I stand from the floor. Once I stopped bleeding, the small amount of coverage I had been allowed was taken from me. Once again, I'm paraded through the estate naked. Forced to endure the lustful stares of the guards we pass in the hallways. When we get to his office, I take my usual spot on my knees. Instead of going onto his computer or phone like normal, he spins his chair to face me and leans forward, resting his elbows on his spread legs.

"Look at me, *mascota*," Silverio commands.

I raise my eyes and meet his dark stare.

"Tomorrow will be an exciting night for us. Do you want to know what happens tomorrow?"

Not knowing what day it is gives me no reference for what tomorrow is. Either way, no, I don't want to know. I don't care what happens tomorrow. But if I don't play along and indulge him, I'm certain I'll be punished.

"What happens tomorrow, Master?"

He runs his fingers through my curls before grabbing a fistful and tugging. "Tomorrow, while Alejandro watches, I will finally taste you and use every hole until I have my fill. And after you're done screaming my name, you'll take your place on my stage with the other *putas* to be sold."

"You can't do that," I yell. "You made a deal with Alex."

Silverio's hand strikes my face with a loud crack. Instantly, my cheek is on fire. I bring my hand up to cover it.

"Watch your mouth, *mascota*. Unless you'd like to experience my whip again?" He raises an eyebrow, watching for my decision.

I drop my shoulders and lower my gaze to the floor.

Knowing he's won, Silverio swivels his chair to face his laptop, turning it on before returning his attention to me.

"Your dominant failed. He didn't get me the information I wanted. Which means you are now mine to do with as I please."

The horror of his statement sends ice through my blood. He's going to rape me and then sell me. I'll never see Alex or my family again. I can't just let this happen. I have to do something.

"Master," I say quietly.

"What?"

If I'm not sold, Silverio will keep me here. It's the only chance I have of being rescued. His laugh fills the room.

"After I have my fill, I'll have no use for you. I have my sights set on a much younger slave to amuse me. Now shut up. I have work to do."

He hasn't said her name, but I know exactly who he has his sights set on—Amelia

I vow to myself that before he has the chance to lay his filthy hands on her, I'll find a way to kill him.

Alex

THE DAY IS IRRELEVANT. Each blends into the next as if there's no beginning or end. It's been nearly two weeks since I last saw Natalie. Since the night, I was forced to carve her body. Two weeks since my vicious claiming. The one that killed our unborn baby. It physically hurts knowing the heartache Natalie's experiencing right now—alone. I've demanded to see her, but my demands were met with refusals and beatings. There have been no other deviations from my daily routine. Each day I'm hauled to the tech building, chained to a chair, where I remain unsuccessfully trying to access Maxim's files for hours. According to the clock on the computer screen, it's now twelve-thirty p.m. Moreno gave me until noon to deliver the information, and I failed. Our agreement has expired.

My time's up.

Leaning forward in my chair, I drop my head into my hands. I feel utterly hopeless. I pick up the laptop from the table and throw it at the metal wall.

"Fuck," I yell, my anguish echoing in the small room.

The laptop screen shatters. Shards of plastic pieces and electronics scatter across the floor. The guard throws the door open, slamming it against the wall. He looks around at the destroyed components of the laptop.

"You'll pay for that," he snarls and cuffs my hands.

I don't resist. There's no reason to fight anymore. My worst nightmare is about to happen tonight, and I have no way to stop it. Moreno's going to force me to watch as he rapes my fiancee. Then he's going to parade her across the stage and sell her to the highest bidder. It'll be as though Natalie never existed. She'll disappear. The future she deserves will be over before it even got to begin. We'll never marry. She won't get a second chance at becoming a mother. Instead, she'll be subjected to the twisted desires the sick fucks Moreno sells women to like. Rather than being treasured, she'll be repeatedly raped and tortured until her owner decides to put her out of her misery.

I don't want to live in a world without Natalie. My hope is Moreno kills me too.

Finally, I'm dragged from the computer room. We go past the warehouse facilities to a building that sparks terror in my core—Moreno's club. Once inside, I'm put in a room similar to the one I was in the night of our scene. Except tonight I won't be going out to Natalie. Instead, I'll watch Moreno do unspeakable things to her before he auctions her.

Alone and depressed, I slide my body down the wall. While I'm sitting on the floor, I reminisce about our relationship.

I came so close to not showing up at Fire and Ice that night. The last thing I wanted to do was babysit the girl who called the cops on my best friend. But my promise to Brandon ended up being the driving force behind why I went. I'll never forget my first glance at her from across the room. God, she took my breath away. From our first touch, there was electricity between us. And she was so curious. Despite everything I'd previously thought, I was drawn to her. After that, I couldn't walk away.

The day she finally agreed to sign the contract and give a Dom/sub relationship a try was the first day I really started living again. And that silly expiration date. She insisted on it, but I knew that wouldn't be the end—it couldn't be. We were too good together.

I remember the look on her face when I proposed to her in Central Park—it was the best day of my life so far. And just a few weeks later, the worst day of my life—when she safeworded. But I worked hard to fix myself and earn her trust again. We were going to be parents.

We haven't had enough time together.

The lock clicks, and the door opens. I don't have to look up to know Moreno and his guards have entered the room.

"You don't look so good, Alejandro."

When I don't respond, I'm kicked in the stomach, causing me to double over.

"I was informed that not only did you fail to get me the information." He crouches down in front of me. "You also destroyed one of my computers."

"As if it matters," I sneer. "I'm sure you won't even miss it."

A fist strikes my jaw. The physical pain doesn't compare to the emotional agony I'm in.

"Get up," Moreno orders as he backs away.

Before I'm fully standing, one of the guards delivers a series of punches to my front, cracking at least one rib. The pain is so intense that I fall to my knees. While I'm down, they continue their assault on my body. I don't bother to protect myself. Death would be a welcome respite.

"Enough," Moreno yells. "I want him alive to watch me fuck his girlfriend tonight."

They leave me lying on the floor, broken but unfortunately alive.

Viktor

BETWEEN THE COMBINATION OF the name Timur gave us and the continuing efforts of someone trying to access our system, we finally caught a break. Dimitri and his men were able to trace the location of the cyberattacks, confirming Silverio Moreno is the man responsible for everything. Last week, Maxim and I assembled a select team of security and medical professionals. We flew to Alex's apartment in New York City, where we set up a home base for our next step—rescue.

Maxim's been trying to bring Moreno down for years. Creating a profile and history for Salvador and Paul, the two plants, was a painstaking process. Their backgrounds had to be iron-clad to pass Moreno's security tests, which are some of the most advanced in the world.

It's taken nearly two years for them to gain trust and work their way into Moreno's buyers' circle. They've showed up, played the part, and purchased *slaves.* Only these girls were the lucky ones. Instead of living a life of sexual slavery and torture, they were brought to Jelena's Hope, where they received medical and psychological care to recover from their trauma. Some were able to be reunited with family. Others were set up with a new life.

Salvador and Paul got a message through to us last week. They were invited to a special get-together about two weeks ago. Moreno had a new acquisition he wanted to show off to a select group of buyers. After being shown pictures, our men confirmed his *acquisition* is Natalie and that she was the victim of a brutal scene at the hands of one of Moreno's men—one that will be dead when I find him.

According to Paul, Moreno spent the rest of the evening bragging about his new *pet*. He was already taking preliminary bids for her and said she'd be available for purchase at his next auction, which is tonight.

Unfortunately, we don't have confirmation of Alex's whereabouts. Moreno mentioned he found a potential new slave trainer, but neither of our men could confirm his identity.

After receiving the information, Maxim hired the best private rescue team money can buy. It's a mix of American and Ukrainian ex-special forces—a team that operates in the grey area of legalities. Given the short timeline, we've been working around the clock. The plan is to infiltrate Moreno's desert compound and extract Natalie and hopefully Alex—alive.

While we're there, we'll also take out Moreno and his men, shutting down his operation. Then, the teams from Jelena's Hope will step in to care for the victims we identify.

Right now, we're on the ground in Mexico, sitting in a dump of a motel outside Juarez, about a half-hour from Moreno's headquarters. It's an easy place to hide in plain sight. This area is used to wealthy men waltzing in either looking for cheap thrills or as a stopover before going to Moreno's. People here have learned to keep their heads down and their mouths shut. No one's even spared us a second glance.

We've rented several rooms, one of which has been turned into our tech room. Dimitri set up his equipment, ensuring we maintain a constant connection with the rest of his team, including Timur, who is back in New York City.

As soon as Timur could sit up, he insisted on being a part of this mission. But he's still weak and would be a liability. The doctors compromised and cleared him to fly to New York, where he's heading the communications. It's not exactly what he wanted, but he's thankful he wasn't left behind.

So far, everything's going as planned. Paul and Salvador received their text earlier, gauging their interest in making a purchase at tonight's auction. They responded by paying the minimum buy-in amount of half a million dollars. So now we are waiting for a confirmation text granting admission. They expect to receive it any minute.

"Got it," Paul says, holding up his cell.

"Mine's here too," Salvador confirms. "It's go time."

We have less than four hours to finalize a very intricate plan. If anything goes wrong, we'll lose our only chance to get Natalie and Alex out alive. Anything other than perfection is unacceptable.

Moreno allows the buyers to bring their cell phones in for the sole purpose of using an app specifically designed for his auctions. Once inside the gates, all cell and Wi-Fi signals are scrambled, rendering the phones useless to contact anyone outside. When the auction starts, one of several recycled internal frequencies is chosen randomly so buyers can use the app to bid and easily pay for their acquisitions.

Paul and Salvador, who are also tech geniuses, are going in equipped with a high-tech phone case they designed that will easily pass Moreno's strict security measures. Once the internal frequency is turned on, they'll activate the satellite phone feature embedded in the case to contact Timur, who will direct me and the army of men assembled outside the compound. They've tested their system at previous auctions and have remained undetected.

Once inside, our goal is to take the perimeter guards down quickly and quietly so our entrance to the facility goes undetected. At the same time, Timur will scramble the guards' frequency, ensuring they can't communicate with each other while. We'll make our way through the warehouse buildings taking out the guards one at a time.

As long as we're successful, the club will proceed as usual. Our goal is to eliminate any reinforcements Moreno may try to call when we enter the club.

On our team are trained mercenaries who will have several tasks, including eliminating everyone inside, finding Alex, and detaining Moreno.

Maxim has given strict instructions to do everything possible to secure Moreno alive. A swift and painless death is too good for him.

My job—locate Natalie and get her to safety.

Our task is nearly impossible, but with Alex and Natalie's lives on the line, failure is not an option.

Natalie

SILVERIO DROPPED HIS BOMB on me, then continued his work as usual. On the other hand, I had nothing but time on my hands to think about every possible scenario for tonight. The problem is, I know the worst I can imagine is nowhere near as bad as it will be.

"Well, *mascota*. It's time for you to get ready for our date tonight." He pulls me to my feet, which are numb from kneeling for hours.

I wiggle as the numbness quickly switches to pins and needles. The movement of my body causes my naked breasts to bounce. Silverio takes the opportunity to grab one.

"I've wanted to touch these since the first time I saw them," he says, twisting and pinching my nipple roughly. "Do you see what you do to me?" He adjusts the erection tenting his pants with his free hand. "I should try out your throat now, a little appetizer before tonight. Would you like that little *mascota*?"

"Go to hell." My words earn a slap across my face.

Silverio pulls my leash, forcing me onto his lap. "You will behave like the perfect little *mascota* for my guests tonight. You will open your mouth when I tell you to suck me." He runs his thumb along my lips before pushing it inside. "You will take all of what I give you. And you will thank your Master for it when I'm done."

I have nothing left to lose and snap my teeth down on Silverio's thumb, infuriating him.

"You bitch." He wraps his other hand around my throat, squeezing tight. "For that move, you'll get twenty lashes before I fuck each of your holes. Then, when I'm done using you, I'll make sure you're sold to someone who'll make you wish you were dead." He laughs and shoves me off his lap.

I'm delivered to Silverio's room by one of his guards, where Amelia waits to help ready me for tonight. She's already drawn my bath and poured aromatic oils in. But, this time, when I slip into the warm water, there's no enjoyment, no relief. Instead, my tears fall, landing like raindrops on the water.

"I'm so sorry, miss." Amelia does her best to console me.

Even though she knows the fate that awaits her, Amelia's putting on a brave face and apologizing to me.

"Alex will save us," I say, but this time my words lack the conviction they held the first time I uttered them. There are only two of us against Silverio and all his men. We're severely outnumbered, and I have no idea where Alex is.

Reality has set in. I'm going to get out of here, but not with Alex. Our lives are about to be permanently altered. Our future, the one that just a few weeks ago was everything we could've ever asked for, no longer holds the promise of happiness.

"I heard the guards talking. From what I could hear, they beat your Alex today. He destroyed something that belonged to Master," Amelia says quietly.

"What else did you hear? Is he okay?" I want to force her to tell me every detail, but she walks away, returning with a towel.

"You need to finish getting ready."

"Please, Amelia. Did they say anything more?"

"They stopped talking when I entered the room."

I take the offered towel and wrap it around my body.

"Alex is strong. I know he's okay," I say, trying to convince myself more than Amelia.

"Yes, miss." She offers me a sad smile.

No other words are spoken as I finish getting ready for the unavoidable night in store for me. Until this moment, I had never felt true hopelessness. After drying my hair, I return to the bedroom to find the same white silk robe on the bed. A pair of white strappy heels sits on the floor.

"What's the point in even putting this on? We all know I won't be wearing it for long."

Amelia doesn't react. She silently holds the robe for me as I slide my arms into the sleeves and tie it shut before putting on the shoes.

"I'll get the guard."

Natalie

THE SCENE PLAYS ON repeat. We enter the club through the backdoor. But this time, we're not alone. Walking down the hall, I hear crying behind the closed doors. There are different guards, men I've not seen, milling around who stare as we walk by. But no one says a word or makes a move to touch me.

Finally, I'm brought to the stage. The curtains are closed, but I can hear the low murmurings of the men gathering on the other side. Tonight, the stage is set to look like a BDSM dungeon. There are several pieces of furniture, including a spanking bench, a pillar with chains hanging from the ceiling, and a bondage bed.

"Strip. Except for the shoes. *El Tomador* wants those on."

My fate may be sealed, but I refuse to cower in fear. With my head held high, I untie the belt and allow the robe to slide off my arms. It falls into a puddle on the floor. The guard kicks it aside and steps closer, removing the leash. He takes me by the arm leading me to the pillar.

"Turn around and bend over."

He grabs my hands, wrapping them around the pillar before securing them to the chains that hang overhead. Then he reaches into his pocket and pulls out a black piece of satin which he wraps tightly over my eyes, stripping me of my vision.

"Don't do this," I whisper. "I'll tell Alex not to harm you. He'll let you go if you help us get out of here." He doesn't answer. Instead, he kicks my feet apart, attaching them to chains fastened to the floor. "Please," I beg.

The bravery I felt earlier disappears and is replaced with desperation. I can't help it. I'll plead and promise. Anything to get out of here untouched and alive. Then I feel his body against mine, his erection pressing into my ass.

"Your begging turns me on, princess." I hear his zipper. "I think I'll have a piece of this before—"

"What the fuck do you think you're doing?" Silverio's voice booms across the stage.

"*Tomador*. I didn't. I mean, I wasn't."

"Take him to a cell," Silverio orders. "I'll deal with him later."

There's a scuffle behind me. I hear the man begging as he's dragged away. What does it say about me that I don't feel an ounce of pity for what I'm sure will happen to him later?

Silverio steps up to me. "It's understandable why Julio couldn't keep his hands off you. Bent over on display like this, you're a sight to behold." He runs his fingers between my spread legs. "Just a little while longer, and I'll be able to sink my cock into you." His fingers tease the outside of my folds. "I'll be back for you soon, *mascota*."

His footsteps retreat, leaving me alone on the stage, and I pray for a miracle.

The announcer instructs everyone to take their seats. The voices I heard earlier begin to subside until the room is silent. The master of ceremonies then describes the evening's events. Once again, it seems I'm the top bill. Following it will be the auction. A feeling of overwhelming dread courses through me. I've run out of time.

The sound of a loud detonation makes my ears ring. The floor below my feet shakes from the impact.

Pop. Pop. Pop.

Gunshots and yelling come from the other side of the curtain.

Everything happens so fast.

A warm body comes up close behind me. I scream and struggle to get free. "Natalie, hold still."

"Viktor?"

"It's me." I feel his warm breath on my neck. "Stop fighting. We need to get out of here fast."

"Where's Alex?"

"I don't know." Viktor releases my hands and then moves to my ankles. I slowly stand up and remove the blindfold, not that it helps me see anything. It's pitch black in here. "Take these off," Viktor instructs and helps me out of my high heels.

The commotion on the other side of the curtains is escalating. It sounds like an army has invaded. There's men yelling in both English and Spanish. Gunshots are being exchanged back and forth.

Viktor lifts me into his arms. "Stay quiet. We're getting out of here."

Grabbing his shirt, I tuck my head into his muscular chest.

I'm putting my complete trust in the man who is no longer just my bodyguard and friend. He's the rescue I hoped for but didn't think would come.

Alex

THE MONITOR FLICKERS TO life. I'm helplessly staring at the scene unfurling in the club's main room. Moreno has the stage set up like a dungeon with several pieces of BDSM furniture. The more sinister items are hidden behind a black curtain, not seen from the main stage area, where a guard is walking with Natalie. Several whips are laid out on the table, some relatively innocent, others more destructive. The worst of which is the cat-o-nines made of chains with barbs on the end. Moreno intends to tear Natalie apart.

This is my fault—I failed. And Natalie's about to pay with her life.

Natalie's stripped and positioned bent over. Then she's restrained to the pillar.

The guard reaches for his zipper and pushes himself up against her. "What the fuck?"

Just as he steps up to mount her, Moreno storms onto the stage. He's livid and barking orders. The man is dragged off—his time remaining on the earth isn't long.

Moreno moves in close to Natalie and slips his hand between her legs. It's almost too much to watch, yet I can't take my eyes off the screen. My body vibrates from uncontrolled rage. How am I going to get through tonight?

"I'm so sorry I couldn't save you, baby girl," I say aloud, even though I know she can't hear me.

The room plunges into darkness, leaving me alone and disoriented in the soundproof chamber. Clutching my aching ribs, I cautiously crawl towards the far corner, fumbling in the pitch-black void. A series of thuds reverberate against the door, followed by a burst of sparks, and the door forcefully swings open. The hallway beyond is also shrouded in darkness, indicating that the entire building has lost power.

Crouched in silence, I hope to remain unnoticed, using the darkness to my advantage. My efforts are interrupted by gunfire and shouting emanating from somewhere in the distance. Panic sets in as I realize the club is under attack. Natalie is out there, a helpless target on the stage, in grave danger. As heavy footsteps approach my hiding place, I hold my breath and brace for the worst.

"There's someone in here," a male voice says. "On the floor, back right corner." I don't move. "Alex? Is that you?"

"Who are you?"

"Maxim sent us. Come on. We're getting you out of here."

I'm sure I must've misheard, so I ask again. "Who are you?"

"We don't have time for that now."

A hand grabs my arm, pulling me up. I groan in pain. "Can you walk?"

"I think so." I try to take a step, but the pain from my broken ribs makes breathing difficult.

They're going to waste too much time on me. "Leave me here. Natalie's on the stage. Go get her instead."

"Viktor's got her. We're getting you out of here." The hand stays firmly attached to my arm. I'm nearly dragged from the room and out of the building.

Once outside, we take cover against the club's back wall. The scope of what's happening around us is overwhelming. An army has invaded Moreno's compound. Gunshots ring out from all directions, and explosions light up the night sky. Now, I understand how rescuers found me in the pitch black. They're wearing night vision goggles which are now flipped up on their helmets. I lean back and try to catch my breath.

"Name's Michael," The man still holding my arms says. "You doing okay?"

"I'm fine. Where's Natalie?"

"She's with Viktor. They left through the side entrance. He's taking her off the property."

"Where are we going?"

"To the main estate. They're holding Moreno there for you."

Viktor

I HOLD NATALIE'S TREMBLING body tight against me as we quickly escape through a side door. I set her down as soon as we're out of the building.

"Don't leave me, Viktor." She fists my shirt, holding tight.

"I'm not going anywhere," I reassure her. Without removing my arm from her waist, I use my free hand to take off my night vision goggles, tossing them over my shoulder into my backpack. "Fuck, you're naked." I was in such a hurry to get her out that I didn't think about her lack of clothes. Despite her protest, I let her go and rip the pack off, dropping it on the ground. With my hands free, I pull my T-shirt off. "Put this on." I help her into my shirt. "Are you hurt?" I scan her for any apparent injuries.

"No," she says softly.

I click a button on the earpiece I'm wearing. "Boss?"

"Do you have her?" Maxim asks.

"She's safe. I've got her." I stop, listening to the orders being given. "Yes, sir. I'll call when we get there."

"Where's Alex?"

"He's with another group from our team," I explain.

"Will you bring me to him? Please?"

I lift her back into my arms, cradling her against my chest. "You and I are leaving. They'll bring Alex as soon as he's ready."

"I can't go without Alex." She punches my chest and tries to wiggle out of my hold.

"Natalie, stop." I know she's scared, but there's fighting all around us. I have to get her out of here and back to safety.

"I'm not leaving without him or Amelia. I promised we'd keep her safe."

"Who's Amelia?" I stop with my back against the side of a building while I scan the area.

"She's a young girl. In Silverio's house. Promise me you'll save her."

"I promise." I adjust my grasp on Natalie. "But right now, you and I are getting out of here."

Satisfied with my answer, she tucks her head back into my chest. I tighten my hold and break into a sprint heading to the black SUV waiting outside the gates.

Alex

AFTER WHAT SEEMED LIKE an eternity, the sounds of war finally subside. The scent of gunpowder lingers heavily in the warm night air. Flanked by Michael's team, we walk toward Moreno's estate. I struggle to catch my breath and keep up with the group. Looking around, I can't help but wonder how Maxim had managed to orchestrate such a successful raid. Not only have they infiltrated Moreno's facility, but they also took out all of his men. Within the span of an hour, Maxim shut down the entire operation.

Michael hands me a cell phone. "It's the boss, sir."

"Hello?"

"Alexander. It's good to hear you," Maxim says, relief evident in his voice. "Before you ask. Viktor has Natalia. She's safe and off the compound."

"How?"

"We will discuss that once we get you home. Right now, your only priority is getting to the villa safely. My men are holding Moreno," Maxim says, pausing momentarily before continuing. "I know you remember our discussion about Thomas. Your actions tonight will have life-changing consequences."

"Moreno's going to die tonight. A slow, painful death."

"Make him pay for what he has done. Then you will be brought to Natalia."

I disconnect the call and hand the phone back to Michael.

"Have a seat." He points to a stone bench near a fountain outside the front door to Moreno's estate. "We need to wait for the power to be restored before going in."

I slump onto the bench. Our respite allows to catch my breath after the grueling walk up the hill.

"What happens now?" I motion in the direction of the buildings still bathed in darkness.

"Several recovery teams will go through each warehouse and scan every individual for trackers, which they'll remove and destroy," he explains, gazing out over the vast grounds. "Any person requiring emergency treatment will be transported by helicopter to secure medical facilities tonight. The rest will wait until morning to be transferred. It'll be a long night for everyone." He pauses for a moment before continuing, "Tomorrow, recovery teams will arrive and assess the needs of those still remaining. They'll gather as much identifying information as possible for each person. Once everyone has been accounted for, they will be transferred to specialized facilities for recovered trafficking victims."

Michael's cell rings, interrupting our conversation. "I have to take this."

While I'm waiting, the power is restored to the desert compound. The haze is just beginning to clear, giving way to a cloudless, star-filled sky. Despite the atrocities that have occurred here, it's a relief knowing the compound is now under Maxim's control. Moreno's reign coming to an end seems to have cleared the evil presence that filled the space just a short time ago.

"I just received confirmation that your fiancé is safely back at the motel with Viktor," Michael says. "She informed Viktor a young girl was being held somewhere in the estate. I'm sending a few of my men to search for her." He places his hand on my shoulder. "Are you ready to pay Moreno a visit?"

I close my eyes and try to take a deep breath. Unfortunately, my broken ribs prevent that from happening, and I wince in pain.

"Do you want me to tape those up before we go in?"

"No," I say firmly. "I've already waited too long for this."

Alex

WHEN WE ENTER THE estate, we're met with a flurry of activity as armed men, all under Maxim's control, move about.

"Did you get the description I sent out?" Michael asks one of the soldiers standing guard at the bottom of the staircase.

"Affirmative. I forwarded it to the teams inside. If she's here, we'll find her."

"Keep me updated."

"Will do, Mike."

We continue walking past the entrance to Moreno's office to the end of the hall, where a hole is blown open. "There used to be a door opened only by retina scan. My guys did a little redesigning to make it more accessible." Michael grins.

The air temperature noticeably cools as we descend a wooden staircase that brings us underground. A chill runs up my spine.

"He hosted special events down here that only select individuals were invited to. It took Salvador several years, but he was finally able to infiltrate that inner circle." We stop at an open door. "Unfortunately, if a girl was brought here, she didn't make it out alive."

As I make my way through the building, I unwittingly walk into a windowless room. Despite its emptiness, my mind conjures up images of the unspeakable horrors that have occurred there. The modern lighting fixtures seem out of place amidst the ghastly surroundings.

Hooks are installed at various points on the walls, with some still holding cuffs. The ceiling is rigged with an intricate track system, complete with chains and suspension bars dangling from it. Bloodstains still mark the floor. My hands shoot out and clutch the door frame for support. There are no words to describe the depravity of a man like Moreno. But tonight, the tables have, and he won't be leaving alive.

I follow Michael to the end of the tunnel, where we stop in front of a medieval-looking door. It's easily eight feet tall and made of vertical wood planks secured by horizontal braces. Iron hinges hold it to the stone that makes up the arched doorway.

"Ready?" Michael turns to me.

Am I ready? The knowledge that once I choose to walk through this door, my life will never be the same isn't lost on me. I'm transported back to the day I stood before a different door, one with Thomas Moore sitting behind it.

After what he did to Natalie and her family, I couldn't see past my rage. Killing him was the only option I could imagine. It was Maxim who impressed on me the life-altering implications of taking the life of another. In the end, I found a small amount of compassion and decided to spare his life in exchange for him going to prison.

But at this moment, as I prepare to face Moreno, I have no compassion. There's no excuse for the hell he's put not just Natalie and me through but also countless others. There will be no bargains made. Moreno will suffer, and then he'll pay with his life. I meet Michael's steely gaze. "I've never been more ready."

I cringe as the metal latch scrapes across its housing, followed by the groaning of the hinges from the weight of the door as it's pulled open. Fighting the searing pain in my ribs, I pull my shoulders back and step across the threshold, prepared to come face to face with the devil himself. This room is more rudimentary than most of the others we saw. If it can even be called a room. The walls are made of brick, and the floor is dirt. It smells musty and stale. My eyes scan my surroundings. Various whips hang on the walls, not the typical kind one would expect to find in a BDSM club. The sole purpose of these whips is to maim the person on the receiving end of their punishing strikes. On the opposite wall are knives and daggers of various sizes. It hits me like a punch to the gut. This is the room where Moreno carves the skin of his slaves.

Then I turn my attention to Moreno himself. Walking further into the room, I stop a few feet in front of him and inspect the job Maxim's men have already done. Blood drips from the corner of his mouth, and his right eye is swollen shut. Heavy chains attached to a pulley system, the same one that's held countless innocent victims, now bind his wrists above his head. Moreno's body is strung, so only the tips of his toes brush the floor.

"Where's the dagger?"

"Fuck you, Alejandro." Moreno spits at my feet.

"Michael, can you—"

"Already on it," he answers before I finish the question.

With my back to Moreno, I walk to his wall of whips and inspect each one. I'm looking for the one that will cause the maximum amount of pain. The same one he was prepared to use on Natalie tonight.

"You aren't man enough to wield one of my tools," Moreno snarls.

Oomph.

I spin around. "Stop," I bark, freezing one of our men mid-punch. "Let him say what he wants. He won't have the option of talking much longer."

He steps back.

Returning my attention to the task at hand, I remove a bullwhip from where it's placed on the wall and test the feel of the dark wood handle in my hand. I run the whip's thong across my palm, noting the quality of the plaited leather. As I reach the end, I examine the sharp razors intricately woven into the fall. This whip has one purpose—maximum destruction of flesh.

I cock my wrist back, pausing briefly, my stare directed at Moreno, whose one good eye is locked on the whip. I'm sure he's wielded this instrument of torture many times on innocent women. He's basked in their screams each time the razors hit their skin. Then, he turns his attention back to me. Fear swirls in his eye. Moreno knows exactly what's about to happen as I flick my wrist back, the tail of the whip flies through the air, landing across his chest with a loud crack. Without pausing, I land several more strikes across his torso and down his legs, tearing the expensive fabric of his clothing and ripping through his flesh. He flinches each time the razors connect with his body. Curses fall from his lips.

"How does it feel to be powerless?"

I begin another round of ruthless strikes allowing the razors' edges to slice through his flesh. Moreno's wails of pain fill the room. With each lash, I feel my humanness slip further and further away. Knowing the weapon I'm wielding holds the power of life and death is a dangerous and heady feeling.

When I'm satisfied with the thoroughness of my assault, I return the whip, now dripping with blood, to its place on the wall.

Turning to Michael, I ask, "Can someone get me a bucket of cold water?"

Michael directs two of his mercenaries to complete the task.

"You know," I walk closer to Moreno. "Now I understand the high you get from using your whips."

"Fuck you, Montgomery." His breathing is labored.

I land a punch to Moreno's jaw, whipping his head to the side. Blood splatters fly from his mouth, landing on the wall. His head lolls forward as he battles to stay conscious.

Michael's phone rings. He exits the room just as two men enter, carrying buckets of ice water.

"You're just in time. Dump one on the bastard. We don't want him checking out just yet."

The men approach Moreno to carry out my order while I briefly exit the room and search for Michael. I find him standing at the end of the hall, talking on his cell phone. While I wait, I lean against the wall and close my eyes. Pain radiates across my chest. Each breath is more painful than the last.

"Are you holding up okay? We can get you to medical if—"

"I'm fine," I say, pushing off the wall.

He holds up his phone. "My men found the girl in a hidden room off Moreno's bedroom."

"Is she okay?"

"They're bringing her for medical attention," Michael says, sliding the phone into his pocket. "The guys said she's just a kid."

"Fuck. I need your gun."

Without question, Michael pulls his pistol from the holster on his waist and hands it to me.

"Take your time with him. Make him suffer." He motions with his chin over my shoulder. "My team wired the estate with explosives. When you're through, we're going to blow Moreno and this house of horrors apart."

With the gun in my hand, I return to Moreno. "Did you miss me?"

He doesn't look up. Doesn't answer.

"We're going to take a trip down memory lane, you and I," I say as I prowl around him like a predator stalking his prey. "Let's go back to our first day as your *guests*. Do you remember what you did to my submissive?"

"I took great joy in whipping her." An evil grin spreads across his face. "I should've fucked her then."

"You touched what didn't belong to you." Clicking the safety off, I raise the gun and aim it at his right hand. The one he used to hold the whip he marked Natalie with and pull the trigger.

Moreno's screams echo in the small room. His body shakes from the excruciating pain, but I don't look away.

Instead, I stand and watch the blood that spills from the carnage that used to be his hand—and I feel nothing. Over the next few hours, I alternate between inflicting pain and dousing Moreno with cold water to keep him from losing consciousness.

Between my malnourishment and injuries, I'm utterly exhausted. My body pleads with me to rest, but my mind refuses to slow down. I settle for taking a break and walk out of the room, with Michael following closely behind. I make my way back through the tunnels and take the steps two at a time, not stopping until I reach the front door of the estate. I open the door and stumble into the cool early morning air, which does little to alleviate the stench of death that still lingers in my nose.

Taking a few steps away from the house, I fall to my knees as my stomach involuntarily empties itself, not realizing there's nothing in it. Each heave sends searing pain through my chest. I try to push myself back up to my feet, but the blackness creeping into my vision causes me to fall once more.

"It's a given Moreno's going to die. You need to see a doctor. I don't want you dying too."Michael grabs my arm, helping to steady me.

Losing all self-control, I tear my arm from his grasp and yell, "You don't understand everything he's taken from me. He stole my fiancée. Then, that bastard paraded her around naked and tethered to a leash—treated her as if she were an animal." I point in the direction of the house. "Because of him, my unborn child is dead." My emotions are a jumbled mess. I'm unable to separate one from the other.

"Dammit. I had no idea. I'm sorry we can't give back what you've lost." Michael puts a hand on my shoulder. "Let's go finish him and get you back to your girl. She's going to need you."

Using the back of my hands, I wipe the tears from my face and try to catch my breath.

Before going back in, I tell Michael exactly how I want this to end.

As we approach the door, one of the men steps forward, holding out the black box that contains Moreno's prized dagger. The group falls silent as I take the box and slowly open it, revealing the weapon within. I lift the blade from its resting place, and my hand trembles as memories from the last time I held it flood back. I force them from my mind and focus on what I must do. For generations, this dagger has represented the purest form of evil in the world. The man who possessed it had used it to extract screams of pain from their victims, all for their own sick pleasure.

When we arrive outside the room, one of the men steps forward. In his hand is the black box that holds Moreno's prized dagger. The men gathered are silent as I open the box and lift the blade from its resting place. My hand trembles as the memories of the last time I held this weapon wash over me. I force them from my consciousness and focus on the task ahead. For generations, this dagger has represented pure evil walking the face of the earth. The man in possession used this implement to elicit the screams of the victims they tortured for their sick pleasure.

The reign of the Moreno family ends today.

Never again will this weapon be used to harm an innocent.

The soldiers guarding the doors pull them open. Then, with the dagger firmly in my grasp, I walk up to Moreno. "Look at me, you son of a bitch." He slowly lifts his head, a snarling grin on his face. "Do you have any last words?"

"Go to hell."

"You first."

Lifting the dagger, I drive it into Moreno's chest. His piercing scream fills the room as I drag the blade down his torso—bones crack, and blood pours out. I reach into his chest with my free hand. Moreno has a flash of recognition. Terror oozes from his pores as I wrap my hand around his heart and rip it from his chest.

In my hand, I hold the useless organ as it pulses.

Once.

Twice.

It quivers.

Moreno's life ends.

Viktor

WE MADE IT OUT of Moreno's fortress and are being driven back to the motel. Natalie's weak and scared. Her body trembles as I cradle her on my lap and rub her back softly. Once we're parked, the driver comes around and opens the back door of the SUV. I slide out with Natalie still in my arms. We're under the cover of darkness and in a seedy town. No one notices or cares that I'm carrying an almost lifeless woman into a motel room.

"We need to get some food into you," I say as I try to set her down.

"Don't let me go." She wraps her arms around my neck, holding on as if her life depends on it.

"It's okay. I won't leave you." I kiss the top of her head, trying to console her.

Without letting go, I grab the blanket folded at the bottom of the bed and sit with her on my lap. She holds me tightly while I open the blanket and cover her before pulling her close to me once again. Then, her tears start to fall.

"Shh. I've got you," I whisper. "I won't let anything happen to you." I gently stroke her hair and quietly hum the haunting lullaby *Bayu Bayushki Bayu*. It's the song my mama sang to me when I was a little boy and would wake from nightmares.

When Natalie's tears finally subside, I turn her so I can see her face. My eyes are drawn to her neck and the leather collar that's locked on it. How the hell did I miss that? I touch it looking for a clasp or a lock but find nothing.

"Moreno put it on me," she says over a sob.

I reach into my pocket and grab my knife. "I'm taking it off." Angling her head away, I slide the knife under the collar and carefully slice through the leather, freeing her. She runs her hand along her neck. I take both the collar and knife and slide them into my pocket. "Why don't you take a bath and get washed up? I'll have one of my men get us something to eat."

"I don't want to be alone."

"I'll be right outside the bathroom door."

"No. Don't close it. You can't leave me alone." Natalie's body trembles from fear.

I take a second to try to figure this out. "I'm going to move you off my lap and go talk to one of my men." I point to the door of our room. "I won't go out, but I need to ask them to get us some food. I'll come right back to you."

"Okay," she says softly.

I shift her off my lap, and she pulls the blanket tight around her. Every few steps, I look back and remind her I'm still here and not leaving. Natalie's eyes remain fixed on my every move. When I open the door, I give one of the men instructions to find us food. The other is to stay on guard outside the door.

"We didn't want to interrupt. But we were told to relay a message that the girl, Amelia, was found. The kid was beaten and raped. She's been brought for a medical evaluation. But they expect her to be okay."

"Thank you." I close and lock the door before returning to Natalie.

Her hair falls over her face, and I gently brush the blonde curls behind her ear.

"They found Amelia."

She looks up at me. "Is she okay? Where is she?"

"They brought her to the doctor. She's got some bruises, but she'll be okay."

"I promised her we'd keep her safe."

"And we will. Let's get you cleaned up. Can you walk?"

"I think so."

She tries to stand, but her legs don't hold her. I'm sure it's a mix of dehydration and shock. I wish the medical team were here to make sure she and the baby are okay, but they're still at Moreno's. Right now, I need to get her clean and warm. Then I'll get some food and fluids into her. I scoop her up once again and carry her to the bathroom.

"It's not much," I say, setting her on the edge of the tub. "But it'll do the job."

I fill the tub with warm water.

"I'll help you get in. Once I'm out of the room, you can take off my shirt. Don't worry if it gets wet—"

"You said you wouldn't leave me alone." She starts crying again.

"Natalie, I can't stay in here."

"Please," she begs, holding onto my arm with all her might. "I'm scared."

"Alex is going to kill me," I mumble. But I don't have the strength or the heart to leave her alone when she's terrified. "Can you take the shirt off yourself?"

She nods before slowly pulling my T-shirt over her head. There's nothing sexual in her movements, and I do my best to keep my line of sight above her shoulders. Gently and carefully, I help her step into the tub and steady her as she slides her body into the water before I turn away, pretending to busy myself with towels. Doing anything to avoid looking at my boss's fiancé.

I've grown to care about her too much. But I'll never let those feelings slip. I'll never act on them.

She can never be mine.

Natalie

VIKTOR'S MY ROCK, MY safe place, and the only thing keeping me from falling apart. I know he's uncomfortable being in here while I bathe. But I need him. I can't be alone. Although I've grown accustomed to my nakedness, Viktor's anything but comfortable with it. He's busying himself with straightening towels and toiletries, anything to keep from looking at me while remaining close.

I slide down the tub until my head goes underwater, shutting out everything except the racing thoughts inside my head. Where's Alex? Is he okay? Why isn't he here yet? How am I going to tell him about our baby? Gasping for air, I shoot up. Water splashes over the sides of the tub from my sudden movement.

"Are you okay?" Viktor rushes over and drops to his knees.

I meet his cerulean blue eyes that are swirling with concern. There's an avalanche of emotions at the precipice of crashing down and burying me. I wrap my arms around my abdomen.

"What's wrong?" he asks, grabbing my shoulders. "Is the baby okay? Fuck, I need to get a doctor here." He starts to get to his feet.

"There is no baby." It's the first time I have uttered the words aloud, and I'm not prepared for the onslaught of grief acknowledging my loss brings.

"What do you mean?" Viktor freezes.

"A few weeks ago. Moreno made Alex—" I choke on a sob. "There was so much blood. I lost the baby."

He pulls me close, holding me tightly. In that moment, the magnitude of our emotions is indescribable. Wrapped in a cocoon of deafening silence, we share a bond of grief I have never felt before. For a brief moment, I allow myself to be lost in the warmth and strength of his embrace.

"The water's getting cold," he says, pulling away suddenly. "Let me get you a towel."

Viktor leaves, and I shiver from the loss of his heat. When he returns, he's holding a towel out for me. I feel a little stronger and stand up and step out of the tub alone. He averts his gaze while I squeeze the excess water from my hair and wrap the towel around my body. Viktor holds my arm to steady me as he leads me back to the bed.

"Sit." I perch on the edge of the bed, holding the towel close, and watch as he opens one of the duffle bags sitting on the motel's dresser. "We thought you might appreciate having your own things." He shrugs as if he's unsure of his actions.

"That was very thoughtful. Thank you."

He approaches the bed with my hairbrush in his hand.

"Turn around." I sit with my legs crossed and my back to him. His touch is gentle yet sure as he combes the tangles from my hair.

"You've done this before?"

"Never."

While he brushes my hair, I realize I don't know much about Viktor's personal life. He's never told me about his family or if he's had any serious relationships. Although I want to ask, I know right now isn't the time for my questions. There's a rapping sound on our door. I jump and almost lose my grasp on the towel.

"Wait here."

Viktor pulls his gun from the holster on his waist as he approaches the door. His muscles visibly relax when he looks through the peephole, and he returns the weapon to its place before looking back at me. "It's our food." He cracks the door exchanging hushed words with whoever is on the other side before closing it and securing the locks. "Dinner?" He holds up the bag and grins.

His smile is contagious, and despite my sadness, I can't help but return it with one of my own. Viktor returns to the bed, sets the bag down, and begins rummaging through its contents.

"We're in luck. They found a street vendor," Viktor says as he pulls the food from the bag. "There's tacos, quesadillas, elotes, and fresh fruit. They even managed to score some churros if you're in the mood for something sweet."

My stomach turns at the thought of eating any of the spicy offerings. "I think I'll stick to this." I grab a banana.

Viktor frowns. "You need to eat more than that."

"I haven't had anything more than beans and rice for weeks. And even that was only if he decided to let me eat."

"Death isn't good enough for that bastard."

I put my hand on his arm. "It's over now. Thanks to you, I'm safe." I set the banana down. "Before I eat, can I get dressed?"

"Shit. Your clothes." Viktor hurries over to grab the duffle bag. "I don't know what Irina packed for you."

He pulls out a variety of shirts, shorts, and pants. I grab one of Alex's T-shirts and bring it to my face. It smells like him. Needing to feel close to him, I slip it over my head before grabbing a pair of yoga pants. Without removing the towel, I put my feet in and pull them up. Then I unfasten the towel and pull it out from under my shirt.

"Impressive." Viktor chuckles and claps his hands.

I pretend to bow. "Thank you." Having my clothes helps me feel a bit more like myself. "Do you know when Alex will get here?"

Viktor tenses. "He's with one of the teams. They'll be here in a bit."

There's more he isn't telling me, and I wait for him to elaborate.

"Eat your banana." He motions to the fruit lying on the bed and then passes me a bottle of water. "You need to get some nourishment, and then you need to rest."

Reluctantly, I take the piece of fruit and take a small bite while Viktor grabs a taco and sits next to me. "Did you ever think we'd be having dinner in a motel room again?"

"It seems to be our thing."

Several silent minutes pass as we share the comfortable familiarity of a meal together.

"Thank you, Viktor. I thought Silverio was going to—"

"Don't go there," Viktor interrupts. "And don't thank me. It's my job."

I resist the urge to roll my eyes at his comment. "Well, thank you anyway." A yawn escapes.

Viktor finishes the last bite of his taco, crumbling the wrapper in his hand.

"You should lay down."

He scrambles to clean up the food packages putting the garbage in a small wastebasket by the dresser.

I look toward the door. "I was hoping to wait for Alex."

"It's been a long day. You need to sleep. I promise I'll wake you as soon as he gets here." Viktor pulls the blankets down and motions for me to get in bed.

"You promise you won't leave?"

"I'll be right here." He goes to sit in an armchair in the corner of the room.

"Can you lay with me?"

"You know I can't."

"I need to feel you next to me. To remind me I'm safe. Please," I beg.

He drops his head in defeat before walking to the far side of the bed. "Alright. I'll stay next to you."

My limbs are heavy, and as much as I want to stay awake until Alex gets here, sleep beckons me. Unable to resist any longer, I crawl into bed. Despite the lumps in the old mattress, it feels like heaven compared to sleeping on the floor.

Viktor pulls the blankets up to cover me, and I slide close, resting my head on his chest. He tenses. His heart is racing. I'm sure he's worried about Alex's reaction, but I'm not concerned. All Alex will care about is that I'm safe.

Viktor puts his arm around me. "Close your eyes. I've got you."

Alex

IT'S AS IF WE'RE frozen in time. No one moves or makes a sound. I remain rooted where I stand in the middle of the room. Staring at the lifeless body hanging from the ceiling—the dagger tightly gripped in one hand. Moreno's useless heart in the other.

Michael comes over to me. "He's dead, Alex. It's over."

I let my fingers fall slack, and the dead organ drops to the dirt floor.

"It's time to go."

My legs are lead weights beneath me, anchoring me to this spot.

"Come on. Let's blow this place up."

Silently, the men file out of the room.

I don't move. An unknown force is holding me here, and I can't leave.

Michael tugs my arm, urging me to go with him. Without conscious thought, my legs move, following him. When we reach the doorway, I look over my shoulder at the carnage behind us. I should be happy that bastard's dead. That there's one less piece of scum walking the earth.

It was justice.

A life for a life.

Killing him was supposed to piece the shattered pieces of my heart back together. But I feel nothing.

We climb the rudimentary stairs, taking our final steps toward the exit. The sun is cresting the horizon, illuminating the once-dark night. As we move away from Moreno's estate, the warehouses come into view. Those who were once prisoners, facing a bleak future, now move freely within the compound's gates.

When we reach a safe distance, we come to a stop, and our group turns to face the villa. A man to my left begins a quiet countdown. "Three. Two. One."

The explosion's deafening sound shatters the desert's silence. Stone blasts apart, and glass shatters. Debris flies high into the air as the ground shakes beneath our feet from the sheer force of the blast. Transfixed, I watch as the rubble falls into piles and the dust begins to settle. In just minutes, the entire estate is destroyed.

Around us, men and women gather in small groups, clutching each other for support. The sound of children's cries fills the air. Moreno's reign of terror is over, but my soul feels no relief. I am nothing more than a cold, dead shell of a man.

"Alex." Michael's voice slices through the dark fog in my head. "Our ride's here. Let's get you back to Natalie."

Silently, I follow him to a black SUV that's waiting for us. As we drive, Michael and the driver talk to one another. Although I hear their voices, their words are nothing more than unrecognizable sounds. I stare out the window watching the landscape pass by in a blur. I don't know where we're going, only that Natalie is there and she's safe.

I should be happy. All I've wanted is to be reunited with her, but after everything I've just done, I'm scared.

In the past few weeks, I've killed two people. The first a heinous monster. I did things I never imagined I was capable of—and I enjoyed them. I took pleasure in administering even a fraction of the torture Moreno has inflicted on countless people. I watched as the life drained from his eyes and felt no remorse for being the one to snuff it out.

The other, my unborn son or daughter, once the symbol of new life and hope, now a victim of my actions. As a father, my role was to protect my child, yet I caused mortal harm. I would give my own life if it meant I could give our child back to Natalie. How can she ever forgive me for taking our baby from her? I am a murderer, a monster. Why would Natalie ever want me now?

The vehicle stops in a dirt parking lot at a rundown motel. Michael leads me to the door of a room.

"It's time to give this to me." Michael reaches for the dagger, but I pull my arm away. "Sasha's going to take it and get it cleaned up." He points to the other man standing with us and then tries to take it again, but I don't release my hold.

This dagger is my lifeline. The only thing connecting me to reality. If I let it go, I fear I'll fall into the black abyss lurking in the shadows, waiting to swallow me whole.

"Alex, if Natalie sees this, it'll scare her. You don't want that, right?" Michael places his hand on top of the dagger's handle. We're stuck in a silent battle. Finally, my fingers open, allowing him to take it. "I'll make sure you get it back."

Michael opens the door. Shuffling my feet, I walk into the room. I'm expecting to see Natalie, but there's no one here.

"Before we go to Natalie, you need to shower and get into some clean clothes."

I walk into the bathroom, my movements robotic, and I stop in front of the mirror. Looking back at me is a stranger, wearing the same black outfit I was forced to wear weeks ago when I committed unforgivable acts. The torn and filthy clothing hangs from my body, and my hair is disheveled, almost matted. My face is covered in coarse, dark hair from not shaving in weeks. Another man's blood is smeared on me from head to toe. Part of me recognizes that it's my image, but the rest feels like I'm viewing everything from outside my body.

Slowly, I strip off my clothes, letting them fall on the cracked tile floor before turning on the shower's knob. Water spurts from the small showerhead. I turn it as hot as it will go before stepping under the stream, hoping it will rinse the filth from me.

My body is hyper-alert, sensing movement outside the shower. I'm at a disadvantage and have no weapons to fight with. Carefully, I move the edge of the shower curtain to see who's there, unsure of what threat I'm about to face.

"It's just me," Michael says calmly. "I'm taking your dirty clothes and leaving clean ones right here." He points to the pile of clothes neatly folded on the counter by the sink.

Quickly, I close the curtain and lean back against the wall. It takes a few minutes for me to catch my breath and stop my body from shaking. When I finally compose myself, I grab the soap and washcloth to cleanse myself of the horrors I've endured. But no matter how hard I scrub, the feelings and memories won't disappear.

Desperate, I get more soap and try again. Over and over, I attempt to wash away the guilt, the memories, and the filth. My skin is red and raw when I finally give up and shut the water off.

While I dress, I listen to the voices on the other side of the door. I hear Michael and an unknown woman's voice. When I open the door, they stop talking and turn my way.

"Alex, this is Milina. She's one of our medics. She's going to tape up your ribs and check you for any other injuries."

"Come sit on the bed so I can look at those cuts on your face." Milina sets a black bag on the bed.

Instead of sitting, I walk to the door. I don't care about my injuries. Regardless of whether she'll reject me, I need to see with my own eyes that Natalie's safe.

Michael blocks my path. "As soon as we get you patched up, I'll bring you to her."

My mind screams no, but my body lets him lead me to the bed.

"This is going to sting," Milina says before using an alcohol wipe to clean the cut over my eye. "I'm going to need to stitch this one. Can you grab my suture kit, Mike?"

Michael digs through the bag, gathering the required supplies. He lays them out on the bed. Milina grabs a vial and a needle, filling it with a clear liquid.

"I'm going to numb it first," she explains as she injects it into the area around the cut.

It may numb the pain from the U-shaped needle she uses to stitch up my head, but it does nothing for the ache deep in my soul.

"Alex?" Milina leans down, coming eye-to-eye with me. "Did you hear me?" Her words float around outside me, but I can't grasp them. Can't respond to them. "Has he spoken at all?"

"No. Not since we left that bastard's house."

"I'm concerned he's in shock." Milina gently removes my shirt and presses on my ribs.

Red-hot pain shoots through me. It's hard to breathe.

"Maxim has a medical team waiting in New York."

"I don't think he should wait that long," she says as she wraps tape around my chest. "He needs to be evaluated now."

I rip the tape from her hand and toss it onto the bed before putting my shirt back on.

Michael looks between Milina and me. "What he needs is his fiancée."

"Michael." Milina crosses her arms in protest. "He needs medical and psychological treatment."

These two can keep arguing. I'm done waiting. I shove past Milina and head for the door.

Michael follows me. "Let's go. I'll take you to Natalie's room."

Alex

MICHAEL'S TALKING. I SEE his lips moving and how he looks at me, waiting for a response. But the thoughts swirling in my head are too loud. I'm unable to hear what he's saying. I can't respond. It's early afternoon, and the heat in this godforsaken place is already oppressive. Beads of sweat run down my face as we walk along the cracked concrete sidewalk littered with cigarette butts and garbage. How the hell did they find this dump? How much farther is Natalie? I want to ask, but words don't come.

We finally get to another rusty white door with two guards posted outside. Michael stops to talk to them, but my focus is past them. It's on the woman inside the room. My heart jackhammers in my chest, and I'm certain it's about to explode. I desperately want to see Natalie, but I also fear her rejection. How will I go on without her in my life?

One of the men knocks, and we wait. Finally, the door swings wide open. Viktor stands there, a huge smile on his face. "Good to see you, Alex."

I walk past him without acknowledging his greeting.

"I didn't want to wake her. She—"

His voice fades into the background. My entire being is laser-focused on Natalie. She's asleep on the bed, her blonde hair fanned out on the pillow around her. Carefully I sit on the bed, trying not to wake her, but she stirs anyway.

"Viktor?" She reaches across the bed, her eyes still closed.

Viktor? Why the hell is she asking for him? I thought my heart couldn't break anymore, but I was wrong. It hurts. Pain sears through my chest. Natalie knows, and she doesn't want me anymore. Her hand feels around the bed and comes up empty. Then, she opens her eyes and sits up quickly.

"Alex?" Her green eyes blink a few times. "Is it really you?"

I'm frozen in time, waiting to see the disgust on her face. Waiting for the rejection I'm sure, is about to come.

"You're here." She throws her arms around my neck, holding me tight. "It's over. It's really over."

Natalie's tears run down my neck as she cries, and I feel the weight of her sadness. Her sobs are the catalyst that breaks through my numbness, allowing me to feel. I break. Tears stream down my face, and my body trembles from the sheer force of emotions I can no longer hold back."

"I'm sorry. I'm so sorry, baby girl. I ruined your body. I scarred you. And our child—I killed our baby." I choke on a sob. "It's my fault. This is all my fault. I don't know how to fix this. I don't know how to fix us."

She pulls back and holds my face in her hands. "Alex. Stop."

"I should've fought harder. I should've done more to protect you. I ruined everything. I failed." I'm unable to stop the purge of emotions.

"Everything you did was to protect me." Natalie wipes my tears. "I'm alive because of you."

"But our baby." I drop my head. "I don't expect you ever to forgive me."

"Look at me," she says softly.

I don't look up. I'm afraid to see the hate in her eyes—the pain I've caused.

"Please, Sir."

Slowly, I lift my face and nearly drown in the depths of her emerald gaze. Because instead of hate, all I see is love and compassion.

"I'm so sorry, baby girl."

"There's nothing to apologize for." She caresses my cheek with her tiny hand. Her skin is so soft against mine. "Alex, we were forced into an unimaginable situation. The choices you were given were impossible. But you acted as my Dominant and did everything in your power to protect me from Moreno's depravity." She takes my shaking hands in hers. "You made sure it was you on the stage that night instead of him. You did that to protect me—to make sure I lived. What happened after that was out of our control."

"I should've—"

"You can't blame yourself."

She wraps her arms around me again, and I cling to her as if my life depends on it. And it does. Without her strength. Without her love. I'm going to fall back into the black abyss.

"I love you, Alex. We're together, and we're safe." She rains kisses on me. "Everything's going to be okay now."

Natalie

Alex is sitting on the bed, I think. I've had this dream so many nights that I'm afraid to believe it's real. He doesn't answer when I say his name. I'm scared when I go to touch him, his image will disintegrate as it has so many times before. But this time, when I reach out, I feel the warmth of his body. It's really him. He's still here. The nightmare is finally over. But then he shatters in my arms. His body trembles as he cries and apologizes over and over. He's broken. I look over Alex's shoulder and see the concerned look on Viktor's face. The man standing next to him whispers something. Then, with one last glance, they leave, closing the door softly behind them.

It's just us.

Alex's expression is tortured as he pours his heart out. He's blaming himself for everything. Hearing the agony in his voice is killing me. Everything that happened was Silverio's doing. He's the only one responsible for the heartache we're both experiencing. Knowing I lost our baby has been indescribable grief. An emptiness like I've never imagined possible. But not even for a second did I blame Alex. I don't know what to do other than tell him how much I love him and hold him. I'm hoping my love breaks through the grief he's experiencing.

Alex finally lifts his head his brown eyes, still filled with tears, meet mine.

"I love you, Alex. Nothing will ever change that," I say one more time before he relaxes and begins to accept the truth of my words.

He leans in and kisses me. It's different from any kiss we've shared. It's desperate, like he's drowning, and I'm his air. His lifeline—the only person who can save him.

"I don't deserve you," he says between kisses.

His words tear my heart in two. "Don't say that. I was made to be yours." My lips meet his once again. I pull him with me as I lay back on the bed. He winces. "Are you hurt?"

"I'm fine. Don't stop."

Grabbing his shirt, I lift it up, revealing his chest. It's wrapped tightly in medical tape, and he has sutures above his eye. I was so concerned with his emotional state I didn't notice them before. "What happened?"

He pulls his shirt down. "It's nothing, just a few broken ribs."

"A few broken ribs? That's not nothing." I don't want to hurt him, so I try to pull away.

"It's not important." He holds me tight. "It's over. Moreno's dead."

Moreno's dead? I want to ask him more. I want to know how Silverio died. But Alex's eyes plead with me not to question him. That right now, what he needs is my love. I take the shirt I'm wearing and pull it over my head. Alex palms my breasts, kneading them before rolling my already hard nipples. His hands skate down my sides to the top of my pants. I lift my hips as he slides them down my legs, tossing them off to the side before he leans over me, kissing me deeply.

Grabbing the hem of his shirt, I carefully help him take it off. It lands near my pants on the floor. Carefully, Alex stands up. Each move looks stiff and painful. He kicks off his shoes before unbuttoning his jeans, removing them and his boxers. My eyes scan his body, assessing each and every cut and bruise. He was beaten, and given the different colors of the bruises that cover his body, he was beaten more than once. Tears fill my eyes at the thought of him being hurt.

"It's over. No more tears, Natalie."

I close my eyes, trying to rid myself of the sadness.

Alex takes the opportunity to position his body over mine. I've missed this feeling. There were many days I didn't think I'd ever experience being loved by Alex again. His lips caressing my lips. His hands roaming my body, touching every inch as he reacquaints himself.

"I've missed you so goddamn much, baby girl."

"I need you." I lift my hips encouraging him.

He runs his fingers between my legs and gives me his sexy smile. I'm already wet and ready for him. Then he slides his erection in ever so slowly. Stretching me inch by inch until he's fully sheathed. His eyes close momentarily.

"You feel so good."

I moan in appreciation, loving the way our bodies fit together as if we were made only for one another. Alex begins to move in a gentle rhythm as he makes love to me. I pour every ounce of emotion I have into each movement and each kiss, using my body to convey my love for him. We climax at the same time, solidifying our reunion.

Carefully, Alex moves off me. We lay together, wrapped in each other's arms, our legs entwined. The nightmare we were forced to live in is finally over. I'm drifting in and out of sleep when a knock on the door startles me.

"Stay here." Alex gets out of bed and slips his pants on. Then, padding to the door, he looks out the peephole before opening it.

"I'm sorry to interrupt, boss."

I release the breath I'm holding when I hear Viktor's voice. Sitting up, I hold the blankets against me to keep covered.

"Maxim's jet is ready. We need to leave for the airport."

"Give us a few minutes."

"You got it." Viktor reaches out and clasps Alex's shoulder. "Glad to have you back, boss."

"Thank you." Alex glances back at me. "And thank you for taking care of Natalie."

Viktor's blue eyes meet mine from across the room. "It's my job, sir."

That simple statement, everything he isn't saying, holds so much meaning. We've formed a friendship unlike any other. I owe him something I can never repay—my life.

Alex closes the door, and I climb out of bed and gather my clothes to get dressed.

"Are you ready to go?"

"I never thought I'd hear you say that." I smile. "Let's go home."

Alex

A PARADE OF BLACK SUVs accompanies us to a private hangar at the Abraham Gonzalez Airport. Viktor helps the rest of the men load everyone's bags onto the plane.

Michael walks over to where I'm standing. "This is where we part ways."

"I can't thank you enough for everything you've done." I motion for Natalie to come over. "Michael, I'd like to introduce you to my fiancée, Natalie."

"I've heard a lot about you." He smiles and reaches to shake her hand, but she surprises us both when she hugs him instead.

"You brought Alex back to me. Saying thank you doesn't feel like enough."

"It's my job, ma'am."

Natalie giggles. "I've heard that somewhere before." She glances in Viktor's direction.

"Did you get—"

"It's all taken care of. Viktor has it."

Natalie looks at me curiously, but I'm not ready to talk about the dagger and what I did. I don't know if or when I'll ever be ready.

"Where are you headed now?" I assumed Michael and his team would accompany us back to New York, but they don't seem to be getting on the plane.

"We're off to our next job."

"Mike, you ready to go?" a man calls from one of the other vehicles.

"Be there in a minute." Michael shakes my hand. "I'm glad to see you're doing better. You two have a safe flight."

I wrap my arm around Natalie's waist and watch Michael walk away. "Let's go home."

Together we climb the stairs into Maxim's jet and get settled in our seats. Viktor, Sasha, and a few more of Maxim's men board the plane after us. We're taxiing down the runway within minutes, and the wheels lift off the ground. I didn't think this moment would ever come, but finally, this whole nightmare will be in our past.

It isn't until the plane touches down at JFK that I can breathe easily again. We're home, and we're safe. It's really over.

"Maxim sent a driver and a car. He's waiting at your apartment," Viktor says as we prepare to exit the plane.

"How did you find us?" I'm trying to put the pieces of our rescue together.

"It wasn't until after Timur woke up. He told us he heard the name *El Tomador*," he explains as we walk across the tarmac to the waiting car. "That was the break we desperately needed."

"Timur's alive? He was so still, and there was so much blood." Natalie's voice quivers. "I thought he was dead."

"He got lucky. The bullet missed his heart by a few inches."

We slide into the car's back seat and sandwich Natalie between us. The lights from the skyline illuminating the night come into view. It's a welcome sight. I put my arm around Natalie, and she lays her head on my shoulder.

"Tired?" I kiss the top of her head.

"My body doesn't know if it's day or night." She yawns.

"I'm sure you haven't slept well in weeks." I know I haven't slept a full night since we were taken. But now that we can finally let our guard down, I feel like I could sleep for a week. And even that probably wouldn't be enough.

"I texted Maxim," Viktor says as we pull into the underground parking garage. "They're awake and can't wait to see you both."

"You shouldn't have woken them.".

"Maxim gave me orders. Take it up with him."

Something's off with Viktor. He's been distant since we left for the airport. I'm sure he's trying to process everything. It can be argued he had the most important job—Natalie. Finding her tied up on that stage must have been hard for him. And then he was the first one she told about miscarrying. Viktor has a lot of responsibility on his shoulders. Usually, he handles it well. He rarely lets his emotions show. Knowing Viktor, he wanted to be in that room with Moreno. Maybe he needs some time off after this to decompress? I make a mental note to speak to Maxim about it later.

We climb out of the car and make our way to the elevator, where I punch in the code for the penthouse.

We're finally home.

Natalie

IF THIS IS A dream, I never want to wake up. The three of us are in the elevator, a normal occurrence I've taken for granted. As I look between the two men who mean the world to me, I'm filled with gratitude. It's hard to believe that I'd said my silent goodbyes to them just yesterday, thinking I'd never see either one again. But now we're safe, and we're home. The elevator doors don't have a chance to open all the way before Maxim grabs us, pulling us in for a hug.

"Alexander. Natalia." His voice cracks. "Welcome home."

"Natalie." Irina wraps me in a hug before pulling back and appraising me. "You're so thin and pale. How are you feeling?"

Did anyone tell them? I look to Alex. He offers me a slight shrug as if he doesn't know what to say either. My gaze turns to Viktor, and he shakes his head no.

"I think we're all tired." I choose an evasive answer, not wanting to ruin our homecoming with the news of our loss.

Movement from the kitchen catches my eye, startling me. I let out a small gasp.

"It's just Dr. Turova," Irina says, touching my arm.

"Welcome home, Natalie," Karina says.

"Thank you."

Alex doesn't leave my side as we make our way into the apartment.

"I know you've just gotten in, and I'm sure you're exhausted," Karina says quietly. "But I'd like to examine you right away."

My body trembles. "I, um—"

"Natalie, why don't we take Karina to our room. We can talk more there."

I nod, trying to hold back my tears. Alex places his hand on the small of my back as the three of us walk to our bedroom.

"I hope you don't mind. Maxim had me set up in here."

The ultrasound machine sits next to the bed, taunting me with the memories of our visit with the doctor. We were so happy watching our tiny baby move inside me. Everything was perfect. Then we left her office, thinking we were heading back to the safety of the compound.

The lights. The sounds. The blood. Horrific memories resurface, and I grab Alex for support.

He leads me to the bed. "Sit." His voice firm yet gentle. "Doctor, while we were being held, I did some terrible things." I cover his hand with mine for support. His voice cracks as he says, "I caused Natalie to lose the baby." Alex walks to the large window keeping his back to us.

"Can you tell me exactly what happened?" Karina sits beside me.

Although the story is painful, I do my best to recount the events of that fateful night. "While I showered, there was so much blood. I continued to bleed for over a week." I wipe the tears from my face.

"I'd like to do an ultrasound."

"Why?" I don't want to see an empty uterus.

"Diagnostically, it's important I check."

Alex spins around and comes back to my side. "Don't you think she's been through enough without putting her through this too?"

"Mr. Montgomery," Karina says patiently. "I understand your concerns, but I have a medical responsibility to my patient. And right now, that involves an ultrasound examination."

"Alex, it's okay." I do my best to reassure him. "If it's too much for you, you can wait—"

"You were forced to grieve this loss alone. I'm not leaving you to do this without me too. Let's get this over with." He glares at the doctor.

She appears unphased by his outburst. I pull up Alex's T-shirt so she has access to my abdomen.

"The gel is going to be a little cold. I apologize."

She places the wand on my stomach, and I turn away from the screen. I can't bear to watch. To see an empty place where my baby should be. Alex keeps his eyes locked with mine as he holds my hand tight. His presence gives me the strength to get through this. Karina's silent as she moves the wand across my abdomen. She clicks a button on the machine, filling the room with a familiar sound.

Swoosh. Swoosh. Swoosh.

I snap my head to the screen. My mind can't process what I'm hearing or seeing.

"Your baby is alive and well," Karina announces.

"I don't understand."

She moves the wand a little lower. "This." She points at the screen. "Is your placenta. It's typically lower in early pregnancy and moves higher as your uterus grows. Yours is still very low."

"What are you saying?" Alex asks.

"What Natalie described didn't sound like a typical mis-carriage, but I didn't want to say anything until I confirmed my suspicions. Natalie most likely suffered cervical trau-ma, which upset the low-lying placenta and caused the bleeding," she explains. "The fact that you were forced to stay off your feet for a few days following the episode was a good thing. It allowed your body to heal."

"I didn't lose the baby?" My head can't wrap itself around what she's saying or what I'm seeing.

Karina smiles. "Your baby's heartbeat is strong and healthy. It measures right on track at almost eighteen weeks."

"Our baby's okay?" I ask again.

"Your baby looks perfect." Karina looks between Alex and me. "Do you want to know if you're having a boy or a girl?"

"Do you want to know?" Alex asks me.

"Yes, please."

Karina moves the wand until she gets the angle she's seeking and then pauses the image on the screen. "It looks like you're having a girl."

For the past few weeks, I believed our baby had died. It was a loss unlike anything I'd ever felt. Finding out our baby is alive has brought back a part of me I feared was gone forever. I'm laughing and crying as I look at the crystal-clear image of our baby girl's tiny hands and feet as she kicks and wiggles around.

"That's my daughter?" Alex asks in disbelief.

I watch Alex's expression as he gazes at the image of our little girl on the screen. The light that had been missing from his eyes has rekindled. Learning our baby is alive has aided in healing the broken fragments inside him. Grateful for our miracle, I redirect my attention to the screen. Karina prints off a fresh set of photographs. The last one she hands us says *It's a girl* in pink ink.

"Wait until Maxim sees this. He'll never let us forget he was right." Alex laughs.

It's been so long since I've heard him carefree. It's a beautiful sound

After I wipe the gel off, we move to the sitting area in our room to complete the rest of our visit. I've suffered from malnutrition and have lost a significant amount of weight, which explains why I'm not showing. Karina gives me some new prenatal vitamins, and we discuss a diet plan that includes extra nutrition and calories so I can slowly gain back the weight I lost.

"I fully anticipate the placenta to continue moving to exactly where it should be. But I'd still like you to take it easy the next few weeks."

"I'll make sure she does. I'll see you out."

"Alex?"

He turns to me.

"Can you get Viktor? I want to show him our daughter."

Viktor

THE LOOK ON NATALIE'S face when the doctor said she wanted to examine her nearly killed me. I watch helplessly as she and Alex bring Karina to their room. I hate that Natalie's already suffered so much, and now she must endure this.

My nerves are on a hairpin trigger, and I need to be alone, so I don't snap. I stalk down the hall to Alex's office, closing the door behind me. Lowering myself onto the desk chair, I unlock the bottom drawer and take out the gift box with the pink and blue bows.

The night Misha and I found their abandoned car, I saved Natalie's ultrasound pictures. Even managed to get them into a little photo album. These pictures are special, and I knew Natalie would be happy that I was able to save them. But now, I don't know what to do with the reminder of what could've been. I drop my head into my hands.

I'm startled when the door opens and quickly sweep the box into the drawer, slamming it shut.

"Is everything okay?" Alex asks.

I jump up from my seat. "Yeah, all good. Did you need something?"

"Natalie asked to see you. She's in our bedroom."

I walk down the hall to their room. Even though the door is open, I knock.

"Come in."

I find Natalie reclining on several fluffy pink pillows—her tear-stained face tugs at my heart.

"Hey."

"Hey yourself." I stop just inside the doorway. And after our interactions in Mexico, I'm unsure what to do or how to act. It's a foreign feeling.

"Come here." Natalie pats the bed.

I cock my head slightly before taking hesitant steps to her side. She slides over, making room for me to sit next to her.

"Are you okay?"

Natalie pulls out a piece of paper she had hiding under the pillow next to her and hands it to me.

I hold the paper, momentarily shocked at what I'm seeing. "Is this?"

"Yes. It's my baby." She smiles, and her eyes light up.

My thoughts return to yesterday. How I held her while she cried in my arms, mourning the loss of her child. The look of torment in her eyes was too much to bear. But right now, her beautiful green eyes are glistening with excitement as she explains everything Dr. Turova told her about what caused the bleeding. "But the baby is alive and healthy."

"Wait here." I jump up and hurry to the door.

"Where are you going?"

"I'll be right back." I hurry back to the office and retrieve the box from the drawer. The thought of giving Natalie this gift fills me with joy. After everything they've gone through, they truly deserve a happy ending. "This is for you." I pass her the box.

"What is it?"

"Open it." I smile.

Carefully, Natalie unties the ribbons and lifts the lid off. She picks up the photo album and looks at me before opening it and flipping through a few pages.

"Viktor," she says as tears fill her eyes. "Where did you find these?"

"You must've dropped them during the struggle. I salvaged what I could. I don't know if I did this right." I shrug. "But I thought it might be a nice surprise when you got home."

"I couldn't imagine anything better." She wraps her arms around me. "It's perfect."

"I'm glad you like it."

"I love it." She releases me and sits back. "Will you help me put these in?"

I take the book from her, flip to the next empty page, and arrange the pictures. When I get to the last photo, I freeze. "It's a girl?"

"It is." She beams with pride.

"Maxim's never going to let you forget he was right." Natalie joins me, laughing. Then my focus shifts back to her and how thin she's gotten. I don't know anything about pregnancy or babies, but I can assume her severe weight loss isn't good. "Are you hungry? Can I get you something to eat or drink? I can order—"

"Viktor. It's the middle of the night. I think we need to get some sleep before you try to fatten me up."

"She's right," Alex says as he walks into the room. "It's time to sleep so your body can focus on growing our little girl."

"I'm going to go down to my place. A hot shower and my bed sound really good right about now." I clasp Alex's shoulder. "Congratulations, boss. I'm happy for you both."

"Thank you. We'll see you later today."

It looks like everyone's already gone to bed. The house is quiet as I make my way to the elevator to go down to my apartment. It's time to wash away this nightmare and get a few hours of sleep.

Alex

THE MORNING SUN'S JUST beginning to peek over the horizon, dispelling the darkness we've been living in these past few weeks.

"What's that?" I point to the box next to her.

"Viktor found the ultrasound pictures I dropped. He made us a photo album."

After all the time they spent together in Northmeadow, he and Natalie formed a close friendship. It seems their bond grew even stronger after their experience in Mexico. They care about each other. I can't lie. Part of me hates what they share and wants to put an end to it—I'm territorial and jealous. But the rational side of me realizes they've shared some traumatic experiences. It only makes sense that they're going to be close. I try my best to hide the conflicting emotions. "It seems he's already smitten with our little girl."

"I think he is."

"Let's shower. Then we need to get some sleep." My eyes are glued to her as she strips, making a small pile of clothes on the floor next to her. Until now, I never understood what people meant when they said a woman glows when she's pregnant. Natalie's absolutely radiant.

"I never thought I'd be so excited to do something as mundane as showering." She grabs her clothes and turns to bring them to the hamper.

The happiness I felt seconds ago fades when I see her back. It's a stark reminder of what we've been through—what I did to her. Natalie continues talking while I stare at the two cuts that are still in the beginning stages of healing. They were deep and needed stitches, but she wasn't allowed medical care. Now she's going to be left with jagged scars that will serve as a permanent reminder of what I did to her. She spins around, and I know she sees right through me, straight to the feelings of inadequacy and guilt that are assaulting me.

"Alex, don't. They're just cuts that'll heal. You kept us safe. That's all that matters."

The love that's reflected in her eyes rights every wrong.

She twists, looking over her shoulder in the mirror. "I was thinking maybe I could get a tattoo after it's healed."

"I think that's a great idea."

"Maybe we can pick a design together?"

"Of course, baby girl."

Once we're in the shower, Natalie lets her hands roam my body, her lips following their path.

I'm rock hard in an instant, but I pull back. "Dr. Turova said no sex for three weeks."

"She didn't say I can't make you feel good." Natalie begins to lower herself to her knees, but I grab her elbows holding her up.

"I'll wait as long as I have to for us to be together. I will not use you for my pleasure."

I don't know what triggers it, but Natalie starts crying. "I was so scared, Alex."

"I know, baby girl. I was scared too. But it's over. I'll never let anyone hurt you again."

We continue our shower, and there isn't a minute where our bodies aren't touching. Natalie's touch is tender as she washes my bruised body. Then, it's my turn. My hands glide over her, reacquainting themselves with every curve. I've never experienced something so sensual and intimate outside of sex.

After we're dry, I close the blackout curtains and climb into bed. I've spent the past month in a primitive cell, forced to lie on a dirty floor. Our soft sheets and fluffy comforter feel like heaven. It's a luxury I'll never take for granted again.

"Please don't let me go. I'm afraid if I close my eyes, you'll disappear."

"I'm not going anywhere," I say as I stretch my arm out, and she snuggles close.

I wait until her body relaxes and her breathing calms before closing my eyes. But for me, sleep never comes.

The clock on the nightstand reads eleven a.m. Natalie's still sound asleep in my arms. As much as I want to, I can't lay here any longer. There's work to be done. I'm certain Maxim's waiting to debrief us. Slowly, I pull my arm out from underneath her. She stirs slightly but thankfully doesn't wake. Viktor warned me about her reactions to having a closed door, so I leave it cracked open.

Before going to the kitchen, I have an important task to take care of in my office. Sitting in my chair, I open the top drawer and take out paper and a pen. Before meeting Natalie, I never thought about the potential risks of working with Maxim. My life is different now, and after what we've just lived through, it's something I realize I must do. As I put pen to paper, I'm certain this will be the hardest thing I've ever done.

After shredding at least five sheets of paper, I'm finally satisfied with the words I've penned. The letter gets sealed in an envelope with Natalie's name and placed with the other essential documents she'll need if anything ever happens to me. With that out of the way, there's one final step I need to take.

On my way down the hall, I check in on Natalie, who's still sound asleep. Then, I go to the kitchen, where I find Viktor sitting at the island drinking a cup of coffee.

"I wasn't sure if you'd be up yet." I walk past him and grab a mug from the cupboard.

"Couldn't sleep," he mutters.

"Me either." I push the button on the Keurig, and with a hiss, the machine comes to life.

Viktor glances down the hall. "Is Natalie still sleeping?"

"She is." I add sugar and creamer before I take a seat next to him. "We need to talk."

"Okay." Viktor turns slightly to look at me.

"Natalie is my world. I owe you everything for rescuing her."

"I was just doing my job."

"Cut the shit, Viktor." He always blows off his actions as *just his job*, but I know this is more personal to him. "Natalie is more than just a job to you. I know you care about her."

"Alex, if you're implying—"

"I trust you with her life," I interrupt him. "And I know you'll always put her first."

"What are you getting at?"

"I need you to promise me something."

"What kind of promise?"

"If anything ever happens to me. I need you to step in and take my place with Natalie and the baby."

"Boss, I know you've just been through hell, but we've got everything handled."

"This situation was a rude awakening. All these years, I've ignored the danger working with Maxim could present. That was fine when it was just me, but there's two more people I need to protect now. It'll give me peace of mind moving forward, knowing you'll be with them if anything happens to me."

Viktor studies my face before running his hand over his shaved head. The thought of Natalie being with someone else makes me feel sick, but I need this commitment from him. He's the only one I know I can trust with their lives.

Several long minutes pass before he speaks. "I promise, boss."

"Thank you."

It's both a relief and a promise I hope to never have to rely on.

Natalie

I WAKE DISORIENTED, MY heart pounding. Squeezing my eyes closed, I try to take a few deep breaths, but my body doesn't cooperate. Panic is rushing through me like a freight train. I can't breathe. I'm suffocating. "You can control this. Find something to ground yourself," I say the steps aloud. Opening my eyes, I look around the room and find something to focus on—the picture of Alex and me on the dresser from Christmas Eve. It's a selfie of us in Central Park right after he proposed. Sitting up, I swing my legs off the bed and touch them to the cool wood floor. Then, I run my hands along the soft blankets next to me. Slowly, the familiarity of the objects helps to calm my over-stimulated senses.

"My name is Natalie Clarke. I'm in my apartment in New York City. I'm safe and loved. I am strong," I speak the affirming words repeatedly, anchoring myself to the present. Little by little, my body begins to regulate itself. My breaths come easier. Next, I focus on the auditory senses. I hear familiar sounds—Maxim's boisterous voice, Viktor's deep timbre, and Alex's carefree laugh. The full realization washes over me, filling me with an all-consuming peace—I'm home.

After a quick trip to the bathroom, I put on a silk robe, tying the belt in a knot before padding down the hall to the kitchen to join everyone.

"Good afternoon, sleepyhead," Alex says when he sees me.

"You should've woken me up." I sit next to him at the island.

"You looked too peaceful to wake. Besides, Karina said you need to rest."

"Oh good, you're awake." Irina hurries into the kitchen. "I hope you're hungry. I made lunch."

"Lunch sounds wonderful. I'm starving."

"Perfect." Irina grabs a plate and starts dishing out food.

"She's been out here all morning cooking," Viktor whispers conspiratorially. "You'd think she was making food for an army."

Out of the corner of my eye, I see the silhouette of a man coming around the corner. "Timur," I squeal. Jumping off my seat, I run over to him, wrapping him in a tight hug. His body stiffens, and I let go quickly. "Did I hurt you? I'm so sorry."

"It's okay." He smiles stiffly.

"I thought we'd lost you."

"It'll take more than a bullet to get rid of me." He winks.

"It's time we get to work," Maxim interrupts.

"Where are you going?" Alex tries to stand, but I grab his arm, stopping him.

"I'll just be in my office. Come and get me when you're done eating." He kisses the top of my head.

"Yes, Sir." I don't want him to return to work already, but I'm sure they have important things to discuss. I watch the men exit the room, leaving Irina and me alone in the kitchen. She wastes no time setting a plate of cucumber and tomato salad before me.

"This looks heavenly." I moan, seeing the fresh food.

"That's just a start, dear." She opens the oven and pulls out a tray.

"Did you make *piroshki*?"

"I know how much you love it."

"You must've been up with the sun to get all this done." I take a bite of my salad, savoring the flavors.

"I couldn't sleep," Irina says before opening the refrigerator and pulling out another plate.

This time the platter has what looks like buns with open centers. Some appear to be filled with cream cheese, others with apples.

"What are they?"

"These are called *Vatrushka*. It's sweet dough with a filling. I used my *babushka's* recipe."

"I don't know what to eat first." I giggle, looking at the decadent foods set out for me.

"Now that it's just us." Irina sits next to me. "How are you, honey?"

I set my fork down and finish chewing my bite of food. I'm trying to buy myself some time before I'm forced to answer. My eyes dart around the room, avoiding eye contact with her for fear that she'll see right through me.

She places her hand over mine. "You don't have to put a brave face on. It is okay to not be okay."

I blink back the tears that once again fill my eyes. "I had a panic attack when I woke up." When I finally give in and look at her, I find her gray eyes filled with compassion.

"We're home and safe, but I can't shake this fear. I'm afraid to trust that it's really over. It's like something bad is lurking in the dark, just waiting for me to let my guard down."

"That's perfectly normal." She rubs my hand gently, soothing me like a parent would a young child. "You've experienced significant trauma. It's normal to struggle with your emotions."

"I know all of that."

"Yes, you've learned how to help others from a textbook," she agrees. "But living through it and finding your own healing is very different."

Tears slide down my cheeks. "Silverio forced Alex to do awful things to me. There was so much blood. I was certain I lost the baby."

"But Alex told us the baby was okay." Irina looks confused.

"Karina did an ultrasound last night. She explained my placenta was low, which was the most likely cause of the bleeding episode. That's when I found out the baby was okay."

"I'm sorry you had to go through that."

"I know I'm lucky. For the most part, I was spared the horrors most of the people there had to endure." I swallow over the lump in my throat.

"You must not compare your trauma with that of anyone else."

I take another bite of my lunch as I let her words sink in. She's right. My trauma isn't any more or less. It's unique to me. I'm going to have to learn how to live with it.

"I'd like to put you in touch with a therapist from Jelena's Hope," Irina offers. "It will be helpful with your recovery."

"I think that might be a good idea."

Irina is easy to talk to, especially about these difficult subjects. I find myself sharing more details about the night in the club with Alex and the scars it left on my back. Then I tell her how close I came to being raped and sold.

"If Viktor hadn't come." My voice trails off.

"The important thing is he did."

I nod in agreement, unable to think about what might've happened. But then, a forgotten detail surfaces, and the panic I thought I had under control rears its ugly head. "There was a young girl. She lived in the house with us."

"Amelia?" Irina asks.

"Yes. Have you heard anything about her?"

"She was brought to a secure clinic just over the Mexican border. She's being treated for some—" Irina hesitates. "Injuries."

"Injuries? What kind of injuries?" She's leaving something out, I can tell.

"Natalie, Amelia was raped."

"No. Please tell me that's not true. I promised Amelia she'd be taken care of."

"Viktor told me everything. As soon as she's medically cleared, Maxim and I will fly her to Jelena's Hope, where I will personally make sure she's cared for."

"Thank you." I throw my arms around Irina.

"Right now, you only need to be concerned with resting and getting stronger."

Natalie

AFTER FILLING MY TUMMY with all the delicious foods Irina made for me, I return to our bedroom to get dressed. It's a hot August afternoon, so I choose a loose sundress, put on some makeup, and pull my hair half-back.

"You look beautiful, baby girl," Alex says from the doorway.

"Thank you." A blush creeps up my cheeks.

"It's a good thing it was me walking past the open door while you were dressing, though."

"I'm sorry. I can't be in a room with the door closed."

"I'm not angry." Alex comes up behind me. "It'll take time for us to get over what happened." I rest my head on his chest. "I have something for you."

"You do?"

Alex takes my engagement ring from his pocket. "I hope you still want to marry me."

"There's nothing that can make me change my mind about becoming your wife."

He slides the ring back on my finger, pausing to look at it. "There's something we have to do today."

"Oh?"

"Your parents have been calling. Everyday."

"What are we supposed to tell them?" Panic begins to come to the surface once again.

"First, you need to relax. You and the baby don't need any more stress." Alex takes my hand and leads me to the bed. "Viktor has been speaking to them. They think we went on an extended earlymoon."

"An earlymoon?"

"Yes, an earlymoon." Alex grins. "You know, a honeymoon before the wedding."

"I see."

"We left our phones at the Soloniks' and went off-grid to spend some quality time together."

"Is that what we're calling spending time with a madman?" I give a sarcastic laugh.

"For this purpose, yes." Alex leans in and kisses my nose. "We took an earlymoon because we found out we were pregnant and knew we wouldn't be able to take a honeymoon."

The smile on his face tells me he's proud of the story he's come up with, and although I hate to admit it, I think it might work.

"Do we have time to call them now?"

"I think now is a perfect time." He reaches into his pocket and pulls out my phone. "Viktor kept it while we were gone."

Darkness clouds his eyes as if he's disappeared into the memories of our past few weeks.

"Hey." I take his hand. "I'm right here."

Shaking his head, he returns his focus to me. "Let's call your parents and give them the good news."

I pull up their contact and touch the green call button.

"Natalie?" My mom answers on the first ring. "Is that you?"

"Hi. Mom. You're on speaker. Alex is here too."

"Stanley," Mom yells. "It's Natalie and Alex. Where have you two been? We've been worried sick about you."

"Alex and I went on an earlymoon." I try to stifle a laugh.

"So we were told," Dad says.

"Hi. Dad." I keep my voice as carefree as possible. "How are you feeling?"

"Better now that we've heard from you."

"I'm sorry, Mr. and Mrs. Clarke," Alex chimes in. "It was a spur-of-the-moment decision. I was in such a hurry and wanted to surprise Natalie. Looking back, I realize I should've called to give a heads up."

"That would've been nice," Mom says, a sarcastic edge in her tone.

"I'm sorry, Mom."

"Where did you two run off to anyway?" she asks.

"Alex arranged for us to use Max's remote cabin," I tell them all about Maxim's compound without telling them we were actually hiding in a heavily guarded fortress before being kidnapped. Instead, I describe a beautiful cabin atop the Baltic Sea's cliffs. "The place is totally off-grid. No phone or internet. It was wonderful." I look to Alex, who nods in approval.

"I'm glad you had a nice time," Dad says, "But please, don't disappear and scare us like that again."

Disappear.

My father says the word so casually, not knowing how close we came to truly disappearing. It's something they never need to know.

"We won't." It's time to change the topic of conversation. I open a text message on the phone and attach one of our ultrasound pictures. "I just sent you a text. Can you check it out?"

I grab Alex's hand, trying to hold back a swirling mix of nerves and excitement.

"What is it?" Mom asks, her voice laced with confusion.

"We're having a baby." I squeal.

"That's why we went away early," Alex explains. "We knew we wouldn't have a honeymoon after the wedding."

I hear crying. "Mom. Are you okay?"

"I wasn't expecting something like this. It isn't right."

"This wasn't something we planned."

"How did it happen then?" Mom snips. "And what am I supposed to tell our friends?"

"I suppose you'll tell them you're going to be a grandmother."

"I can't believe my little girl is going to be a mom," Dad says.

"I am, Daddy. Alex and I are thrilled. We hope you both will be as well."

"Well, we weren't expecting this, so it's going to take a little time to get used to the idea," Dad says calmly. "But I'm sure we'll be just fine once the shock wears off."

"We need to reschedule the bridal shower. When are you coming home?" Mom's tone is clipped.

"We just got back to New York yesterday," Alex says. "Natalie had a few complications—"

"What kind of complications?" Mom interrupts.

"I had some bleeding. I've seen an excellent doctor who assured us that everything is okay. I have to take it easy for a few weeks, but she and I are healthy."

"She?" Dad asks.

"We're having a baby girl."

"As soon as Natalie gets the all-clear, we'll fly out."

"Do whatever you need to keep my daughter and granddaughter safe."

"You know I will, Mr. Clarke."

A yawn slips out.

"You sound tired," Mom says, her voice softening slightly. "Alexander, make sure Natalie's getting enough rest."

"I will. We'll call you tomorrow."

Alex

"You heard your mom." I wag my finger, trying to do my best impression of Charlotte. "It's time for your nap."

Natalie laughs at my poor comedy skills.

"I've barely been up a few hours," she protests.

"Doesn't matter. You need to rest."

"Can I interest you in *resting* with me?" She bats her eyelashes.

"I have to go out for a bit."

"Please don't leave me." Natalie clings to my shirt.

"Hey, baby girl." I move her back so I can see her face. "I won't be gone long, I promise."

"I don't want to be alone," she begs.

"Lie down." I pull the light blanket from the bottom of our bed over her. "I'll get Viktor and have him stay here with you until I get back."

"Thank you, Sir."

"I'll be back soon." I lean down and kiss her. "I love you."

"I love you too."

Leaving the bedroom door open, I search for Viktor and find him still in the office with Maxim and Timur.

"Can I steal Viktor for a little while?"

Viktor looks to Max, who gives a nod of approval before joining me in the hall.

"I have some errands to do. Natalie's lying down but doesn't want to be alone."

"I'll stay with her," he answers before I ask him.

"Thank you. I shouldn't be long."

I pull into the parking lot for the businesses in Chelsea. My destination—Fire and Ice. Shortly after we got back together, I designed a collar for Natalie and was planning a ceremony. But then we ended up in Russia, and everything spiraled downhill. Shake it off, Alex. I silently remind myself as I pull open the door to the club.

It's a Wednesday evening. The only thing going on is a beginner class in the main room. I quietly walk in just as Star prepares to dismiss the students into their small groups. She smiles and holds up a finger. When the last of her students exit the room, she walks across the club's wood floor—her stiletto heels clicking with each step.

"Alex." She hugs me. "I'm so glad you're back. How's Natalie?"

"She's pretty shaken up. But she'll be okay."

"When Anthony told me." She puts her hand over her heart. "I'm just glad Maxim was able to get you two back."

"Actually, he got three of us back." I grin.

"Three?"

"Natalie's pregnant." It's the first time I've told anyone outside our family.

"Oh, Alex. I'm so happy for you both. Let's go to my office to talk."

We continue chatting. "It was a surprise for the both of us, but we're incredibly happy."

"When is she due?"

"The beginning of January."

Star has a huge office space. Half of the room is a typical setup with a desk where she conducts the club's business. The other half is a sleek sitting area with red leather furniture. She sits on the sofa and motions for me to sit across from her.

"Do you know what you're having?"

"It's a little girl." I beam with pride.

"You're so screwed." Star laughs. "She's going to have you wrapped around her little finger the second she's born."

I laugh along with her. But the reality is we came so close to losing the baby. I already know I'll do anything to make sure she's not only well-cared for but also safe and happy.

"I'm assuming you're here about something else, though." She raises an eyebrow at me.

"Do you have the collar?"

"I do." The experienced Dominatrix rises gracefully. She pulls a small key from her pocket and unlocks one of the desk drawers. Reaching in, she takes out a black jewelry box. "I hope you don't mind that I peeked."

"What did you think?"

"It's breathtaking." She passes me the box and returns to her spot on the sofa, crossing her legs.

Instead of opening it, I set the box on the glass table in front of me.

"What's wrong?"

A sick feeling stirs in the pit of my stomach as flash-backs of Moreno play in my mind. "He put a collar on her," I grit out the words. "He put her on a leash and made her crawl around. He treated her like an animal." I drop my head in my hands.

"I'm so sorry, Alex," Star says quietly. "Look at me." I can't lift my head. The memories are too much. "Alexander," she says sternly. "Raise your head and look at me."

Slowly, I lift my head. My vision is blurry from the tears that are now falling.

"That collar meant nothing." Star perches on the edge of the table and picks up the jewelry box. "This has meaning. This collar represents the Dom/sub bond you and Natalie share."

"I know, but—"

"There are no buts, Alex. Moreno will get what's coming to him. I'm sure Maxim will see to that."

"He's already dead. I killed him."

Star nods, undaunted by my admission. "Good." She pushes the box into my hands. "Open it."

With a deep breath, I lift the lid. "It's stunning."

The collar is a silver chain, not much thicker than a traditional necklace. It's discreet in appearance, so Natalie can wear it every day without garnering unwanted attention. Set in one end of the chain are two gemstones: a Peridot, Natalie's birthstone, and an Amethyst, my birthstone. The ends of the chain attach to a heart lock with the words *baby girl* inscribed on it. Once it's locked around her neck, it won't come off without the key I'll be wearing.

"She's going to love it," Star assures me.

"Do you think I'm doing the right thing? Given what's happened, should I wait?"

"What does your heart say?"

Rarely do I listen to my heart. It's a foreign feeling to make a decision based on pure emotion. "It tells me to do it now. To replace the terrible memories with something wonderful."

"Then you already have your answer."

"I'll call Anthony and tell him we're a go for Friday night. Can you make sure Brandon gets this for the ceremony?" I hand the box to Star.

"I'll take care of the rest of the details," Star reassures me.

Natalie and I are lucky to have such a supportive community to rally around us.

Alex

"EVERYTHING'S ALL SET. WE'LL see you Friday." I disconnect the call with Anthony before getting into the elevator. The collaring ceremony's in two days. It's last-minute, but I shoot a quick text to my father. He's been on cloud nine since my earlier text about the baby.

(Me) Natalie's collaring ceremony is Friday evening at Tony's place. I know it's last minute, but is there any chance you and Luna can fly in?

(Dad) I'll do everything I can to get us there.

Everyone's sitting in the living room when I get upstairs.

"How was your nap?" I go straight to Natalie.

"It was good. I feel much better now."

"I'm glad to hear that."

"Where did you go?"

"My impatient little sub. You'll find out soon enough." Natalie sticks her lip out in a pout.

"You're cute." I kiss her forehead. "But that won't work. Something smells delicious." I change the subject.

"That is my wife working her magic in your kitchen," Maxim says proudly.

"I offered to help, but she refused. I'll go crazy if all I can do is sit with my feet up for the next few months."

"Rest now, Natalia," Maxim advises. "When that little one comes, you will no longer have the luxury of rest."

"Dinner's ready," Irina calls from the kitchen.

"Let us eat." Maxim stands and, as usual, is the first one in the kitchen.

I offer my hand to Natalie, helping her from the couch. "You're glowing, baby girl."

"I'm so happy to be home and to know our little girl is okay." She places her hand on her stomach.

We join our extended family in the dining room. Irina is a master in the kitchen and has filled the table with various mouthwatering Russian dishes.

"I can't thank you enough for this." I motion toward the spread of food.

"It's my pleasure," Irina says before taking her seat next to Maxim.

Natalie waits while Irina makes Maxim's plate, showing deference to his place in the lifestyle before she makes mine.

When she's through, Maxim announces, "Everyone, please make your plate."

Viktor and Timur don't waste a second piling their plates high.

"Should we tell them now?" I whisper to Natalie.

"Yes." Her eyes light up.

"We have an announcement to make." I get everyone's attention.

The room grows quiet. All eyes are now on me.

"As you know, we had an ultrasound yesterday." I place my hand on Natalie's thigh under the table. "Dr. Turova assured us our baby is strong and healthy. She also informed us we're having a little girl." My heart swells with pride.

"A *moya vnuchka*," Maxim boasts. "I knew it."

"I don't know how." Natalie laughs. "But you were right."

"We didn't officially find out the gender of our babies before they were born. But Maxim knew both times."

"Somehow, that doesn't surprise me."

The rest of the meal is filled with baby talk and all the shopping Irina and Natalie plan to do before the Solonik's return to Russia.

"It sounds like I need to start converting one of the guest rooms to a nursery sooner rather than later," I say to my fiancé, who is absolutely radiant.

When I bought this penthouse, I never imagined I'd share it with a woman, let alone a child. But now that it's happening, I can't imagine my life any other way.

Natalie

Being back in New York is like a dream come true. It's taken a few weeks, but we're finally falling back into a familiar routine—something that's helped keep my anxiety at bay. Yesterday, I had my first video session with my therapist from Jelena's Hope. Even skimming the surface of what I endured was hard to do. However, my therapist assures me we'll work through it at my pace and that I'll be okay. Recovery will be a bumpy road. It always is. But I'm confident that with the help of my support system, I'll triumph over my fears.

After my session, we had quite the online shopping spree for baby Montgomery. Irina is taking her role as *babushka* seriously. While we're shopping, I get a text from Alex.

(Alex) Don't worry about cooking. We're going out tonight for a farewell dinner.

Maxim, Timur, and Irina are leaving for Russia tomorrow. I don't want them to go, but I understand they have lives to return to.

(Natalie) Where are we going?

(Alex) It's a surprise.

A surprise means the unknown, and the unknown is terrifying. I've lived the past nearly month of my life with 'surprises.' I put my phone away and try to concentrate on baby shopping instead of the fear clawing at my insides.

I've just finished my shower and am standing at the mirror, wrapped in a towel, attempting to apply my makeup.

"You're shaking. What's wrong?" Alex asks when he walks into our room.

I push the mascara wand back into its tube and set it on the dresser. "Not knowing where we're going is messing with my head. I know you want it to be a surprise—"

"A surprise isn't meant to scare you," he says patiently. "We're going to *Italiano Desiderio.*"

"You didn't have to tell me." I look down, disappointed with myself.

"I know I didn't." He pulls me into his arms. "It won't be scary forever. We both have some issues to work through, and we'll get through them together."

"But I've ruined your surprise."

"Oh, baby girl," he says with a sexy grin. "You haven't ruined anything. Now put on your black lace dress so we can get to dinner."

"I love you, Sir." I plant a kiss on his lips.

"I love you too, baby girl."

This time, my hands are steady as I apply my mascara. I style my hair in a simple updo, leaving some loose curls to hang softly around my face. Then, I find the dress, a mermaid style, floor-length evening gown Alex told me to wear, and put it on. Solid black lace covers me to my knees, where the fabric transitions to sheer lace. It's sexy yet not overly revealing. As I slide it on, I notice my breasts are already fuller than usual, enhancing the tightly fitted bodice and the deep V neckline.

"Can you help me zip this?"

"Sure." I turn around, and Alex slides the zipper up slowly.

"It feels a bit tighter than usual." I run my hand over my stomach.

Alex puts his hands over mine. "You can blame Irina's cooking and the baby you're growing." He kisses my neck before returning to buttoning his shirt.

When we're finished, we head out to the living room, where our guests are dressed equally as fancy.

"Everyone ready?" Alex asks.

We make our way to the garage. Maxim and Irina go with Timur in their rented car, and Viktor drives our vehicle as we head to the restaurant for our goodbye dinner.

Alex

EVERYTHING'S ALL SET FOR the ceremony tonight. Natalie thinks we're going out to have a farewell dinner for our Russian family. Instead, everyone's coming to celebrate us. Dad and Luna were able to get a flight in late last night. Lana and Brandon flew in earlier in the week. They've laid low since Natalie thinks they're still visiting Lana's extended family in Russia.

Collaring a submissive is a significant step in a Dom/sub relationship. It's not to be taken lightly. In many ways, this step is more serious than our upcoming marriage. I'm more nervous than I've ever been. I want everything to be perfect tonight.

"There's no one here," Natalie remarks as we enter the empty restaurant.

"Must be a slow night." I shrug, feigning indifference.

"Alex. Natalie." Anthony comes around the corner. "It's so good to see you both."

He wraps Natalie in a hug. "I hear congratulations are in order."

"They are." Natalie smiles. "Thank you."

"It's good to have you back." Tony reaches to shake my hand but decides to go for a hug instead.

"It's good to be back," I assure him.

Tony exchanges greetings with Max and Irina before turning back to us.

"Since it's such a beautiful night. I took the liberty of setting your table in the garden. Follow me."

Am I doing the right thing? Or is it too soon? My heart pounds as I place my hand on the small of Natalie's back. We follow Anthony through the restaurant and out the glass doors leading to the garden.

Natalie

WHEN WE GET TO the restaurant, it's empty. I'd be more suspicious if we weren't out with Maxim. He has a habit of booking out entire venues to avoid crowds and security issues. But after what we've just been through, I have a newfound appreciation for his actions. Tony leads us to the outdoor seating area, but instead of stopping, we turn in the opposite direction.

"Where are we going?" I ask Alex quietly.

"You'll see."

I squeeze Alex's hand, fighting the anxiety that's trying to steal this moment. It takes a conscious effort to remain grounded in the present. I try to focus on everything around me, like the flagstone path we're walking on. The creeping thyme with its delicate purple flowers growing between the stones. I'm careful where I step, trying to avoid sinking my heels in the dirt. On both sides of the walkway are lush gardens of all-white flowers. The blooms are meant to be shown off by the moon's light. I recognize the Japanese lilacs, night-blooming Jasmine, and gardenia, among many others. Their sweet fragrance fills the air. Behind the flowers are miniature trees adorned with soft twinkling lights.

"It's a moon garden," I murmur.

"Do you like it?" Anthony asks.

"It's magical. I love it."

A tall wrought iron gate stands at the end of the path, guarded by two imposing men. I recognize them as the security guards from Fire and Ice. When we approach, they pull the gates open, letting us pass. The metal clangs behind us. I look over my shoulder and find the gate is closed, and the men have resumed their post.

We stop walking and are shrouded by darkness. I look around but can't see anything. Why are we here? Chills creep up my spine as I try to convince myself the dark isn't going to swallow me whole.

"Are you ready?" Alex's warm breath tickles my neck.

"Ready for what?"

The second the words leave my mouth, lights flicker on, illuminating the open space. We're standing in a circular garden, and all our friends from Fire and Ice are lining the circle's edge. The Dominants are standing with their submissives kneeling at their feet. Maxim and Irina step out from behind us and take their place by Sam and Luna. Brandon and Lana are next to us, completing the circle.

"What's going on, Sir?"

"No more talking, baby girl."

Alex steps away from me and walks to the center of the circle.

"Natalie, please join your Dominant," Brandon instructs.

Lana grabs my hand and squeezes it as I pass by.

Alex motions toward a small black silk blanket on the ground in front of him. "Kneel." He reaches out to steady me as I lower to my knees before him, my gaze cast downward.

"Look at me." Alex's voice is deep and commanding,

I lift my eyes and meet the loving gaze of my Dominant.

Brandon walks up to Alex and hands him a black box. He stays next to Alex as he lifts the lid so I can see what's inside.

I gasp when I see the beautiful collar displayed on the black velvet. In the center of the box is a heart-shaped lock inscribed with the words *baby girl.*

A deluge of emotions, both good and bad, overwhelms me. I close my eyes and try to regain control over my thoughts. Before we were taken, Alex and I talked about me wearing his collar. It was the next step in our Dom/sub relationship, and we were both looking forward to it. But then, a few weeks ago, that monster unwillingly locked a collar around my neck and paraded me around like an animal. I know this isn't the same, but after everything we went through, after being forced to wear a collar I didn't want, am I ready for this?

Alex clears his throat before he speaks. "I'm thankful for each of you who came tonight to share this special evening with us. The last few weeks have been the scariest of my life. Not only was I unsure if I'd live to see another day, but my submissive, the most precious person in my life, was in grave danger. Even though we're back safely, we're both still healing." Alex's voice cracks. "I had this collar made before all that happened. Since we've been back, I've struggled with how to proceed. I wasn't sure if I should let more time pass before offering a collar to my submissive, fearing it would trigger her."

Tears are sliding down my face listening to Alex speak. When he looks at me, he reaches down and wipes my tears.

"I sought the advice of a wise friend." He looks up and smiles at someone behind me. "Who explained to me that the piece of leather Natalie was forced to wear was meaningless—it held no significance in our lifestyle or relationship. This collar in my hand is the one that holds meaning and commitment, the only one that matters. I decided to take a chance and seize the moment because no one is guaranteed a tomorrow. I didn't want to let another day go by without my submissive knowing how much I treasure her. How much it will mean to me if she accepts my collar."

My eyes follow his every movement as Alex takes the collar and lock from their place and hands the box to Brandon. He takes it and returns to his place in the circle.

"Natalie, as your Dominant, your heart, your safety, your life are mine to care for. I'm honored that you've chosen to submit to me. I cherish that submission. Tonight, I'm asking you to take your commitment to us one step further. I'm asking you to wear my collar." I cling to his every word. "By accepting this collar, you demonstrate your commitment to our relationship and your willingness to submit to me both physically and emotionally. You promise to obey me and accept my guidance, knowing I will care for and protect you in every way. Moreover, this collar represents my commitment to continue to train and support you, always respecting your boundaries and helping you grow in your submission. Above all, I promise to cherish and protect you for as long as we live. So, Natalie, I ask you now. Will you accept this collar and all the promises it symbolizes?"

His words weave deep into my heart, knitting together every broken piece. "Yes, Sir. I will."

Alex places the silver chain of the collar around my neck. He attaches the heart lock on the front and snaps it closed. "Thank you for your gift of submission, baby girl."

I place my hands in his as he helps me to my feet. Tears stream down his face as he says, "You are mine."

"i am Yours, Sir."

Alex pulls me tight against him, wrapping me in the strength and love of his embrace.

Our guests approach, offering their support and congratulations. These people are our chosen family, a strong community that has rallied around us. Sheltering us with their love and support.

After we get through the last of the line, Tony announces the food is being served. He motions for everyone to follow him through a pergola overflowing with white wisteria. The other side opens to a reception area where tables are set under a tent. Fairy lights are strung on the tent roof, twinkling in the night, and soft music fills the air.

"It's the wedding reception venue. Alex, this is incredible. How did you do all this?"

"Star was instrumental in helping me."

"Remind me to thank her later."

Alex leads me to our table, which is set apart from the rest. In the center of the table is a vase with a single white rose. Alex pulls my chair out just as Anthony approaches our table to personally serve our food.

"We'll be having a traditional seven-course meal," he says as he sets down our first plate.

It's a beautiful antipasto for two, complete with fresh meats, cheeses, and several varieties of olives. Alex and I taste some of each. I can't decide which is my favorite. Tony approaches with our next course. He sets a bowl of soup in front of us.

"This is my creamy tortellini soup."

I taste the first spoonful and moan in delight. "Tony, this is the best thing I've ever tasted. I'm going to want this every day."

"I can make that happen." He smiles and leaves us to finish.

The next course is shrimp fettuccine alfredo, followed by a Caprese salad. Two of my favorite dishes.

"I don't know if I can eat another bite," I say. "I feel like I'm going to explode.

I'm still having a hard time increasing my calorie count. Tonight's meal is the most food I've been able to eat.

"That was the bulk of the meal. Only do what you can," Alex says, taking my hand.

The next course is a light offering of fresh fruits. Followed by dessert, cannoli, and coffee.

Once the meal is over, we're treated to exhibitions from some Dom/sub couples from the club. My favorite is the fire play display.

"Have you ever tried fire play?" I ask Alex.

"No. Why?"

"I really like it."

Fire play wasn't something we discussed when we negotiated our contract, so I'm not sure about Alex's thoughts
on it.

"I'm not super comfortable doing it, but I'm willing to talk
about it. After you have the baby."

"I can live with that."

What I assumed would be a simple farewell dinner
turned out to be an unforgettable night that will stay with
me forever. As I run my fingers over my collar, any doubts
or uncertainties I had are dispelled. Wearing Alex's collar
around my neck fills me with pride and serves as a constant
reminder that I belong to him. It's a beautiful and meaningful symbol of our bond, and I'll cherish it forever.

Alex

LIFE APPEARS TO HAVE returned to normal or at least a new normal. While I go into the office, Viktor stays with Natalie. It's the only way I can walk out of the house without worrying about her safety.

I'm grateful that Brandon, even from Russia, was able to keep the business up and running. Especially after I disappeared without warning. Being back in the office the past few weeks, I've come to a new realization. My heart is no longer in advertising. I've been toying around with the idea of a major career change. I think I'm finally ready to talk to Natalie about it.

Right now, I'm supposed to meet Natalie at her obstetrician's office. It's her twenty-week ultrasound and check-up. When I rush into the waiting room, she's already there with Viktor at her side.

"I'm sorry I'm late." I kiss her cheek. "I got stuck on a call."

"It's okay. The doctor's running late."

The office door opens. "Natalie?"

"That's us." She smiles as she stands. "Do you want to come in for the ultrasound, Viktor?"

His face pales. "No thanks. If it's okay, I'll head back to the apartment. There are some things I need to get done."

"Sounds good. We'll see you later."

Viktor exits the waiting room as we go into the back office with the nurse. After checking Natalie's vitals and weight, we get settled in the ultrasound room to wait for the doctor.

"Do you think everything's okay yet?"

"I sure hope so. Because I don't know how much longer I can keep my hands off you." I adjust my erection, and Natalie laughs.

There's a knock on the door a second before it opens. "Good afternoon," Dr. Young greets us. "Are you two kids ready to take a peek at your little one today?"

"We sure are," I answer.

Natalie adjusts her clothes so the doctor can access her tummy. She's followed Dr. Turova's advice to the letter and is slowly gaining back the weight she lost. She's now sporting an adorable baby bump.

"Have you felt any movement yet?" he asks while setting up the scan.

"Sometimes it feels like there are butterflies in there. The books say that's the baby moving?" she asks, unsure.

"That's what they tell me too." He chuckles.

The doctor starts with the routine part of the exam—all the measurements to make sure the baby is growing appropriately.

"Here's what we're looking for." He points to the screen. "The placenta is nice and high, right where it's supposed to be."

Natalie sighs in relief.

With the diagnostic portion of the ultrasound done, Dr. Young switches the view to 4D.

The image of my baby daughter is crystal clear. I'm in awe. "Look at her little nose. She's beautiful, like her mama."

Natalie laughs as our daughter does acrobatics. "She's sucking on her toe."

"You've got quite an active little girl in there," The doctor says as he finishes the ultrasound and hands me the printed pictures.

Baby Montgomery is going to fill her entire photo album before she's even born.

"I'll give you a minute to clean off, and then we'll talk in my office." With that, he exits the room.

Natalie uses the provided towels to wipe off her tummy before fixing her pants and shirt. Then we go to Dr. Young's office, where he's already behind his desk waiting for us.

"Everything looks great. The placenta previa is completely resolved, and the baby's growth is right on track."

"Am I able to travel now?" Natalie asks, a hopeful tone in her voice.

"Yes, this would be the perfect time to take any trips you have planned."

"What about sex?" I ask.

Natalie's cheeks turn red at my candor.

Dr. Young chuckles. "You're clear for sex. Natalie may be uncomfortable at first, so go slow."

"I'll be cautious," I assure him.

"Do you two have any other questions?"

Natalie looks at me. Uncertainty is written on her face.

"Yes, we do," I say confidently. "We were referred to you because you're a kink-friendly physician."

"Yes, that's true." The doctor leans back in his chair, steepling his fingers. "Let me reassure you both that this is a judgment-free place. I want you to feel comfortable speaking freely and asking your questions."

"We're in a BDSM relationship. As her Dominant, I have to be certain that anything we do is safe for her and the baby."

"The first thing I advise all my expectant couples is to practice good communication. It's even more important now than pre-pregnancy," the doctor explains. "Natalie, your body's going through many rapid changes, which will impact your comfort level. So things you were previously okay with may not be okay right now. And things you are okay with today may not be okay in the coming weeks."

"Are there any activities that are off-limits while she's pregnant?"

"Do you have anything specific in mind?"

"Is bondage okay?" Natalie asks.

"Yes. With some modifications."

Dr. Young explains that the obvious areas, like Natalie's abdomen, must be excluded to not restrict blood flow to the uterus. Refraining from having her fully on her back or tummy is also important. "I'd suggest you avoid full suspension because it puts too much pressure on your limbs and could cause serious complications. Those are the most important things to consider. Other than that, use common sense, communicate openly, and you'll be okay."

"What about impact play?" I inquire.

"Impact play is safe." The doctor smiles. "Again, the abdomen is off-limits, as is her lower back. Any area that may impact the uterus."

"Thank you, doctor." I'm surprised by how few restrictions there are. "We appreciate you taking the time to answer our questions. I think that's all we have right now." I look to Natalie, who nods in agreement.

"If anything comes up before your next appointment, you have my number."

"Do you want to grab a bite to eat?" I ask Natalie on the way out of the doctor's office.

"These days, I'm always hungry."

"There's a quiet little place a few blocks from here. Are you up for a walk?"

"I'd love that."

The air is beginning to change, the heat of the summer is starting to give way to early fall. Hand-in-hand, we walk down the busy Manhattan streets until we find a corner café. It isn't a tourist destination like many other restaurants in the city, so there aren't any crowds. We should be able to talk in relative quiet.

"You can get us a table, and I'll order."

Natalie chooses a secluded table in the back corner. It's perfect. The conversation we're about to have is important, and I don't want to be interrupted.

While we eat, an awkward silence stretches between us. I'm struggling to find the right words for what I'm about to propose. I don't know if there's a perfect way to say it, so I blurt it out. "The past few weeks, I've had a lot on my mind."

"Okay." Natalie sets her sandwich down. "Is everything alright?"

"Yes," I assure her.

Her shoulders relax.

"I'm going to be stepping away from my company."

"Oh?" Natalie cocks her head. "I thought you loved your job?"

"I do. I did." I stammer over my words. "But my heart's no longer in it. I'll still hold the majority of the shares, but I'll be putting Brandon in charge of the day-to-day operations. That'll leave me free to pursue other ventures."

"Such as?"

My palms are sweating, and I wipe them on my pants. Here goes nothing. "I want to open a recovery center, a branch of Jelena's Hope, but here in New York."

Natalie's expression gives nothing away, and I hold my breath in nervous anticipation.

Natalie

I'M SPEECHLESS. ALEX WANTS to walk away from the company he worked so hard to build, to make a success so he can help others.

"I thought maybe it was something we could do together. I'll use my business skills, and maybe you'd be willing to use your training as a therapist."

The idea of using the skills we both have and being able to use our experience to help others is more than I could've ever imagined.

"You are an amazing man, Alexander Montgomery," I say, reaching across the table to take his hand. "You have the most generous heart, and I'm in complete awe. I would love to do this together."

The tension falls from his face, replaced with his sexy smile.

"It's going to be a big change for us. I wasn't sure what you were going to say. I didn't know if—" He hesitates. "If, after everything, it would be too much for you."

"We're going to see the after-effects of the worst of humanity. I'm not going to lie and say I think it's going to be easy. There'll be many hard days," I say and place my hand on my tummy. "But if we can make this world a little safer for her, it's something we have an obligation to do."

"I love you, Natalie Clarke," Alex confesses.

"And I love you."

"I'd like to talk to Brandon right away. Would you call and see if they're available to come over tonight?" Alex pulls out his phone. "While you do that, I'll book a flight to Missouri.

I grab my cell and call Lana.

"Hey, girlfriend. How did your appointment go?"

"Everything's great. I got the all-clear."

"That's awesome." She puts her hand over the phone and relays the message to Brandon. "Does that mean you'll be leaving us to visit your parents?"

"Alex is booking the flight now." I can't take my eyes off the incredibly sexy man across from me. "Are you and Brandon free to come over for dinner tonight?"

"Hang on, let me ask." Lana puts me on mute. "We're free. What time?"

We decide on a time and say our goodbyes.

"Flights booked." Alex puts his phone away.

While we finish our lunch, Alex excitedly tells me about his ideas for the recovery center. It'll be a huge undertaking, especially with a baby coming in a few months, but I have no doubt we'll be able to handle it. I'm impressed with the amount of research he's done. He's already started applying for the permits and licenses we'll need to get started.

"I've been looking at real estate," he says as we walk back to the car. "One building, in particular, stands out. It would allow us to have our office and primary residential spaces in one place. I'd like to show you on our way home."

I share his excitement. My mind's already racing with the possible services we can offer the survivors. All the different therapy options we can use to help them recover from their trauma and begin a new life—a free life.

It takes nearly forty-five minutes for us to drive a few miles across town. Finally, Alex pulls the car to the side and points out a 1930s Art Deco-style building overlooking Central Park West.

"The building has round-the-clock security at the door and a state-of-the-art video surveillance system. There's enough space on one floor to set up administrative offices, medical, and therapy rooms. The top three floors of the building will be used for residential units."

"I see one problem," I say, looking out my window at the tall building.

"What is it?"

"Real estate in this area costs millions. We don't have that kind of money at our disposal."

"I've already spoken to Maxim. He's willing to front the costs."

"Wow." I knew Maxim had money. I guess I never thought about how much. "That's very generous of him." I look at the building, the sunlight reflecting off its windows. "I love it. When the survivors first get here, they'll be very vulnerable. Being able to stay within the protective walls of the center to access all their treatments is important."

"Exactly. And as they progress in their treatment, they'll move to transitional housing," Alex adds.

"Allowing them to learn to maneuver in the world while still having protection." It's a great plan. "How do we buy the space?"

"I'll call the realtor and attorney and have them start the process."

It's hard to believe it was only two years ago when I came back from Northmeadow heartbroken and stumbled upon Brandon and Lana in our apartment. At the time, I could never have imagined being here right now. I'm collared and engaged to the most amazing man in the world. And I'm pregnant with his child and about to embark on a life-changing adventure. My mind drifts back to the cab driver, Shusuke. I'll never forget the kind man and the words he said, *"Your heart is broken now. It is blessing when wrong person leaves your life. Don't let hurt turn to anger. Tonight is start of new journey. Now right person comes."* I'll admit, I didn't believe him. I wish I could find him and tell him how right he was.

We start the drive back to our apartment. Alex calls Maxim from the car and lets him know Jelena's Hope NYC is a go. Maxim assures Alex he'll take care of the financial end and get the necessary paperwork to the attorney.

"Natalia. I have someone here who has been asking to speak to you."

"Who is it?"

"She is an impatient little sub, Alexander." Maxim laughs.

"Natalie?" I hear a sweet little voice with an Australian accent.

"Amelia? Is that you?"

"It's me. I'm in Russia with Mr. Max and Miss Irina."

"How are you, sweetheart?" Being pregnant has my emotions on hyper-drive. My eyes fill with tears—happy tears.

"I have good days and bad days. Therapy's hard, but it's helping. And Miss Irina's very nice."

"They're good people, Amelia."

"Mr. Max scared me at first," she whispers her confession.

"He can be big and loud. But he's one of the kindest men you'll ever meet. He and Irina will make sure you're never hurt again."

"It's the first time I've felt safe in a long time. Almost like I have a family."

"I'm so happy for you, honey."

"Mr. Max said he's going to get me a cell phone, so I can call you whenever I want." She hesitates. "If that's okay with you?"

"I would love that."

"Okay. Mr. Max says he'd like to speak to you again. Catch you later."

"I thought you might like to hear from her." Maxim comes back on the line.

"Thank you, Max. It means a lot to me. What's going to happen to her?"

"Irina and I would like to formally adopt her."

"For real?" I squeal.

"For real," Maxim chuckles. "We've spoken to her therapist about the best way to bring it up. We will be speaking with Amelia about it soon."

"I don't know what to say. Thank you doesn't seem like enough."

"It is I who should be thanking you." Maxim's tone turns serious. "Amelia cannot replace my Jelena, but adopting her gives my wife and me a second chance at parenting. We have the resources to give this young lady opportunities she didn't have just a few weeks ago. We will also assure her a safe and happy future."

I wipe at my tears. Since I've gotten pregnant, it seems I cry at everything.

"We're so happy for your family," Alex says. "I'll let my attorney know to look for your email, and we'll be in touch soon."

Alex

WHEN WE GET HOME, we cuddle on the couch to watch a movie. As usual, Natalie falls asleep halfway through. Her nap is perfectly timed. I need to make a phone call without her overhearing, so I grab the blanket off the chair and cover her before going to my office.

"Alex," Charlotte answers the phone. "How did Natalie's appointment go today? Is everything okay?"

Charlotte has been slowly warming up to the idea of becoming a nana.

"Everything went great. The doctor said everything is exactly where it should be, and she's clear to travel."

"Oh, thank God," she says, relieved. "I've been praying for that."

"Thank you." I may not be a religious man, but I won't turn away her mom's prayers. "I have us booked on a flight for Sunday."

"Stanley and I can't wait to see you both."

"I have a favor I'd like your help with. But I don't want Natalie to know."

"Okay," Charlotte says hesitantly.

I give her the details of my plans, and although it'll be a lot of work, Charlotte's totally on board.

"I'll start working on it immediately," she assures me.

"Thanks. If you need anything, just call."

With that handled, I open the food delivery app and order dinner. It's already been a long day, and I don't want Natalie to have to cook for everyone tonight.

Last week I had my attorney draw up the necessary paperwork allowing Brandon to step in as the CEO of Montgomery Advertising. All he has to do is say yes and sign his name to make it official. I grab the folder containing the contract and go to wake Natalie. Brandon and Lana should be here any minute. When I get back into the room, I see Natalie beginning to stir.

"What time is it?" she asks.

"Almost seven."

"Oh my God, Alex." She jumps up, and the blanket falls to the floor. "Why didn't you wake me? I have to get something ready for dinner."

"Relax, baby girl." I walk over and pick up the blanket. "I ordered take-out."

"Still." She pouts. "You shouldn't have let me sleep all afternoon."

"You need—"

"I know." She rolls her eyes. "I need to rest."

"Did you just roll your eyes?" I set the folded blanket on the back of the chair.

"Maybe." She bats her lashes.

"It's a good thing you napped." I take slow, measured steps in her direction. "Because you're going to need it after our guests leave tonight. It's been a long time since we've been together." I pull her close to me, so she can feel my erection. "I plan—"

The ding of the elevator's arrival interrupts us.

"Saved by the bell." She smiles and sashays to the foyer to greet our guests.

Alex

THE KITCHEN ISLAND IS full of steaming Chinese take-out cartons. Brandon and I shoot the breeze while Lana and Natalie gush over Baby Montgomery's newest photos.

"This is so good." Natalie groans after taking a mouthful of noodles and vegetables.

Lana laughs. "I've never seen you enjoy food so much."

"I am eating for two." Natalie grins.

"Lana said you two are leaving for Missouri this weekend. How long are you staying?" Brandon asks.

"Only a few weeks. We promised Charlotte she could have a small bridal shower while we're there."

"Has she settled down about the baby yet?" Lana asks.

"Kind of," Natalie says between bites. "Mainly, she avoids the topic, and that's fine. Right now, I don't need any more stress."

When we're done eating, the girls clean up, and I grab the folder before moving to the living room. Brandon and Lana take the loveseat while Natalie and I sit on the couch.

"This is the real reason I asked you over tonight." I hold up the manilla folder.

"What is it?"

I take out the paperwork and pass it to him, giving him a few minutes to read it.

"You're kidding, right?" He sets the packet on the glass coffee table.

"I'm dead serious."

"What is it?" Lana asks.

"Alex wants to step down from his company, and he wants me to take over as the CEO."

"Are you kidding?" Lana looks between Natalie and me.

"I'm not kidding. We're planning to start a new venture together."

"Care to elaborate?"

"We're opening Jelena's Hope NYC."

"I don't know what to say." Brandon looks stunned.

"All you have to say is yes and sign the contract." I pull a pen from my pants pocket and slide it across the table to him.

"Aren't you afraid this might put a target on your back?"

"Judging by recent events, I think the target's already there. But for this, there'll be state-of-the-art security in place. Dimitri's already on it. So I have no doubts about our safety."

Brandon picks up the pen and clicks it nervously. I don't know why he's stalling.

"The new position comes with a raise. If that helps sweeten the deal." I quirk my eyebrow.

He flips through the packet with overexaggerated movements until he reaches the signature page and signs with a flourish. "I would have signed either way."

We all share a laugh.

In all seriousness, I'm relieved. Brandon's been by my side since day one. Under his leadership, I have no concerns about the company's future. Which frees me to give my full attention to getting Jelena's Hope NYC off the ground. It's bittersweet happiness I'm feeling. I'm excited to work side-by-side with Natalie. But I wish there wasn't a need for such a place. The sad reality is human trafficking remains a lucrative business for those who seek to steal and destroy lives. As long as people, and I use that term loosely, are willing to pay, trafficking will never cease to exist. There'll be a continued need for people like Maxim and Nicholai, fighters who seek to shut down as many rings as possible. And there'll be a need for places like Jelena's Hope to exist for identified survivors to access the treatment they need to heal.

"What does the timetable look like?" Brandon asks, handing me the pen.

"I plan to speak to the employees and contact my personal clients over the next few weeks." I lean forward to sign the contract making the transaction official. "By the six-week mark, the transition will be complete."

"That sounds doable."

"Are you planning on working at the center, Nat?" Lana asks.

"We haven't talked about all the details. But yes, I plan to be on the staff as much as I'm able."

"I'm so proud of you. You could've let your experience in Mexico ruin you, but instead, you're going to change so many lives because of it." The admiration in Lana's voice is genuine.

"It hasn't been easy," Natalie says quietly.

It hasn't been easy.

The truth is Natalie has had a very hard time. Everyday things like dark rooms and closed doors are triggers for her and have caused major panic attacks. We've also been working through her apprehension with blind-folds, starting with a few seconds and allowing her to remove it without needing permission. She needs me to be strong, so I hide my fears. But each night, I wake from nightmares that put me right back in Moreno's club, hurting her. Over and over, I see the blood on my hands and relive the feeling of killing our unborn daughter.

"I know Silverio's dead, but the memories can be so vivid—so real. Every day, sometimes more than once a day, I have to make a conscious decision not to let the memories get the best of me." Natalie swipes at a lone tear making its way down her cheek. "I have to be stronger than the memories."

Witnessing Natalie struggle is a heart-wrenching ex-perience. As a man and a Dominant, I feel a responsi-bility to shoulder her burden, but I know it's impossible to erase the pain she's endured. The first few days after our ordeal, she pleaded with me to pack our bags and flee to a remote island in the Caribbean, where we'd be safe from harm. I hated telling her no, that running away would not solve anything. We might be physically safe, but it wouldn't erase the memories.

Instead of living in constant fear, we've decided to turn our harrowing experience into something positive. We've realized that we can no longer ignore the evil that exists in the world and assume that others will take care of it. Maxim, Nicholai, and many others are fighting against traf-ficking, but we must also do our part. Although my com-pany helps transfer information, it's not enough now. The fight has become personal, and it has led to the creation of Jelena's Hope NYC.

Rather than cower in fear, we want to turn our trauma into a force for good and make a meaningful difference in the world. We know it won't be easy, but we're committed to the cause and won't stop until we see an end to trafficking crimes.

I have a baby daughter coming into this world in a few short months. I owe it to her to do everything I can to make the world a safer place to live.

Alex

"NATALIE," I CALL FROM the kitchen. "Are you ready? If we don't leave now, we'll miss our flight." I pace back and forth. Nervous energy pulses through my veins, and I'm ready to explode like a pressure valve.

"I'm ready." Natalie strolls into the room, wheeling her suitcase behind her.

"Let me take that." I grab the handle.

Viktor gets up from the couch. "Let's get this show on the road."

Thankfully, the traffic isn't too bad, and we're able to make up some time. While Viktor arranges long-term parking with the valet, I get our bags out of the car.

As we're hurrying to our terminal, I break the news. "We're going to have to stay at your parent's house."

"What? Why?"

"Your mom texted this morning. She went to the cottage to air it out and found it infested with spiders."

"Eww." Natalie shivers.

"She called an exterminator, but they can't come out until Wednesday. Then we have to wait twenty-four to forty-eight hours to go back in."

"Why can't we stay in Viktor's cottage?"

"Same story there. Spiders. Lots of them."

"Where's Viktor going to stay?"

"Your mom offered me her couch."

"The couch?" Natalie shakes her head in disbelief. "This trip is going to be a disaster."

Oh, baby girl, if you only knew. The last thing this is going to be is a disaster.

The weather was great, and we had a smooth flight. Now, we're in our rental car on our way to the Clarke's house. It's a good thing Viktor's driving because I'm busy answering non-stop messages.

"Who's texting you so much?"

"It's the attorney. He's making sure he has all the details for the transition." That's not totally untrue. This particular text is the attorney. All the other texts she doesn't need to know about.

Viktor pulls into the Clarke's driveway and turns the car off. Natalie leans forward to grab the door handle and freezes. Her hands quickly go to her abdomen.

"What's wrong?"

Natalie grabs my hand and puts it on her stomach.

"Do you feel it?" She looks at me expectantly.

My gaze shoots to where my hand presses against her stomach. Soft bumps hit my hand from the inside. I'm awestruck as more little thumps hit my hand.

"Alex? Do you feel the baby kicking?"

"I do." I finally manage to get words out. "That was incredible."

"That was the first time I've felt her kick so strong."

I've been addicted to this woman since I first met her. Soon after, I learned she struggled with her body image due to Tommy's inability to appreciate her inner and outer beauty. Over the past two years, I've worshiped her body, teaching her that every inch of her is beautiful. Thankfully, she's finally accepted it and has confidence in her appearance. But this, what her body's doing now as it's growing our baby, is beyond comprehension. "You're amazing." I lean over and kiss her.

"What do you mean? I didn't do anything."

I put my hand back on her belly. "You're growing our child. That's the most incredible thing in the world." I don't break eye contact, mesmerized by the depth of the green in her eyes. "I hope our daughter gets your eyes."

Tapping on the window interrupts the moment we're sharing.

"Are you two ever getting out?" Charlotte's bent down, hands cupped over her eyes as she peers into the car.

Viktor's behind her, shaking his head. Even he can't stop the force that is Charlotte Clarke.

"Maybe we should've called Marshall?" Natalie laughs.

I kiss her one more time before opening the car door and stepping out. "Charlotte. It's so nice to see you." I hug her.

"We're so glad you two are here." She squeezes me back and whispers, "Everything's going as planned."

Natalie comes around the car before I can respond.

"Look at you. You're positively glowing." Charlotte hugs Natalie. "I'm still not thrilled about your order of events," she says and dabs at her eyes with a tissue. "But I'm excited that I'm going to be a Nana. Wait until you see the blanket I'm crocheting."

"Thank you, Mom. I'm sure it's beautiful."

"Come on." Charlotte takes her arm. "Dad's inside and can't wait to see you."

Charlotte's already going a mile a minute and is dragging Natalie into the house.

Viktor and I stay behind to grab the bags.

"You sure about this, boss?"

"It'll all be worth it on Friday."

Alex

WHAT WAS I THINKING, agreeing to spend the week at her parent's house? Natalie was right. I should've called Marshall. He and I have kept in touch and now have a business relationship.

Marshall had a dream for his motel but couldn't secure the funds to make it happen. So, as a thank you for his taking care of Natalie while she stayed there, I invested in his motel. The rooms were remodeled during the off-season, and I designed an advertising campaign to attract tourists. He's doing a great job running his now clean and modern motel. I should've gotten rooms there. But, instead, I'm going crazy here. The walls in this old house are paper-thin, and Natalie's bedroom is next door to her parents. And did I mention she only has a twin bed? Sleeping in rather uncomfortable positions has been the only thing on the menu.

When I come downstairs, Viktor's already waiting in the living room. He follows me as I go in search of Natalie and find her sitting on the front porch swing, enjoying a glass of sweet tea with her dad.

"Viktor and I are going to head over to the cottage to check on the progress." I kiss her on the cheek. "We shouldn't be too long."

"Are you sure it's safe?"

"They fogged yesterday. Hopefully, it's gotten rid of the pests." I keep up the ruse. "We'll check it out and open the windows to air it out."

"See you boys later," Stanley calls after us.

"She's really buying the spider thing," Viktor says dryly.

"Natalie hates spiders. It was a guarantee she wouldn't want to be anywhere near the place if there was even a chance at coming in contact with them." I chuckle.

"Tony texted. They landed safe and are already at the lake."

"Perfect." Somehow, even on short notice, everything's coming together seamlessly.

We pull up to a flurry of activity at the lake house. Leo's in the driveway directing people who are unloading their vehicles to set up for tonight.

"You guys look busy."

"There's a lot of work to be done in a short time," Tony says between directing people carrying food into the house. "Someone keeps scheduling these big events at the last minute." He chuckles.

"On that note, I'm going to head to the security room to check on everything." Viktor doesn't wait for a response before hurrying off.

"Since I'm that someone, where can I help?"

Tony pulls out his phone and unlocks the screen before handing it to me. "I have pictures of the flowers. I need you to take a look and give your okay."

"Svetlana really came through on these," I say as I scroll through the pictures. "Good thing she had access to Natalie's *kinkterest* boards."

Tony freezes mid-movement. "Her what?" His brows furrow. I don't know whether it's from confusion or extreme interest.

"Pinterest." I nearly double over laughing. "Those two manage to find some pretty kinky stuff on there."

"Damn. I thought I was missing out on something new." Anthony shakes his head and returns to his task while I look through the pictures.

The first photos showcase the tables and centerpieces, which feature three vases of different heights filled with clear crushed glass and illuminated by small LED lights at the bottom. Purple orchids are beautifully arranged in a vase that's filled with water. A small floating candle adds an extra touch of elegance.

The following image is Lana's simple yet classy bouquet made of purple orchids. When I swipe to the next picture, I admire the bride's stunning bouquet, featuring a mix of purple orchids in varying shades and white Calla lilies cascading down in an elegant design. Lastly, we see the boutonnieres for the men, each adorned with a single deep purple orchid.

"They're perfect." I hand the phone back to Tony.

"Excellent." He swipes his fingers over the onscreen keyboard. "I just gave the final approval to the florist. The flowers will be delivered first thing in the morning."

"Have you heard from Brandon and my dad?"

"Yes. Both have landed and are en route as we speak."

"I can't believe this is actually happening." This surprise wedding will be considerably smaller than the ceremony we had planned for next year, but I couldn't wait. I don't want another day to start and finish without Natalie being my wife. "She was okay with the surprise collaring ceremony. I hope I didn't go too far planning a surprise wedding."

"Natalie's going to love it," Tony reassures me.

Several tables have been arranged on the patio, each adorned with a single white rose, just like the beautiful centerpieces we used for our collaring ceremony. To provide warmth and illumination as the evening air cools, faux stone propane fire columns have been strategically placed around the area. It appears that the finishing touches are being applied to the tables in preparation for tonight's dinner. "How much longer do you need?"

"Give me an hour to finish the food," Tony answers confidently.

"Sounds good. I'm going to make sure the guest rooms are ready."

Tony starts walking away, then stops. "Alex," he calls over his shoulder.

"Yeah?"

"Stay out of your bedroom. Her dress is in there."

I text Charlotte with an update.

(Me) We'll be ready for you in an hour.

(Charlotte) I'll let Stanley know.

Next, I send a text to Natalie.

(Me) The cottage has been cleared for us to go in.

(Natalie) Are you sure there are no spiders?

(Me) I'm positive.

(Natalie) What about the chemicals? Are you sure it's safe?

(Me) The exterminator said your mom overexaggerated the infestation. He didn't have to do as much as he anticipated. He left the windows open to air it out overnight. We just hung up, and he gave the all-clear.

(Natalie) I don't know. Maybe we should wait, just in case?

(Me) Do you trust me?

(Natalie) Of course, Sir. It's the spiders I don't trust.

I laugh aloud, drawing a few curious looks from people walking past.

(Me) I wouldn't tell you to come back if there were still spiders or any danger from the chemicals. Your parents agreed to drive you over so I can get our room ready. I'll send Viktor back to get our things later. Oh, and wear that pretty new dress you bought. The one thing we don't have here is food. We'll go out for dinner tonight.

(Natalie) Yes, Sir. See you soon.

With that done, I start toward the guest rooms to ensure we're ready for our company.

Natalie

"WHO WAS THAT?" DAD asks.

"It was Alex." I set the phone in my lap. "He said the cottage is spider-free, and we're staying there tonight." I fiddle with my hands nervously.

"That's good news."

"I guess so."

"What's wrong?"

"Do you think they got rid of all the spiders?"

My dad nearly doubles over in his seat, laughing. "I don't think your overprotective fiancé would let you go back if there were still spiders."

"I know." I scrunch my face. "But spiders, eww." I shiver, then stand and kiss my dad on the cheek. "I'm going to go change. Alex said we're going out for dinner."

"That sounds like a great idea. I think I'll take your mom out, too."

When I get to my room, I find the soft pink maternity dress Alex requested I wear. It's a thin gauzy fabric that hangs loose and stops just above my knee. Looking in the mirror, I run my hands down my front, pulling the fabric tight to emphasize my little round tummy. "You're starting to make your presence known, Baby Montgomery." I rub my hands over my belly and am rewarded with a kick. "I can't wait to meet you, sweet girl."

My curls are a bit unruly today, so I pull my hair back into a long ponytail, grab my sandals, and head downstairs to see when we're leaving.

Mom and Dad are sitting on the porch. "Are we ready to go?"

"As soon as we finish our coffee," Mom says, picking up a mug and taking a sip. "It's such a beautiful afternoon, isn't it?"

"Yes." Now that I know Alex is waiting for me, I want to go to him right away, but my parents are dilly-dallying with coffee. "Maybe I should call Viktor to come and get me?"

"Don't be silly." Mom waves me off. "Your father and I are looking forward to the ride, but there's no hurry. Sit down and relax for a few minutes. I made you chamomile tea." She points to a cup on the little metal table next to her.

I sigh loudly, not trying to hide my impatience as I plunk into the wooden rocker. "Thank you."

I text Alex.

(Me) Are you sure you or Viktor can't come to get me? My parents don't seem to want to move.

(Alex) There's no hurry. Anyway, it'll do them good to get out for a while.

(Me) At the rate they're moving, we won't be leaving until after the baby is born.

(Alex) LOL Enjoy your time alone with them. It's going to be the last trip here for a while.

I gently rub my tummy. The next time we're here, our baby will be with us. The thought fills me with both excitement and trepidation. The realization of how much our lives are about to change hits me like a ton of bricks. Once Baby Montgomery arrives, our days of impulsive outings will be gone. We'll have to plan for another little human being, packing and bringing along all the things babies need, even for short outings. We'll have to schedule our days around her nap and feeding schedules.

As I touch the lock on my collar, I wonder how we'll maintain our lifestyle. I have no idea how other Dom/sub couples balance their relationship as a couple with their responsibilities as parents. It seems daunting. We won't be free to go to Fire and Ice clubs or do scenes whenever we please. Our focus will be on our little girl. Her needs always coming first.

I know we're not the first Dom/sub couple to become parents, but the thought overwhelms me. I wish there were classes or resources available to help guide us through this transition. Maybe I can reach out to Irina for advice. She and Max raised Lana while living the lifestyle. I'm sure she could offer some valuable guidance as we prepare for this new chapter in our lives.

"Natalie." Mom's voice startles me.

"Yes?"

"Daydreaming about your little girl already?"

"I am." That and so much more.

"Dad and I are ready to go."

I jump up before they change their minds. "I'll get these." I grab our cups and bring them to the sink.

Mom helps Dad into the car. He's stronger than he was the last time we were here. He can walk short distances in the house with his walker, and he's able to get into the car with minimal assistance. As soon as I get into the back, Mom pulls the car onto the road.

Finally, we're on our way.

My parents are officially old. It may be a Thursday, but clearly, we're out for a Sunday drive. After what feels like an eternity, we turn onto the gravel driveway leading to our cottage. When we pull up, I see several unfamiliar cars in the driveway.

"What's going on?"

"I have no idea," Mom says too quickly, giving away the fact that she knows something.

She beeps the horn, and seconds later, Alex opens the front door. He's dressed in khaki pants and a light blue button-down shirt. And he's wearing the sexiest smile on his face.

Making his way to the car, he opens my door and helps me out.

"Welcome home, baby girl."

"What is all this?"

"Let's go see." Alex opens the door for my dad, who's wearing a matching grin.

"You're all in on whatever this is, aren't you?"

All I get in response are smiles and laughs.

"Patience, Natalie," my dad says as he moves from the car to his chair. "You were never good at waiting for a surprise."

"That hasn't changed," Alex adds while pushing dad's chair across the path leading to the front door.

I grab the screen door and hold it open so Alex can push the chair inside. Walking in behind them, I freeze. In my kitchen are Tony and several sous chefs. By the aromas wafting through the air, he's been busy cooking.

The French doors that lead to the patio are open. There are tables surrounded by fire pillars, the flames flickering from the soft breeze coming off the lake. Milling about outside is our friends and family.

"Alex?"

"Yes?"

"Why is everyone here? What's going on?"

He turns to me and takes my hands in his. "I don't want to wait any longer to make you my wife." My hands tremble in his grasp. "Tonight, we're having dinner with our friends and family. Tomorrow we're getting married."

I blink back tears. "You did all this?"

"I had a little help." He motions to my parents, who are watching from the other side of the room.

"You two knew about this?"

"We did," Mom says proudly. "You have an amazing man there."

My heart is bursting with love for the man next to me. "I don't know how you did this," I whisper. "But it's perfect."

"You haven't even seen it yet."

"I don't have to see it to know."

He leans in and kisses me. "Let's say hi to everyone before I change my mind and keep you all to myself tonight."

"I like the sound of that."

When Lana sees me, she runs up and squeezes me in a hug. "Can you believe he did this?"

"I'm still trying to process everything." I'm over-whelmed by everything I see.

"Before we start our meal," Alex says, getting every-one's attention. "I want to take a moment to express my gratitude. I would never have pulled this off on my own. Even with such short notice, you've all helped create something incredible. Without each one of you, none of this would be possible. From the bottom of my heart, I thank you."

When Alex finishes his speech, Tony signals to one of his staff to begin serving the meal. This evening's dinner is light and delicious. But sharing this special time with our friends and family is even more precious.

After the dishes are cleared, everyone lingers, talking and enjoying the evening.

"Natalie, can you come with me for a second?" Mom stands.

I look at Alex, and he nods in approval.

"Where are we going?"

"You'll see." Mom gives me a rare smile.

I follow her into the house, trying to figure out what she could possibly have up her sleeve. We stop outside our bedroom. Mom takes a deep breath before turning the handle and opening the door. She moves aside so I can walk in.

"Oh, Mom." I hurry over to our bed and run my hands along the antique lace. "It's Grandma's wedding dress."

Mom walks over and puts her arm around me. "Do you like it?"

"I love it." With a trembling hand, I brush away the tears cascading down my cheeks.

"Let's try it on. Mrs. Fisher will be along shortly to make any last-minute alterations."

I hug her tightly. "This is perfect, Mom. Thank you so much."

When I was a little girl, I loved sleeping at my grandma's house. She'd pull out her photo albums and tell me the stories of the pictures and the people in them. My favorite was when she took out her wedding album. Each time I told her I wanted to wear her dress when I got married. She'd light up and tell me about the day she married my grandpa, Isaac.

The year was 1942. It was just after the Japanese attacked Pearl Harbor. Although he was only seventeen, Grandpa had his father's blessing and joined the army.

"Anne, they're planning to send me to Europe. I don't want to leave without having you as my wife."

"That was my romantic proposal." Grandma laughs. "I was only sixteen when I married your grandfather. We were married fifty years when he passed away." Her eyes fill with tears. "It was just a few months before you were born. How I wished you could've met him."

One day when I was sixteen years old, Grandma brought me to her room. She opened her closet and took out a box. Inside the box was her wedding gown.

"I won't be here when you're getting married," Grandma says.

"Don't talk like that."

"Natalie, I'm eighty-three years old. My days on this earth are coming to an end." She takes my hand in hers. "Try the dress on. I want to have the memory of seeing you in it."

So, I did. Grandma helped me zip up the ivory gown, and together we stood in front of her full-length mirror. Tears sprang to her eyes.

"My sweet granddaughter. You've made me very happy today. One day, you'll wear this dress when you marry the man you love. I pray you'll have many happy years together."

That was the last time I saw my grandma. Unfortunately, she passed away a few days later. It's a memory I'll treasure forever.

I didn't bother to ask my mom about the dress. After all these years, I thought it would be too fragile to wear.

"When you showed me the pictures of the dresses you liked, I immediately thought of Grandma's dress. I didn't want to say anything until I took it out of storage and found out if it was still wearable.

If I try to talk, I'll break down. Instead, I pull my dress off and prepare to try on my wedding gown while Mom retells the treasured story.

"My great-grandma, Viola, hand-made this dress for my mom, your grandma," she says as she holds the dress out for me to step into. "She used some of the lace from her wedding gown to make this one." I turn around so she can fasten the tiny pearl buttons on the back. "Natalie. What is this?" She runs her finger along the length of the scar on my shoulder.

I swallow over the lump in my throat and give her the explanation Alex and I came up with if anyone asked about it. "When we were on our vacation, we went hiking. I had a run-in with a vicious tree branch. It was really sharp and cut me pretty good."

"Yes, it did. You're lucky you didn't get an infection."

"Alex would never let that happen." I need to change the subject. "How did you manage to alter the dress? The lace is so delicate."

"Lots of prayers and Dolores," Mom says and steps back. "Turn around and take a look."

As I turn slowly towards the mirror, I take in the sight of the ivory A-line gown with its empire waist, a perfect fit for my growing tummy. The lace bodice, despite its age, feels surprisingly soft to the touch, with pearls delicately sewn along the waistline. I can only imagine the patience it took for my great-grandmother to attach each pearl by hand, a testament to the love and care that went into crafting this dress. The flowing chiffon length of the dress drapes elegantly down to kiss the floor, completing the ethereal look.

"Didn't this have long sleeves?"

"It did." As I stand before the mirror, my mom comes up behind me, and we gaze at my reflection together.

It's reminiscent of that day with my grandma. Tears fill my eyes again.

"It's summer. Long sleeves would've been too warm. I also hoped to make the dress a little more modern for you. Mrs. Fisher took a layer of fabric from underneath to make the sleeves." Loose chiffon falls perfectly on my arm, creating an off-the-shoulder design. "Turn around and look at the back," Mom instructs.

The lace on the back of the dress has a keyhole opening. The train is attached by several pearl buttons and is a mixture of layers of chiffon and the same lace from the dress's bodice.

There's a knock on the door.

"Come in," I call.

"It's just me and—" Lana gasps and hurries into the room. "Natalie, your dress is incredible."

"I know," I say, looking in the mirror again. "I can't believe I'm getting to wear my grandma's dress."

"Dolores," Mom greets her friend. "Thank you so much for coming tonight."

Mrs. Fisher is all business as she sets a bag on the bed and walks to me, appraising each inch of the dress. "It looks like I need to tighten the shoulders just a bit, but other than that, I think it fits perfectly." She reaches into her bag and takes out her pincushion. "Hold this." She pushes the little red tomato into Lana's hand as she goes about her task of adjusting the dress.

"Is there room for one more?" Leo asks from the doorway.

"There's always room for you."

"Girl, you are drop-dead gorgeous." He leans in, kissing me on the cheek.

"Thank you, Leo."

"Okay." Mrs. Fisher steps back. "Take it off so I can stitch it."

Lana begins to undo the buttons, and I allow the raglan sleeves to slide down my arms.

"Natalie," Mom screeches. "There's a man in the room."

Leo and I have changed in front of each other before, so I didn't even think about it. But I understand my mom's objections.

"I'll turn around and close my eyes, Mrs. Clarke," Leo says.

"Kids," Mom says, exasperated.

Lana, Leo, and I laugh while Mom and Mrs. Fisher look at each other and shake their heads.

"You can turn back around," I tell Leo after I've got my sundress back on. "Do you need me to stay to try the gown on again?"

"It'll be a perfect fit when I've finished." Mrs. Fisher already has a needle and thread in her hand.

"Can I get you anything to eat or drink?"

"No, thank you." She doesn't look up from her sewing. "Go enjoy your party. I'll finish this and be on my way."

"I'll stay with Dolores. You kids go have fun."

"Thank you, Mom. This is the best gift you could've ever given me."

Alex

THE THREE AMIGOS EMERGE from the house. My attention is immediately drawn to my fiancée, whose cheeks flush a rosy hue as she giggles at something Lana whispers in her ear. Just then, Natalie catches my gaze and beams at me with her radiant smile. It's hard to believe that tomorrow, this stunning woman will become my beloved wife.

Charlotte and Stanley are the first to leave. Natalie and I walk them to their car. "Thank you both for all your help. I couldn't have done this without you."

"It was our pleasure," Charlotte says and hugs me.

"Drive safe." Natalie kisses her parents goodbye.

With my arm around Natalie, we watch until their car is out of sight.

"I can't believe we're really getting married tomorrow."

"It's real, baby girl." I take her hand as we walk back into our house. "Tomorrow, you'll become Mrs. Montgomery."

"Tomorrow can't come soon enough."

We rejoin our guests, who are laughing and talking around the fire.

"What did we miss?" I ask.

"Lana's just telling us how Natalie first learned about the lifestyle," Luna says.

"I was hoping she would've forgotten that by now," Natalie groans.

"How could we ever forget that?" Brandon asks. "I thought for sure I'd be calling Alex to bail me out."

We tell stories until late in the night. Eventually, Natalie rests her head on my shoulder. "Are you tired?"

"I am."

"We're going inside. My bride-to-be is ready for bed."

"We should all turn in," my father adds. "Tomorrow's going to be a big day."

"Girls in one house, boys in the other," Lana announces.

"Says who?" I ask, laughing.

She puts her hands on her hips. "You can't see the bride on her wedding day until the ceremony."

"You have a bossy little sub there, Brand."

"She can be bratty at times." Brandon swats her ass, and she yelps. "But she's right. Time to say goodnight. You can't see Natalie until the wedding."

"Some friends you are." I roll my eyes. "Come on, baby girl. I'll walk you to our bedroom door, and we'll say our goodnights."

"Viktor, maybe you should stand guard in case he tries to sneak into her room," Brandon jokes.

I throw him the finger and laugh as I lead Natalie into the house.

I reach for the handle on our bedroom door, but Natalie puts her hands on my chest. "Sorry, Sir. You heard the rules. We need to say goodnight on this side of the door," she smirks. "Besides, my dress is in there."

"I'll keep my eyes closed," I tease.

Natalie stands on tip-toes and wraps her arms around my neck. "This is going to be the longest night of my life."

"After tonight, I'm never letting you out of my sight again." I kiss her. "I'm only a phone call away if you need me."

"I love you, Alexander Montgomery."

"And I love you, Natalie Clarke."

With a final kiss, I walk away. The next time I see Natalie will be when she's walking down the aisle. When I get back outside, Tony is finishing extinguishing the fire.

"Night, everyone. Come along, kids," Luna says and motions to Lana and Leo, who are sitting, heads together, giggling like children. "Let's go find the bride."

"He gets to stay in the house?" I pretend to whine.

"He's just one of the girls," Tony jokes.

Leo and Lana link arms as they follow Luna into the house, shutting the back door behind them.

"Boss, do you want me to stay in the main house tonight?" Viktor asks.

"The security system is on. You're off the clock tonight."

Viktor nods, pretending to accept that he's not working. But if I know him, he'll have the monitors on all night, keeping an eye on the house. The four of us walk to the security cottage together.

"I hope you don't mind," Tony says. "I'm going to head straight to bed. I'll be up before the sun to start cooking."

"Thank you for everything." I shake his hand.

"It's my pleasure. Night everyone."

"I'm heading to my room, too," Viktor adds. "See you in the morning."

TARA CONRAD

Dad's the last man standing. I hope he's not ready to rush off to bed. "Do you have time for one more drink?"

"Sure."

I grab two beers from the fridge and pass him one. Dad follows me to the couch. It's been a long time since we've spent any time alone. Tonight, it feels important to have this time together.

"You gave us a good scare."

"I'm not going to lie. I wasn't sure we were going to make it out of there."

"I don't know what I would've done if I lost you." Dad's voice cracks.

"I owe everything to Max and Viktor. If it weren't for them, we wouldn't be here."

A few minutes of silence pass between us.

"Your mom would be very proud of you."

"I wish Mom could've met Natalie."

"She would've loved her." Dad smiles sadly. "She's here with us, though. I can feel her."

Now feels like the perfect time to tell him we chose a name. "Natalie and I would like to name our baby Rose Anne, after mom and her grandma."

Dad sets his beer on the side table and sits back. He doesn't say anything for the longest time. I'm beginning to think he doesn't like the idea.

Finally, he turns in my direction, and I notice tears streaming down his face. "Rose Anne Montgomery, that's the most beautiful way to honor your mother's memory."

My dad has never been the type to wear his heart on his sleeve. Not even when we said goodbye to my mom did he show any signs of tears. Watching him cry now is unbearable. The tears I've been holding back for so long now spill out.

"Mom would want you to move on," I say quietly.

Dad looks up. "What do you mean?"

"With Luna." I wipe the wetness from my face. "If you want to marry her. I know Mom would approve, and so do I."

His features soften. "Luna was only ever supposed to be my submissive. She and I discussed it at great lengths while we were vetting each other. I never intended on falling in love."

"I know all about that." I chuckle.

"Yes, son, you do." Dad smiles. "I love Luna very much. But that doesn't mean I stopped loving your mother."

"You don't have to explain it to me," I reassure him. "I know you'll always love Mom, but she's been gone for a long time. It's okay to share your heart again."

"When we met, I was an emotional mess. I hadn't healed from your mother's death and couldn't see ever falling in love again. Luna never pushed. Never forced anything. She's always accepted her position as my submissive and nothing more. But over the past few years, something changed between us."

I lean forward, recognizing the significance of this conversation.

"I realized that her submission and unwavering patience are her gifts of love. She helped heal my heart, and I fell in love with her."

"Have you told her?"

Dad laughs. "Would you believe me if I said no? I've been too scared to admit it aloud."

"After what Natalie and I went through in Mexico, I've learned not to take a single day for granted."

"I'm afraid she'll see it as a betrayal of our contract," he admits.

"I've seen the way she looks at you. She's as in love with you as you are with her."

"I don't know."

"You need to tell her, Dad. Give her the chance to openly love you back."

"Maybe you're right. It's time to let Luna know how I feel."

We finish our beers while discussing my plans for Jelena's Hope NYC. Dad already offered to become an investor, something I've very thankful for. It's going to take a village to get this project off the ground and running.

Dad looks at his watch. "It's either late or early. I'm not quite sure at this point. But this old man needs to get some sleep."

"Thank you for everything, Dad." I swallow over the lump in my throat. "I wouldn't be half the man I am today if it wasn't for you. I love you." I hug him.

"I love you too. I'm very proud of you, Alexander."

I watch Dad walk down the hall to his room and realize what a lucky man I am.

Grabbing the blankets and pillow I left on the chair, I spread them on the couch before settling in for sleep. The last night I'll do so as a single man.

Natalie

LANA, LEO, AND I shared my room last night. I don't remember what time it was when our slumber party wound down, but I'm sure I was the first one asleep.

This morning, I crawl out from the middle of my best friend sandwich, careful not to wake either of the sleeping beauties at my side, and go to the bathroom for a hot shower. I take my time drying off and putting product in my hair, praying my curls will cooperate with me today. Then I slide on the white silk robe Lana gave me last night with the word *Bride* embroidered on the front. She also had ones made for her and Leo embroidered with *Bride Squad*. Leave it to my bestie to think of all the little details.

I tiptoe back through my bedroom, close the door, and head straight to the kitchen. I'm hoping to score a coffee before the day gets into full swing. When I walk into the room, I see Luna beat me to it. She's already sitting at the kitchen table, cup in hand.

"Good morning. I didn't know anyone was up yet."

"I hope you don't mind. I helped myself to a coffee."

"Not at all." I open the cupboard and take out a mug. "That's what I came out for too."

Luna jumps up. "It's your wedding day. Sit down and let me wait on you."

Luna makes me a cup of French-vanilla-flavored good-ness before she sits back down.

"Thank you for being here. It means a lot to me that you came."

"It's an honor to be included. I wasn't sure, being Sam's sub, if Alex would want me here. I didn't want to overstep."

I grab her hand from across the table. "Alex and I both want you here. You're part of our family."

"Thank you, sweetheart. That means a lot to me."

Our moment alone is cut short when Tony bursts in with homemade pastries and bagels.

"Good morning, ladies." He kisses me on the cheek. "You look well-rested this morning, pixie."

"And you brought breakfast." I grab a cream cheese Dan-ish and a chocolate chip muffin from the tray. "You're a lifesaver."

Luna and I continue chatting while we eat and finish our coffee. When we're done, I grab our empty mugs, bringing them to the sink. "I'll wash these, and we'll get out of your way."

"You'll do no such thing. It's your wedding day." He shoos me away from the sink. "Go get ready to marry that sexy man."

I give him a peck on the cheek. "Thank you, Tony." Then, turning to Luna, I ask, "Shall we go wake up Lana and Leo?"

As we're walking down the hall, my bedroom door opens. Leo stumbles out in his boxers, his robe draped over his arm. "Good morning," he mumbles.

"Good morning, sleepyhead." I laugh.

"You're awfully chipper this morning." He rubs his eyes.

"I've already had my coffee."

He kisses my cheek. "I'm going to the guest room to shower, and then I'm getting myself a cup of caffeine."

Luna and I walk into my bedroom to find the bed empty. The bathroom door is open, and the shower water's running. "Looks like everyone's already up. And they made the bed."

"Seems that way."

"Good morning," Mom says, walking into the room behind us.

"Morning, Mom."

"Morning, Charlotte." Luna and Mom exchange hugs. "I'll give you two some time alone."

I grab Luna's hand. "You don't have to go."

"There's something I need to do. I'll be back in a few minutes." She closes the door softly behind her.

"I can't believe my little girl is getting married today." Mom's eyes fill with tears.

"Don't start crying already." I pass her the tissue box from the bedside table. "Where's Daddy?"

"He's in the other cottage with the men. Oh, did you know there's an army of people on their way here?"

"No. I'll be right back." I rush to the living room.

Looking out the window, I see what she's talking about. Several ladies and a few men unload cars, each pulling rolling luggage behind them.

"Looks like your hair and makeup team is here," Anthony says over my shoulder.

"My what?"

"Alex hired hair and makeup to pamper the bridal party." He opens the door letting everyone in. "Good morning, ladies and gentlemen. This is our bride, Natalie."

We exchange hellos.

"Where can we set up?"

"How much space do you need?"

"We need one area for mani and pedis and another for hair and makeup," a beautiful dark-haired woman says.

The kitchen and living room share an open floor plan. With all the activity in the kitchen, we'd be in the way out here.

"Use the guest room for nails and the master for hair and makeup." Anthony jumps in, saving me.

"That works for us."

"Thank you, Tony."

"No problem, pixie."

"Follow me. I'll show you to the rooms."

The entourage follows behind me and begins setting up their equipment. The photographer arrives shortly after to document our afternoon of pampering. Throughout the day, Tony delivers light snacks and refreshments to our rooms.

While I'm getting my hair done, my phone pings with a text.

(Alex) I'll meet you at the end of the aisle right before sunset.

(Me) I'll be there. <3

Time seems to have flown by, and before I know it, it's time to start getting ready. My mom is donning a light blue dress that flows down to her ankles. I'm surprised she allowed the stylists to not only put her hair in a fancy updo but also to do her makeup.

"You look beautiful, Mom."

"It doesn't even look like me," she says as she examines herself in the mirror.

"I can't wait to see the look on Dad's face when he sees you."

"He won't even notice." She waves her hand, blowing me off.

"If he doesn't, I'll check his pulse."

We both laugh.

Lana comes out of the bathroom. "Can you help me with my dress, Mrs. Clarke?"

"Sure, honey. Turn around." Mom zips up her dress. "You look stunning."

Lana's wearing a deep purple chiffon dress with a sweetheart neckline accented with off-the-shoulder sleeves that mimic mine.

"Brandon's going to go crazy. You'll be walking down the aisle next," I say, imagining my bestie's wedding.

"I don't think so. Marriage is not in my plans."

"Not in your plans? What do you mean, dear?" Mom asks.

"Natalie, can you help me with my bowtie," Leo interrupts.

"Let's see what I can do. Sit down." I stand next to him by the bed and adjust his tie.

I don't know what Lana's talking about. She's told me she wished Brandon would propose to her. I'm going to have to try to get her alone so we can talk.

There's another knock on the door.

"I'll get it," Mom says. She opens it just a crack to see who it is before pulling it all the way open. "Luna, don't you look beautiful."

"And you are a gorgeous mother-of-the-bride."

"Speaking of the bride, I think it's time we get her dressed." Lana grabs my gown.

"I'll step outside while you change," Leo offers.

Lana holds out my gown for me to step into. I open my robe, unashamed of my near-nakedness. My dress leaves no room for a bra, and my panties are barely there—white lace in the front and a string of pearls in the back.

"Those pearls are so hot. It's a good thing Alex won't know what's underneath until later."

"Svetlana," Mom scolds.

"Sorry, Mrs. C." She shrugs. "But it's the truth. He's going to go crazy when he undresses her tonight."

Mom's cheeks turn bright red. Luna slaps Lana's arm and laughs.

I step into the dress and pull it up just as Lana's phone rings.

"Saved by the bell," Lana chirps and hands her job off to my mom while she grabs her phone from the dresser.

I make a few last-minute adjustments while mom fastens the buttons.

"You can come back in," I call to Leo.

"You're even more beautiful today. If I wasn't into men—"

Lana puts the phone on speaker, thankfully interrupting Leo.

"How is my little girl today?" Maxim asks

"I'm good, Papa."

"Turn on your camera. Mama and I want to see your dress."

"Svetlana," Irina gushes. "You look beautiful."

"Thanks, Mama." Lana turns the camera around. "Say hi to everyone."

We all say a collective hello to Maxim and Irina.

"Natalia," Maxim says. "You are a most stunning bride. I wish we could be there to celebrate with you today."

"So do I."

"I'll have them on video the whole time. They won't miss a second."

"Hi, Natalie." Amelia pops on the screen.

"Hi, sweetheart." I smile and wave. "How's everything going?"

"I'm starting to get used to it here. Miss Irina is teaching me Russian, or at least trying to."

"I hope you do better than I have." Russian is not an easy language to learn. I can manage a few words to get by, but mostly I rely on Alex to do the talking for me.

"You look like a princess, Natalie."

"Thank you."

"When will I get to see you?"

"I'm not sure," I answer honestly. "We'll talk to Max and Irina and see what they can do, okay?"

"Yep. Gotta go."

We spend a few more minutes talking with Max and Irina before Mom reminds us of the time.

"I have to finish getting ready. I don't want to be late for my own wedding."

"*Pozdravlyayem vas oboikh I nadeyemsya, chto u vas budet mnogo schastlivykh let vmeste,*" Maxim says.

I look to Lana to translate.

"He said congratulations to both of you. And they hope you have many happy years together."

"Thank you, both."

Lana disconnects the call, promising to call back when the ceremony starts.

"I can't believe I'm about to marry Alex."

"And it's all thanks to me." Svetlana smiles proudly.

I grab Lana's hands. "I'm so grateful you asked me to go to Fire and Ice with you that night," I say quietly. Despite all my efforts to not get emotional, my eyes fill with tears.

"We just spent hours getting our makeup done. There will be no tears yet," Lana jokes.

Mom walks over, interrupting our moment. "It's time to put your veil on. Come sit down."

Carefully she sets the delicate crown on my head. The photographer has her hold the pose for a picture.

"It's the exact veil I wanted." I bring my hands to the crown touching it gently. "How did you know?"

"Aren't you glad I know your Pinterest password?" Lana laughs.

The crown is an intricate weave of ivory flowers, pearls, and Swarovski crystals. Attached to the crown is luxurious tulle that pools at the back of the dress.

"It's your something new," Mom says.

"I have your something borrowed," Lana says, handing me a box. "Open it."

"It's stunning." Inside is a silver chain with a teardrop-shaped diamond.

"My mama wore it on her wedding day. She said she'd be honored if you'd borrow it for your wedding day." I touch my collar. "Don't worry." Lana reaches into her bag. "I have the key."

"How did you get it?" I ask quietly as she works to unlock it.

"Alex wasn't happy at first. But when I explained why, he gave me the key and his permission to remove it for the ceremony." She takes my collar and the key, placing them in the jewelry box. "I'll make sure this gets back to Alex. Turn around."

After she fastens the necklace, I look at it in the mirror. "It's beautiful."

"I have your something old. Well, it's actually from Sam," Luna says and hands me another smaller box. I open this one and find a pair of diamond earrings. "These were Alex's mom's earrings. She wore them on their wedding day. Rose made Sam promise to save them and give them to the woman Alex chose to marry for her something old."

Tears prick my eyes. "This means so much to me."

"We forgot your something blue," Lana says.

"I hope I'm not overstepping, but I have your something blue." Luna hesitantly hands me a small box. Lifting off the lid, I find a blue crystal angel and a locket hanging from a small silver chain. When I open it, I see a photo of Michael on one side and a woman I don't recognize on the other. "That's Alex's mom, Rose. They're both your guardian angels."

"Luna, I don't know what to say." A teardrop slips down my cheek.

"If I have your permission, I can attach it to your bouquet. Both Michael and Rose will be with you on this special day."

I wrap my arms around her. "This is the most special gift you could give me. I'll treasure it long after today."

"Thank you for allowing me—"

"Luna, you're part of our family. Today wouldn't be complete without you here." I look around the room at my friends and family who've made today so special already. "I can't thank you enough. I love you all so much."

Now everyone is dabbing at the tears in their eyes.

"Enough of this crying, ladies," Leo says, wiping his eyes. "You'll ruin my makeup."

His comment makes us all laugh. Another knock on the door interrupts us.

"I'll get it." Leo hurries to the door.

He opens it to let Tony, whose arms are full of white boxes, into the room.

"Where can I set these?"

"On the bed. What's in them?"

"Your flowers." Tony puts the boxes down and spins around. "pixie." He stops mid-step and takes me in head to toe.

I feel a blush creep up my cheeks.

"You're breathtaking. Alex is a very lucky man."

"You've ogled the bride enough. Out you go." Lana shoos Tony out of the room, closing the door behind him.

I wish they'd leave the door open. Each time it closes, I fight the feelings of suffocation and fear. But if I asked, it would draw too many unwanted questions from my mom. Lana's watching closely and provides a much-needed distraction.

"Let's take a look at these flowers." Lana's already opening the boxes.

Inside the first two boxes are wrist corsages for mom and Luna. A third small box holds a deep purple orchid for Leo that I pin to his jacket. The photographer moves around us as I straighten the flower, capturing every second.

"Here's my bouquet," Lana squeals. "It's gorgeous." Her flowers are orchids in various shades of purple. Not only is it beautiful, but the fragrance from the flowers is heavenly. "Open yours," Lana urges.

I open the final box and lift out my bouquet. It's exactly like the pictures I saved. This is probably the only time I'll be thankful someone else knew my password.

Luna walks over and attaches my guardian angel to the ribbon on my bouquet.

Looking around, a feeling of warmth flows through me. Generations of women, some of whom are no longer with us, have played a role in making today special. Their love surrounds me right now. The baby must feel it, too, because she starts to kick.

"It's time," Leo announces. "Are you ready to go get married?"

There's nothing I want more.

Natalie

WE MAKE OUR WAY out to the living room. Lana walks behind me, holding up my train, so it doesn't catch on the floor.

"You look stunning," Dad says when he sees Mom.

"Oh, Stanley." Mom waves her hand at him.

"You're as beautiful as the day I married you."

Mom leans down and, in a rare public display of affection, kisses his cheek. "I love you, you silly man."

I'm glad the photographer was right there and got it all on film

The front door swings open, and Viktor walks in. When he sees me, he freezes. "You're the most perfect bride. Alex is a lucky man." He kisses my cheek. Clearing his throat, he says, "We're ready to start."

"We're ready, too," Lana answers.

"I'll see you out there." Viktor takes one final look at me before leaving the room.

Lana sidles up to me. "If I didn't know better—"

"Don't," I say, interrupting her. "We've been through a lot together, that's all."

"Whatever." She rolls her eyes. It's obvious she doesn't believe me.

"Time to go, ladies." Leo throws open the French doors with a flourish.

Instrumental music floats on the breeze. When I peek out, I see a string quartet off to the side. I don't know how Alex pulled this together, but he didn't miss anything.

Sam walks through the open doors, stopping to compliment Luna, then coming to me. "My son chose a wonderful young woman to become part of our family." He kisses my cheek.

"Thank you."

"Are you ready?" he asks Luna.

"Always," she responds, sliding her hand through his bent arm. Together they walk outside and down the flower-petal-covered path to take their seats.

"May I?" Leo asks mom, offering her his arm.

"You may," she says.

Leo leads mom down the aisle, whispering something in her ear and making her laugh. I'm thankful my parents accepted Tony and Leo without too many questions. I wish they'd have accepted Michael and Evan the same way. I'd have my brother here with me today.

"Are you okay?" Lana interrupts my thoughts.

"I'm missing my brother, but I'll be okay."

"I'm sure he'd be very happy for you." Lana gives me one last hug before walking down the aisle to stand beside Leo.

Alex

I CHECK MY WATCH for the hundredth time. Maybe it needs a new battery or something. The hands of the clock don't seem to be moving. Returning to the mirror, I stab at tying my bowtie, which is proving impossible because of my trembling hands. Get it together, Alex. It's not the first time you've worn a tux. But it is the first time, and the only time, I'm getting married.

There's a knock on the door a second before it opens. Viktor stands in the doorway. "Are you ready, boss?"

Spinning around to face him, my shoulders slump. My arms hang useless at my sides.

"You're a mess. Get your ass over here."

I've never been that guy. But I guess there's a first time for everything. Reluctantly, I shuffle over to Viktor, who takes charge, tying my bowtie with practiced ease.

"Thanks for having my back," I mumble.

He gives it a tug making sure it's straight before stepping back. "I'm ready. You're ready. Let's get you to your girl."

I grab his shoulder. "Wait a minute."

"What's up?"

"Thank you." I stop to swallow over the lump in my throat. "We wouldn't be here today if it wasn't for you."

"It's all good, boss," Viktor smirks but then shocks me by pulling me in for an uncharacteristic hug.

"Are you two done with your love fest?" Brandon laughs from the doorway. "The ladies are ready."

Brandon's smart-ass banter lightens the mood. With my wardrobe issues fixed, I'm able to regain my composure.

"What are we standing around for? It's time for me to get married."

Natalie

I LOOK OUT THE doors and see Alex and Viktor, who are caught up in a private conversation. Alex looks gorgeous in his black tux, and I can't take my eyes off him. Finally, he looks up and sees me for the first time. A sexy smile lights up his face. I never thought I'd say it, but I'm thankful Tommy cheated on me. What I thought was the worst night of my life was actually the first night of my forever.

"Are you ready to go get married?" Dad asks.

"I am."

Dad wheels himself onto the patio. I follow behind. Panic sets in when we get to the edge of the concrete. I didn't think about this part. How am I going to get his wheelchair through the grass? I look around, expecting to see someone coming to help, but no one makes a move.

"How are we going to—" I stop mid-sentence and watch as Dad locks the wheels of his chair. He places his hands on the armrests and pushes himself to a standing position.

"Daddy." My hand covers my mouth.

Taking a step forward, he extends his hand, and I place mine in his. "Did you think I wouldn't walk my little girl down the aisle?"

I'm speechless. Tears blur my vision. This is so much more than I expected.

The quartet begins to play Pachelbel's Canon in D, and we slowly walk down the aisle.

Yesterday, when Alex told me we were getting married, I didn't have time to think about any of the details. I guess I assumed someone would push Dad next to me. It wouldn't have been the original plan, but that didn't matter anymore. The most important thing is Alex and I are alive, safe, and getting married.

When we reach the end of the aisle, Alex steps forward. Dad joins our hands, placing his on top. "I'm trusting you to take good care of my daughter."

"You have my word. I'll protect her until my last breath."

Dad kisses my cheek before sitting next to Mom. Lana steps up and takes my bouquet.

Then, Alex and I take the final steps and stand before Viktor.

Alex

CANON IN D PLAYS just as Viktor and I get into place. Looking up, I catch the first glimpse of my bride. Her eyes meet mine, and I forget to breathe. She's stunning. For a few precious seconds, there's only her and I. Then panic registers on her face. Although I'm prepared for what's about to happen, she isn't. Natalie gasps when her dad stands from his wheelchair and offers his hand to walk her down the aisle.

A few days after I asked Charlotte for help, I got a phone call from Stanley. He told me about his progress in physical therapy and that he'd be walking for our wedding. He also swore me to secrecy so he and Natalie could share this special moment.

When they finally reach the end of the aisle, I step forward. Mr. Clarke puts his daughter's hand in mine. The symbolism of a father handing over the responsibility of caring for and protecting his daughter to another man. I give him my word that as long as I'm breathing, I'll protect her with all I have. When I look into Natalie's eyes, we both know the truth to my statement.

I've already killed to save her life—to keep her mine.

"Natalie, today, my life joins with yours. You are the strength I never knew I needed. The piece of my heart

I didn't realize was missing. There's no one else I want to build a forever with. I promise to love you with all I am—for all eternity."

Natalie

"*Alex, you love me in ways I never dreamed possible. You are my every dream come true. My light in the darkness. You taught me what being loved truly means. I promise to share my whole heart with you and to show you my love every day. I promise you, my love, my husband, to forever be by your side.*"

"You may kiss your bride."

Alex flashes me his sexy smile before he leans in and places a chaste kiss on my lips. He pulls back just enough so I can look up into his deep blue eyes. "Shall we give them a show?"

He doesn't need my permission, but I smile and nod anyway. Placing his hands on my waist, he pulls me tight against him. Gentle and passionate, his lips meet mine. I open, granting him access, and he dips me in his arms as the kiss turns more demanding. Viktor clears his throat, a not-so-subtle hint for us to end our kiss. Then, Alex threads his fingers with mine, turning us to face our guests.

"Ladies and gentlemen, it's my honor to present Mr. and Mrs. Alexander Montgomery."

My gaze travels across the yard, where a small gathering of our family and closest friends now stand, applauding. Lana's holding her phone out so Maxim, Irina, and Amelia can be a part of this moment. Most of those in attendance know how close we came to not being here. It makes this moment all the more special.

Alex leans over and places one more kiss on my lips before leading us back down the aisle. Our guests toss handfuls of birdseed at us as we pass. Instead of going to the reception tent, he leads me into the house and straight to our bedroom, where he locks the door.

"You're a stunning bride, Mrs. Montgomery."

I smile when he says my new name. "You don't look so bad yourself, Mr. Montgomery."

"I wish we could skip right to the honeymoon." He backs up, appraising me with hooded eyes.

Chills cover my body, and I bite my lower lip. I'd like nothing better than to peel his clothes off and spend the rest of the evening celebrating our marriage—alone.

"I have a surprise for you." Alex reaches into his pocket and pulls out a small box with a silver ribbon tied in a bow.

"Another surprise?" I take the box. "Do you want me to open it now?"

"Yes."

I untie the ribbon and lift the lid. Inside are two silver rings. A pearl dangles from a small chain on each one. "They're beautiful. But how do I put them on?" I've never seen a pair of earrings like them.

"Let me help." Alex reaches behind me and opens the first few buttons of my gown. The bodice loosens enough to slide down, my breasts spill free.

"Aren't they for my ears, Sir?" Uncertainty fills my voice.

Alex laughs. "No, they aren't." He steps back and takes one of my breasts into his hand, kneading it gently. "I

checked with the doctor to make sure these are safe."
He lowers his head and takes my nipple in his mouth,
licking and sucking, eliciting a soft moan from me. He
releases it and takes the ring from my hand, placing it
around my nipple and squeezing it, so it clamps tightly.
Then he lavishes the same attention on the other breast
before adorning it with the jewelry.

His heated gaze travels over my body. "You are so
beautiful."

I don't think I'll ever get sick of how his eyes fill with
lust when he looks at me. Alex makes me feel sexy and
adored. I shimmy back and forth, making the pearls sway.
Their weight causes me to become even more aroused.

"baby girl, you need to stop that." He adjusts the prominent erection visible through his pants. "We have a back-
yard full of guests expecting us to be at our wedding
reception."

Right now, I'm not caring about the people waiting
for us. I'm wet from arousal and want him to continue
undressing me. Batting my eyelashes, I move closer and
snake my arms around his neck. "Surely, just a few more
minutes wouldn't hurt." I run my tongue across the seam
of his lips.

"You're quite the temptress, Mrs. Montgomery." Placing
his hands on my shoulders, he pulls the bodice of my dress
up and turns me around to button it. "When I rid you of
this dress." He kisses my exposed neck. "I plan to bring
you pleasure." He kisses my shoulder. "All night long." His
hands slide down my arms, and my head falls back onto
his chest. "I don't want any interruptions while I'm making
my wife scream my name." He steps away, and my body

immediately misses the contact. "But right now, we have guests."

I blow out a frustrated breath. Alex's ministrations have ensured my body will remain aroused all night. "You, Sir, are a cruel man."

"I always make good on my promises." He smirks.

It takes me a few minutes to straighten my dress and remove the veil. Once I'm finished, Alex unlocks the door, and we walk down the hallway.

Lana's waiting for us in the kitchen. "I was wondering how long you two would be." She puts her hands on her hips, a cheeky smile on her face. "Do you want to take the train off now?"

"I almost forgot."

"I bet." She waggles her eyebrows.

Lana makes quick work of unbuttoning the long train. "Thank you. The dress is so much lighter now."

"I'll go hang this up. I'll be out in a minute."

"You're the best."

"I know," she calls over her shoulder as she hurries down the hallway.

Hand-in-hand, Alex and I walk across the yard. The tent for the reception is set up closer to the water. I was so caught up in the ceremony I didn't even look down here. Yet, what I see takes my breath away.

"Do you like it?"

A string quartet is positioned in the middle of the tent, which will later become the dance floor. Their music fills the air with sweet melodies. Surrounding the central area, each couple has their own table adorned with ivory linens and centerpieces that coordinate beautifully with the flowers in my bouquet. For the moment, we're able to remain unnoticed and watch our loved ones as they mingle, laugh, and sip champagne, enjoying the exquisite hors d'oeuvres.

"It's perfect," I whisper.

Anthony, acting as the master of ceremonies, notices we've arrived and asks everyone to take their seats. We settle at our table as servers emerge from the house carrying silver trays overflowing with food. Dinner is a formal, plated event starting with pacific oysters as the appetizer. Alex winks at me as he raises an oyster shell to his lips and swallows. The movement of his mouth is sensual, and my core clenches in anticipation of what magic his mouth will do later. Over the next few hours, we're served several more courses, each dish more delicious than the previous one. When the meal is through, the servers clear away the remaining dinner plates.

Brandon stands to make a toast.

"Ten years ago, Alex showed up in New York City, a transplant from Seattle. As fate would have it, we bumped into each other at a local establishment." Brandon pauses and smiles. "We hit it off instantly. He's become more than just a friend—he's my family. Two years ago, the beautiful woman at his side also came into that same establishment. That night, when yours truly introduced you to each other, it was clear there was an instant connection—I take full credit for this marriage." Our guests share a laugh. "On a serious note, it's been a privilege to watch your relationship evolve into the love you share today. I speak for all of us when I say how happy we are for you both." He turns to our guests and raises his glass. "Please join me in wishing Mr. and Mrs. Montgomery many years of happiness."

A symphony of chiming champagne flutes announces the group's collective toast.

Tony calls us over to a table holding our wedding cake. Like everything else, it's an elegant design consisting of four white tiers. Dark purple orchids cascade down one side. With both of our hands on the knife, we cut a piece from the bottom layer.

"Vanilla?" Alex laughs.

"French vanilla with edible glitter," Tony chuckles.

Alex and I each take a small piece and, with arms entwined, feed each other. I moan when I taste the decadent cake. "You'll be doing a lot more of that tonight." Alex leans in close and licks a piece of frosting from my lip. "Delicious."

Before I can respond, Tony calls us to the center, where the string quartet has been replaced with a DJ. "May I have the bride and groom for their first dance?"

Ed Sheeran harmonizing with Andrea Bocelli's smooth tenor begins to play. The Italian rendition of "Perfect," a romantic tale of two lovers, fills the night. Alex places his hand on the small of my back and holds me tight against him while he quietly sings the lyrics to me, just like he did the first night I danced in his arms. Swaying to the music, our bodies move together as one.

If this is a dream, I never want to wake up.

"You are mine," Alex whispers when the song ends. "I love you, baby girl."

The next song is an upbeat tune, and our guests join us on the dance floor. I'm having the time of my life dancing with my friends. Even Alex, who's usually serious, is smiling and laughing while he's dancing with us.

When the music changes to a slower melody, it takes me a minute to recognize the song "Dance with My Father." Last year I came very close to losing my father, the man who right now is proudly walking on his own to meet me on the dance floor. Alex steps aside as Dad takes my hand. I can't stop the tears from sliding down my cheeks.

"I can't believe my little girl is a married woman," Dad says as we move slowly to the music. "You chose a good man."

"I had a good example."

"I was far from perfect, sweetheart. I made so many mistakes." He's now shedding his own tears. "If only I could go back and do things different, better. Maybe Michael would—"

"He's always right here." I put my hand over my father's heart. "I'm sure he's watching and knows how much you love him."

Dad's unable to speak through his tears. He nods and pulls me close as we finish our dance. When the music ends, I walk Dad back to his table.

"Thank you for the dance, Daddy."

"Thank you, my sweet daughter."

I nearly collide with Viktor when I turn around. "I was coming to ask for a dance, but you look worn out."

"I am."

"Why don't we sit this one out."

I loop my arm in his, and we walk back toward our table, grabbing water at the bar along the way.

We stop walking when I see Alex and his father standing outside the tent. I watch as Sam pulls him in for a hug. Alex's body shakes as he cries in his father's arms. There was only one other time I saw Alex this emotional. The memory nearly wrecks me, and I hold onto Viktor for support.

"He's a Dominant, Natalie, but he's also a man. Over the past two months, you and he have been through more than most people experience in a lifetime. Alex has been bottling up his feeling for too long. It's time he lets it all go."

Alex has been my rock while I've been recovering from the trauma in Mexico. But Viktor's right. He hasn't taken any time for himself. To heal from the things he experienced. It's a moving sight to see my Dominant seeking the safety and comfort of his father.

"Let's give them a few moments alone," Viktor says as he pulls out my chair for me to sit. "Do you need anything else?"

"I wouldn't mind more cake." I grin and put my hand on my belly. "We're both kinda hungry."

"Stay here. I'll go grab it."

Viktor's back in a few seconds with two plates of cake. We enjoy our dessert while we watch everyone on the dance floor. Leo even managed to get my mom out there with them.

Viktor's back in a few seconds with two plates of cake. We enjoy our dessert while we watch everyone on the dance floor. Leo even managed to get my mom out there with them.

Alex walks up behind Viktor. "I'm gone for a few minutes, and you're trying to steal my bride already?"

"Just catching up and having cake." Viktor takes his plate and leans down to kiss my cheek. "Congratulations again."

"Enough." Alex jokingly pulls Viktor away from me. "I think I'll take my bride back now."

Viktor shakes his head and walks away.

"Has Viktor ever had a girlfriend?"

"No idea. He doesn't talk about his personal life."

"May I dance with my wife again?"

"I thought you'd never ask."

I'm dancing with Lana when Alex comes up behind me, wrapping his arms around my waist.

"Are you ready to go, baby girl?" He nuzzles my neck, reigniting my earlier arousal.

"Yes, Sir." I spin around in his arms. "I have to throw my bouquet first, though."

There are only two single ladies lined up behind me as I toss the flowers over my shoulder. Lana quickly steps out of the line of fire. Luna easily catches it, her cheeks turning red.

Then, Alex surprises me by scooping me into his arms. Our guests whistle and cheer as Alex carries me to our cottage for our first night as husband and wife.

The End

Epilogue

EVERY ONE OF THEM is oblivious to my presence across the lake. But I'm here, hidden from their view, a mere spectator on the sidelines watching their lives play out. But not for long. Alex believes he's the knight in shining armor, a gallant hero who's saved the princess from the fire-breathing dragon and now gets to live happily ever after—but this isn't the average fairy tale. In this story, the dragon hasn't been defeated. He's lurking in the shadows, waiting for the perfect time to strike and exact his revenge

While they've been living their happy little life, I've been busy putting my plan into place.

The clock is ticking.

The plan's in motion.

Alex and Natalie won't see me coming.

Everything in their perfect little world is about to come crashing down around them, and there's nothing anyone can do to stop it.

You can find all of Tara's books (ebooks and signed paperbacks) on her website: https://taraconradauthor.com/shop/

Fire and Ice Series

Fighting with Him: https://geni.us/FightingwithHim

Living for Him: https://geni.us/LivingforHim

His Melody: https://geni.us/HisMelody

Her Nightingale: https://geni.us/HerNightingale

Shattered Dreams https://geni.us/ShatteredDreams6

Coming Soon: **Fractured Lives (pre-order today for .99)** https://geni.us/FracturedLives**Release Date: June 27, 2023**

Coming Soon: **Mended Hearts (pre-order today for .99)** https://geni.us/MendedHearts**Release Date: August 29, 2023**

Real Life Romance World

Real Life Romance: Gilbert and Elizabeth

https://geni.us/GilbertandElizabeth

Real Life Romance: Duke and Percy

https://geni.us/DukeandPercy

ABOUT THE AUTHOR

Tara Conrad is a married to her high school sweetheart, best friend, and Dominant, George. They've recently celebrated their 28th wedding anniversary and are more in love today than ever. Tara has always loved reading, especially romance—she's a sucker for a happily ever after. It was from George's encouragement that Tara started her career as an author. With each day that passes, she's more thankful for his encouragement and help with every step of this journey. Tara hopes her readers love the books she's written to date and encourages you all to stay tuned for what's to come in the months ahead.

Keep in touch with Tara to see what she's releasing next and where you can meet her at an in-person event.

Human Trafficking Resources

National Human Trafficking Resource
Center 1-888-373-7888
Text Help to 233733 (BeFree)
PSP Tip Line 1-888-292-1919
Contact local police

ONLINE RESOURCES

• www.dhs.gov/bluecampaign
• www.facebook.com/bluecampaign
• nhtrc@polarisproject.org
• www.traffickingresourcecenter.org

ACKNOWLEDGMENTS

I still can't believe I'm getting to live my dream as an author, and it's all thanks to—YOU. Each of you who's taken a chance on a new author. Who picked up her book and fell in love with Alex and Natalie. I'm excited for you to read the last part of their story—make sure to bring your tissues with you. *Living for Him* is an emotional roller-coaster ride, but one that I believe is so worth reading. I'm going to miss spending so much time with Alex and Natalie.

George- You are my everything! You are why I fell in love with writing again. I love every second of this incredible journey we're taking together. Our walk and plots, our late nights while you listen to endless drafts of my books. Your backward editorial notes on those yellow papers. All of our trips to signings where I'm begging you to turn around, all the while you're encouraging me to keep moving forward. I love you more than words can express, and I'm looking forward to many more books with you!

To my kids- Thank you for all your support while I'm writing. I appreciate the dinners and the extra chores you each pitch in with. I love that you come to all my signings and are my biggest cheering section. I love you all!

Dr. C- Once again, thank you for the medical consults, this time so I could kill off a character in a medically believably way. You will always be a rock star trauma surgeon in my book!

Janelle- I'm so glad we met, and you offered me a home at your store. You and your entire staff mean the world to me. I look forward to each of my visits there. Your support and friendship are very special to me.

Dana- Thank you for beta reading. I appreciate your honesty—when it's good and bad. My books are better because of your help.

Made in the USA
Middletown, DE
26 June 2023

33759705R00236